1. John McNutt
2. Wash Butterfield
3. Isaac Grimes
4. Leazer Grimes
5. Hoss Martin
6. Lew Shingle
7. Maggie Cooper
8. Seth Talbot
9. Elph Waterhouse
10. Judge Carnahan
11. Tom Eccles
12. Lem Crocker
13. Col. Cochran's Inn
14. Jim Sollers
15. Joel Bedford
16. Buckhorn Tavern

The Salt *and the* Savor

The Salt
and the SAVOR

A NOVEL
by Howard W. Troyer

NEW YORK

A. A. WYN, INC.

1950

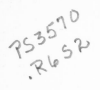

Printed in the United States of America
American Book–Stratford Press, Inc., New York

TO MY MOTHER

Preface

THIS book about frontier life in Indiana was inspired by
the life and recollections of Uncle Perry. I came to know
Uncle Perry when he was a man of eighty-seven. He was
still youthful, slender of build but strong-shouldered, gray-
haired with long, iron-gray mustaches, kindly-eyed, and vol-
uble. After the Civil War, he had worked in the lumbering
camps of northern Michigan for several years and then, following the bent of the times, had gone on west. Later on he
had come back to Milford township and married Lucinda and
after the panic of 1893 they homesteaded together in Oregon.
By the time he came back to the neighborhood once more, in
1934, he was to us living there little more than a name.

Mud Corners is no longer on any map and the post road
has long since become a national highway cluttered with tour-
ist cabins and gasoline stations at every crossroad, but for the
two of us, driving down some country lane lost in the shadows
of the late afternoon, the Indiana frontier—the log-rollings
and husking-bees, the horse thieves and counterfeiters, life in
the meeting house and country store—returned again. Uncle
Perry was a storyteller by nature, always lively, though fre-
quently garrulous and digressive, and often profane. Every
landmark—crossroad, burial ground, set of farm buildings,
meadow land and hillside—recalled an incident. Life hadn't
been all hoecakes and honey, he said, but it had been mighty
good just the same. It was an era of strength and virility, of

hardship and poverty, of loneliness and defeat, but also of courage and of faith. In the little village of Mud Corners, cut off from an outside world, the realities of men living and thinking and working together must have been singularly acute. And in the life of such communities lay the roots of much that we believe in and cherish today.

Every incident related has historical authenticity, of that I have made certain. It is necessary to add, however, that both Uncle Perry and I have taken liberties, his perhaps because of a lapse in memory and mine more deliberate. No attempt, for instance, has been made to abide by the historical record in the naming of characters, and any resemblance in behavior depicted to that of the ancestors of living persons is purely fortuitous and coincidental.

I should like also to acknowledge the generous assistance of others: of Mrs. Hazel Hopper and Mrs. Marguerite Anderson of the Indianapolis Division of the Indiana State Historical Library; of the members of the staffs of the Carnegie libraries at Kendallville and La Grange; of Mrs. Maxine Johnston of Rome City, whose gracious hospitality permitted me to examine the voluminous scrapbooks of her father; of Mr. and Mrs. Gerald Galpin for their kind permission to examine unpublished Civil War diaries; of Stanley Pargellis, through whose interest and the generosity of the Rockefeller Foundation I was given a grant as a Fellow in Midwestern Studies by the Newberry Library of Chicago; and, as always, of D. G. T., whose help and encouragement have been immeasurable.

HOWARD W. TROYER

Appleton, Wisconsin

Acknowledgments: I am indebted to the editors of *The Antioch Review* and *The University of Kansas City Review* for their kind permission to reprint stories which have appeared earlier in their publications.

Contents

[xi]

The Salt *and the* Savor

Chapter 1

HOW UNCLE PERRY *came to chew tobacco, and as far back as he could mind*

AS FAR BACK as he could mind, Uncle Perry was living in the village of Applemanberg with Old Leazer Grimes.

Leazer was a rollin' stone and what moss he got, come from marryin' and buryin'.

Uncle Perry couldn't rightly remember how old he was when he became a member of Leazer's household, but the records show that he was born in 1847 and was therefore five years old in 1852, the year his mother died. Diadamie Tucker, already a widow with a son and two daughters, had married Perry's father, Jeremiah Harman, a widower with five children, the year before Perry was born. Jeremiah had died when Perry was two, and a year and a half later his mother had married Leazer Grimes. Leazer must then have been a man of thirty-five or more, for he had already been twice married and had a family of four children—Noah, Isaac, Charley and Ettie—by his second wife.

How many of the children from these interlocking marriages set their feet under the table after Leazer married Diadamie, Uncle Perry couldn't say, though he minded w⌐ enough that Old Leazer always said it was another fellov 's good times that ate him out of house and home.

Old Leazer never did have any more 'n he could stuff in his pants pockets, and even then they wasn't full.

At any rate about a year after Leazer married Perry's mother, he left his own boy, Charley, and the two older Tucker girls on the old Eli Gunn farm, where they had all been living, and moved to the village with his wife and the younger children, where he set up keeping store.

Fifteen years earlier Len Appleman had built the first store in Applemanberg. For help in the log-rolling he had ridden over to the Indian encampment across the river from the grist mill at Mongoquinong, and had promised the chief a whole keg of whiskey for a day's work. Along about sunrise the next morning there were some thirty bucks dismounting in his yard. First thing they wanted, too, was the keg of whiskey. Len set it out in the open, so that they could see he meant to mind his word, and then he told them the first fellow that would so much as lay a hand on it, he'd bash in his head with a handspike. When they were through with the work, Len knocked in the head of the keg with his axe. The Indians nearly killed each other getting up to the keg. Some of them scooped it up with their hands. Some of them stuck their heads right down in the keg and lapped it up like a dog. Before dark every buck man of them was rolling in the grass, dead drunk.

Then Len and Stiles Gilmore went overland to Toledo, or Vistula as they called it then, with two ox teams to fetch the goods. A hundred and six miles it was one way, and it took them twenty-one days.

The log building was still standing when Leazer came to town, but it was a blacksmith shop then. Len had built a second store along about 1846, a frame building with rough-sawed poplar siding, and that was the one Old Leazer took over.

It was Uncle Perry's job to help out in the store, and the first time he really came to know who he was himself, there he was toting in wood for the old cast-iron stove, or fetching rain water for the family washing from the old uncovered hogshead standing by the back corner where it caught the water from the eaves spout.

Earlier than that he couldn't mind much, though he recalled it was the summer after they'd moved that he had whacked off the end of his big toe on his right foot, chopping kindling for his mother. He bled like a stuck pig, he said. His mother sent his half sister, Nancy, for a bandage and Old Leazer spit tobacco juice on the wound to stop the blood. Then Leazer took some fresh tobacco, wet it down good, and tied it onto the toe for a poultice.

He could remember, too, something of the death of his mother the next autumn when he was five. He could mind that he felt something was wrong when his mother didn't come to supper one night, nor to breakfast the next morning, and later on when Nancy took him in to see her all laid out, it came over him all of a sudden that she was dead. On the day of the burying all of the children came up from the farm and that with the neighbors pretty well filled the little house.

"Get outside," says Leazer.

And Perry did. No one could find him when they got ready to leave for the burying ground, and it wasn't until

[5]

that night when it was all over that one of the older boys happened upon him in an old, empty, tipped-up rain barrel into which he'd crawled and cried himself to sleep.

After his mother's death, Uncle Perry stayed on with Old Leazer, who became his legal guardian, for another year or so. The chore Perry dreaded most while he lived with Leazer was going down to the farm to fetch the fresh-baked bread. His own half sisters, Lissa and Esther, were living on the farm then with Granny Grimes, Leazer's boy, Charley, and Charley's sister, Ettie. Every Monday and Thursday Esther baked the family bread in the old brick bake-oven back of the house. On those days, late in the afternoon, it was Perry's task to turkey trot the two and a half miles to the farm, stuff a dozen or so loaves in a flour sack, and swinging it on his back, return to the village. The road led down to Turkey Creek, across the bridge, and then south along the bank of the stream for three quarters of a mile, before it swung off sharp to the right for the last mile and a half to the farm.

On the days when Uncle Perry got to go early in the afternoon, he didn't mind. Then he would loiter along the creek, roll up his ragged trouser legs and go wading, or if he'd had time to sneak a piece of string and an old bent fishhook, he might dig himself some bait and go fishing. He came to know every deep pool and spring-fed inlet along the stream, and the bushy growth of sumac and hazel gave him ample place to hide if Leazer or one of the boys might happen along. But when Leazer did find out, he put a stop to that.

"Lazyin' and loafin' I don't allow my own children," he says. "From now on if you ain't back in an hour and a half, I'll warm your butt."

Twice after that Uncle Perry forgot and got a raking down with the hickory stove poker. Then Leazer didn't let him go until it was late enough in the afternoon, so that if he quiddled along at all, it would be dark before he got back. Uncle Perry was six then, and he had heard enough stories about wildcats and wolves so that he was mortally afraid of being out after dark. After that he didn't need to be warned.

One day late in the summer Leazer was gone, however, and his older half sister, Nancy, the one person in the household who seemed to care about Perry, allowed he could go early.

"Leazer'll be back by candle-lighting," she says. "Just hump along and be sure to get home before he does."

That afternoon Perry took his string and hook along, and cutting himself a willow pole, went fishing. In one of the pools along the stream he caught sight of a twelve-inch bass. Over and over he baited the hook, only to have the fish slide off the broken barb. Suddenly he became aware of what seemed like a shaggy gray dog crouching in the brush on the opposite side of the stream, watching him. Then it came to him it was a wolf. Dropping his pole, he crawled out through the brush and raced full-split down the road.

It was almost dark by the time he reached the farm. While Esther was putting the loaves in the sack, he sought out Charley in the barn.

"So you're late again?" says Charley.

"I see a wolf," says Perry.

"The old man'll warm you up good and plenty tonight," says Charley.

"I see a wolf," says Perry.

"You're lyin'," says Charley. "Get on home. Ain't no wolves around here no more."

"I be scared," says Perry.

"Get on home," says Charley, "or I'll take a gad to you."

Perry picked up his sack and started for home. He ran all the way until he came to where the road turned and fol-

[7]

lowed the creek. Then he walked along slowly, ears open to every sound. He could hear the water where it rippled over the stones, and the steady hum of crickets. Halfway along the stretch he heard something move in the brush, and turning back, he saw the wolf trotting boldly into the road some distance behind. Afraid to run, Perry stood stock-still and waited. The wolf slowed up, slunk over towards the brush, and then stopped and looked at him. Perry could see the bared teeth and hear a low snarl. In a minute or two he started backing away very slowly up the road, and when he thought he had gone far enough, he turned around and ran, screaming for help.

He had dropped the bread, but he was too scared to think of that before he met Hoss Martin, who came running down from his house towards the road.

"Where you going, Perry?" says Hoss.

"I be scared," says Perry, crying. "I see a wolf."

Picking him up, Hoss carried him back to his house, where Hannah Martin washed his face and offered him supper. He worried down some weak tea and smear-bread, and then Hoss hitched his horse to the buggy to take him home. When they were ready to go, Uncle Perry remembered the bread.

"Leazer can get the damn bread himself," says Hoss.

Leazer never said a word when Hoss brought Perry into the house. Perry could see Nancy had been crying, but she didn't say anything either and took him quietly off to bed. The next morning he felt right good, he said, for when Leazer came home with the slashed and torn sack without anything but a few crumbs in it, he told them it was a wolf all right—they could tell by the tracks—and Perry didn't get the beating he'd figured on. Besides that, it got to be quite a story, told all around, and everyone that came into the store said he'd done the right thing, and in the end he felt himself mighty numerous.

"The one thing he needs now," says Hoss Martin one day, laughing, "is to learn to chew tobacco."

Perry was ready to take that seriously.

In the interior of the store both walls were lined with wooden shelves, and in front of the shelves along the right side ran a low wooden counter. In the middle of the room sat a cast-iron stove, and alongside it was a big wooden box full of sawdust, which Leazer allowed his customers might use for a spittoon during the winter when a steady stream into the stove itself might have put out the fire. Next to the counter on the right-hand side stood a huge sorghum hogshead with a wooden lid, and just above it on the counter itself lay half a dozen whiskey kegs whose spigots Uncle Perry said he used to keep clean by licking them when Old Leazer wasn't watching.

Directly behind the whiskey kegs in a compartment of the wooden counter, Leazer kept his long, twisted pigtails of home-grown and home-cured tobacco. In the bottom of the compartment lay some fig tobacco, waste from the cutting and stray leaves which became unraveled, and when Leazer wasn't looking Uncle Perry would raise the lid quietly and snitch some tobacco crumbs for himself. The tobacco burned his tongue some, but when he could grab enough of it for a real chew, he liked to slip outdoors, and, dodging around to the back of the store, direct a stream of spittle against the butt end of a log or a stone, as he'd seen the older men do.

One day as Perry came sneaking out from behind the counter, Leazer happened to hear him.

"Perry!" he bellows from behind a row of boxes, where he was replacing some goods on the shelf.

Uncle Perry said he was that scared he froze to the floor

and couldn't either move or answer him. Leazer bellowed again and then coming out to the middle of the store, he picked up the old inch-thick hickory cudgel he used as a poker for the stove.

Uncle Perry didn't know whether it was because he was that scared or because he had taken such a large chew he couldn't think of any way to get quick rid of it, but when he saw Leazer reach for the poker, he kind of gulped, and before he knew what was happening, he'd swallowed the chew.

"You chewin' tobacco?" Leazer shouts at him.

"No, I ben't," says Perry, finding his voice.

"Perry, you lie to me and I'll take the hide right offen your butt."

"I ben't lyin'," says Perry.

"Open your mouth!" says Leazer. "What's that stuff you been chewin'?"

"Sorghum," says Perry. "I was a-lickin' the sugar offen that sorghum lid."

"Don't let me catch you doin' that agin! You keep your licker away from there," says Leazer. "And don't ever let me catch you chewin' tobacco. It'll make you sicker 'n the bite of a rattler just to touch your tongue to it."

"Yes," says Perry.

But when he had time to think, it worried him. He didn't dare to ask any more about it right then, but a few minutes later when Leazer was opening the stove door to spit in it himself, he got his grit up.

"Tom Eccles says he always swallers his chew. What happens when you swaller it?"

"Kills you," says Leazer without turning around.

That set Perry to thinking, and the more he thought about it, the more scared he became. He knew it would make him sick all right, for his stomach was already burning like a poultice, but he hadn't exactly figured it was going to kill a fellow. He knew Old Leazer would lick him if he told him what he'd done, and he knew Leazer would be sure to catch on if he got sick. So the first moment the old man turned his back, he skipped out of the door, dodged around the house when no one was looking and headed through the timber for Turkey Creek. He knew a dozen places down by the bridge where they'd never find him.

When he got to the bank, he crawled into a thicket of hazel brush and lay down flat on the ground. He figured if he was going to get sick, he'd just as soon be by himself, and if he was going to die, by the time they'd find him, they couldn't tell whether he had been chewing tobacco or not.

But he didn't get sick. He lay out there for hours waiting for it to come on, but nothing came. Once he thought about Charley's dog, Rover, and how after the dog had swallowed some rat poison, he'd retched and thrown up all over the yard, and how Charley said that was the only thing that had saved the dog's life. So he tried tickling his throat with a piece of weed, but even that didn't do any good. Then he just lay there and pretty soon he fell asleep.

When he woke up, it was after dark and he crawled out to the bank and followed the creek out to the road. When he got back to the house, Old Leazer wasn't home, so he edged in the back way, quiet as a woodmouse, and wouldn't say a word to anybody where he'd been. He got cudgeled the next morning for having run away, but by that time he didn't mind so much any more.

He knew that he wasn't going to get sick and that a chew of tobacco didn't hurt anybody. From that time on he chewed regular, so he said, come Sunday, come Monday, every goddamn day of his life.

Chapter 2

How Leazer Grimes *married the Widow Tidrick, and Uncle Perry ran away*

I<small>T WAS WHEN</small> Old Leazer married the Widow Tidrick that Uncle Perry's boyhood world fell apart like the staves of an old rum puncheon, marked, numbered, and ready for shooking. In a way, though, you couldn't hold it against Old Leazer.

A marryin' always come to follow a buryin', and a buryin' a marryin'—that's the whole twist and tuckin' of it.

There were three weddings that winter, all told. The first was Esther's, one of the Tucker girls, and Uncle Perry's half sister on his mother's side. Esther was known throughout the neighborhood for the bread she baked. Never again this side of heaven's own bakeshop, Perry said, would he touch his tongue to anything like that, butter-crusted and honey-sweet, spread spatter-thick with raspberry jam.

Lissa was no kitchen queen like Esther, but she was a right handy girl in the farmyard. Every year she set two or three dozen turkey hens, driving the young ones out to the scratchings in the woods all summer long. Sometimes, when they weren't too busy in the store, Old Leazer would let Perry go down to help her out—a chore he loved, spending all day in the woods, picking wild berries, chasing squirrels, or watching a grouse hen covey her young.

During the summer the turkeys roosted on top of their own box nests, or in the trees, or even in the haystacks and along the top of the zigzag barnyard fence. In the winter they would freeze their feet doing that, and every fall the whole flock would have to be caught and shut up for a week in the old log chicken house till they got roost-sense and returned there by themselves at sundown.

At the time of the first cold snap that fall Perry went down to the farm with Old Leazer to help catch the turkeys. That was done by shining them with a lantern, like in jack-hunting deer, and then reaching under and grabbing them by the legs. It was his job to carry one of the lanterns or to hold a half-dozen turkeys in each hand, carrying them back to the log house. It was scary work and once when a young gobbler fluttered his wings and curled around till he could peck him in the hand, Perry dropped a whole half-dozen of them. Old Leazer swore and gave him a good hefty cobb on the butt, but he didn't mind that. It was dark when the turkey hunt began, and in the hustle and bustle of coming and going, the light of the lanterns moving in and out of the shadows, and the hobble-gobble of the birds there was a lot of fun and excitement and a feeling that a fellow was earning his salt.

After they were through, there was a late supper of bread and jam, and Old Leazer about to go home, allowed that

Perry might stay there and fetch the bread up to the store the next afternoon. It was in the morning while he was eating breakfast that Esther told him.

"I'm getting married, Perry," she says.

"What's *married?*" says Perry.

"I'm going to live with Isaac and keep house for him like Mom did for Leazer," she says.

"Be you goin' to die like Mom did?" says Perry.

"Some day," says Esther, laughing, "but I hope not right away."

Marriage was something new for Perry, though it didn't seem so all-out strange, since Isaac was one of Old Leazer's boys, and his own half brother on the other side of the family. Isaac had been working as a cabinet maker for two or three years then, but Perry had seen him once or twice, the last time when his mother had died and been buried. After that the children had been pretty well scattered—there were thirteen of them, more than the little house in Applemanberg could hold even if they slept spoon fashion on the kitchen floor. Those who could work were farmed out among the neighbors and relatives for their keep, but Perry had stayed on with Old Leazer and his half sister, Nancy, who kept house for him and the pod of younger children Leazer couldn't get shut of.

Why it was that Nancy kept house for Old Leazer rather than one of the other girls, Uncle Perry couldn't say, though he was sure it was a way-up good thing for him that she did, and he could hardly wait till he got home that day to tell her about Esther and Isaac.

"For a wonder now," she says, "that's good. Little enough any of us will ever get working for Leazer."

Nancy was only sixteen then, but she had a lot of gumption and a faculty for keeping house. She redded-up Old Leazer's place, washed the clothes for the family, mended and ironed, churned the butter, and cooked the meals, besides helping Old Leazer out in the store and playing mother to Perry, the little titman of the household. She used to shear his long black hair, cut down the clothes of the older boys, patching and mending them for him, and often stand between him and the hickory gad when an empty woodbox or an unrun errand roused up Old Leazer's wrath. "Lazyin' and loafin' I don't allow my own children," Leazer would shout. "Let the little shirttail earn his keep."

A bark and a growl and a kick in the butt filled out a day's talk fer Old Leazer.

It was a month or so after the turkey hunt that the first wedding took place down on the farm. Perry could remember the long table set up in the kitchen, loaded down with roast turkey and sugar-cured ham, corn pone and egg bread, mince and pumpkin pies, plum puddings and cakes. Later on he sat on an old chest, watching Tom Eccles play the fiddle, while his older half brothers swung his older half sisters around and around in the parlor.

Ole Dan Tucker clomb a tree,
His Lord and Master fer to see;

Tom would sing in a high-pitched voice while he sawed away with his grasshopper jerk,

De limb it broke and Dan got a fall—
Never got to see his Lord at all!

Then the dancers would join in on the chorus:

Get out o' the way, Ole Dan Tucker,
Get out o' the way, Ole Dan Tucker,

Get out o' the way, Ole Dan Tucker,
You're too late to get your supper!

On that day Noah Grimes, another one of Old Leazer's boys, had come home from Elkhart county, where he worked out as a hired man. When he saw what was going on, and that Lissa was just as trim a daisy as Esther and right handy in field work, he took a shine to her and less than a month later there was a second big wedding. Once more the table was loaded down with eatables and once more Tom Eccles played the fiddle, while Perry's half brothers swung his half sisters around the room. Those were pleasant days to remember later on after Nancy was gone and Perry was left alone with the Widow Tidrick and Old Leazer.

That was after the third wedding had taken place, though Uncle Perry knew nothing about that one until the night Old Leazer brought the Widow and her two children home to live with him in Applemanberg. Perry had been busy helping Nancy—sweeping the house, scrubbing the floors, and filling the woodbox. At supper time that day she had packed her clothes and gotten ready to set out with her bundle.

"I'm going away to work for Minot Gilmore's," she says. "Leazer is marrying again, and I don't feel to keep on here. You be a good boy, Perry, and mind Old Leazer."

He walked along down the road with her as far as the Turkey Creek bridge, where she kissed him good-by. He played there a while and when he got home, the new family was already sitting at the supper table.

"Hump along and wash," says Old Leazer, "or we won't be a-waitin' fer you."

"Who's the little tramp?" says the Widow Tidrick to Leazer while Perry was washing.

"That's Diadamie's boy," says Leazer.

"Can't you find a place fer him?" she says.

"I reckon not," he says. "I kind of promised Diadamie I'd look out fer the little shavetail and he helps out some in the store."

"John and Willie ain't no clutterbucks. That's somethin' they can do," she says, looking at her own children, the younger one about Perry's age but taller.

Uncle Perry didn't know whether she thought he wasn't listening or that he wouldn't understand what they were talking about, but he knew then that things were never going to be the same. He came over to the table, but he couldn't eat his victuals, and when Leazer snapped him on the forehead with his fingers for not setting to, he burst out crying and ran outside. Leazer came out to get him after a while and sent him to bed. He was gentle with him then, and for a day or two roused him out every morning when he himself got up, and took him along over to the store, where he set him to sweeping up the place or fetching in wood for the stove.

Then Leazer would go home for breakfast, leaving him in the store, and after he came back, Perry would go home for his own. It wasn't long, however, until it was John who went along to the store, while Perry had to stay and help out around the house, washing dishes, carrying rain water, fetching in wood for the stove, and pulling weeds in the garden patch behind the house.

Willie was his mother's cosset and he always got the easy thing to do. If they were washing dishes together and one of them dropped a dish, Perry was the one who got cuffed for it, and if they were fetching in rain water or wood and had a rough-and-tumble on the way, he got the fault. He was afraid of the older boy, John, and steered clear of him, but even though Willie was gandier than he, Perry could hold his own at kicking shins, pulling hair, or blacking up an eye.

Whenever that happened, Perry got a hiding with a hickory gad when Old Leazer got home, though the Widow wouldn't let Leazer lay a hand on Willie.

One morning when Old Leazer left for the store, he set the boys to hoeing dock and pulling thistles in the garden. Hoeing the dock was easy enough, but the thistles spread by runners and the roots had to be pulled out clean. The boys were to take turns with the hoe, but when it came Perry's time, Willie wouldn't let go of the handle. They argued, called names, and then with both boys grabbing the handle, Perry kicked shins. In the tussle the hoe hit Willie on the head, the rusty bite cutting a gash over his left ear. Willie bled like a comb-hackled rooster and set up a howl that brought the Widow running from the house.

She took one look at Willie and started after Perry who stood there too scared to run. Grabbing a loose picket from the fence, she hit him over the head, and when he stumbled and fell down, she kept on lamming him on his back and shoulders.

"Stop!" he screams. "You're killin' me."

"I'd just as lief," she says, hitting him again.

"I'll tell Pap," he says.

"Pap?" she says. "Leazer ain't your pap. You ain't got no pap. You're Perry Harman and you ain't got a thing in the world but your name."

And with that she grabbed Willie and led him inside.

Perry lay there a while, feeling for his bruises. Then it came to him he had something new to figure out. He knew that Esther and Lissa's name had been Tucker before they married the Grimes boys. Nancy's name was Harman like his own, but Nancy told him one time that her mother's name had been Adelia, and his mother was Diadamie. Charley and Ettie's name was Grimes like Old Leazer's. He reached

[*18*]

in his pocket for a handful of frayed tobacco leaves he'd snitched from Old Leazer's store a day or so before and filled his mouth with crumbs. All the rest of them like Ettie, and Charley, and Nancy, and Laura, and Lissa, and Esther, had a mom or a pap, or a brother or a sister or someone like Isaac or Noah to get married to, but he was just a stray. He stood up slowly, went over, and picked up the hoe.

After a spell Willie came back out with a piece of cotton outing tied around his head.

"You got a pap?" says Perry, leaning on the handle.

"Sure," he says, "Leazer's my pap now."

"Why ain't he mine?" says Perry.

"You ain't got no ma," says Willie.

"My ma's dead," says Perry.

"You never had a ma," says Willie, remembering something he'd heard his older brother say. "You wasn't born a-tall. A crow just dropped you on a stump and the sun hatched you out."

That was pickery and wormwood for Perry. He turned towards Willie, circled the cud with his tongue, and spat the brown stream full in his face. Willie covered his face with his hands, jumped up and down like a whipsaw, and let out a screech. The old lady came running once more, but this time Perry knew better. He cleared the picket fence before she could lay a hand on him and dusted around the house for Turkey Creek. Just at the corner he ran smack into Old Leazer who was coming home for dinner. Before he knew what was happening, Leazer had him by the seat and held on.

"What's a-goin' on here?" he growls.

He took him along back of the house where the Widow Tidrick was washing up Willie with a bucket of water from the old draw well. Perry couldn't get a word in edgewise, though it wouldn't have done him any good, likely, if he had.

Old Leazer yanked him over to the woodpile and laid on with the hardest licking he ever had in his life. The gad broke three times before Leazer was through, but Perry never cried once. He knew by that time that nobody there gave a dried apple damn for him, and there was no point in a fellow's showing up his hurt. He just stayed outside when the others went in to dinner and when the yard was clear, he lit out.

It's a bitter-weed thing, but when a feller's got to ridge up his own row, the sooner he finds out, the better.

Chapter 3

How Uncle Perry *found his way to Pretty Lake*

and first met Minot Gilmore

I hear say they got a summer place down to Pretty Lake now. They tell me some fellers from Fort Wayne come in down there, cut themselves a road through the timber, cleaned out the brush, and built themselves summer houses on the shore of the lake. Gettin' back to nature, they call it. Gettin' back? Hell! They ain't never been there. They even got their privies inside.

ON THE DAY he cut a shirttail for Turkey Creek, Uncle Perry hoped never to see Old Leazer and the Widow Tidrick again. Leazer wasn't but a penny-pinching old fumblefist and the Widow was as mean and hateful as a short-horned, up-tailed cow.

All he thought of at the time was that he wanted to get away. That was the last double-twisted thrashing Old Leazer would ever give him, and the hickory gad, broken into pieces, could lay there by the woodpile for a hundred years and rot. When he reached the bridge down below Applemanberg, he turned and followed the left bank upstream towards Pretty Lake. He didn't really know where he was going, but he'd heard a lot about the place even then. Hoss Martin was a mighty big hunter and he'd been nigh everywhere. "It's a forty-year wilderness down there," Hoss had said in the store one day, "but the overhead leaves are that thick the manna droppings don't come through."

It's a funny thing the way what a feller never thinks about comes home to him.

A quarter of a mile beyond the bridge Perry came to the clump of hazel where he'd lain out waiting for what didn't come the time he had swallowed his chew, and a little later he passed the deep pools where he'd gone fishing on days he had gone to fetch bread from the farm. A mile or so further on, the land along the stream became marshy, and Perry, afraid of rattlers and quicksand, found a place to wade the creek, came out to the Turkey Creek road, crossed over, and headed for the uplands lying between Mud Corners and Pretty Lake.

Circling a pothole tangle of swamp grass and briar, he climbed a long, billowing, sandy hill covered with a heavy growth of timber. It had been hard going, broguing through the swale grass and briar, but here there was plenty of fallen timber to climb over and crawl under. He was dog-tired and hungry as a weaned pig, and his shoulders ached from the blows Old Leazer had given him. Before he raised the hill, he crossed a small opening with a few wild blackberries still on the vine, but he was so tired that before he had eaten more than a handful, he sank down to rest for a minute. Then the tears came and he cried himself to sleep.

When he woke up, it was getting on towards candle-lighting time. For a minute he couldn't move, he was that stiff and sore, and the salt taste was still strong on his tongue. But he knew that he could never go back. By god, he was Perry Harman, and what he had to count on was himself. He got up and looked around. He was far enough in from the road so they'd never find him, even if they looked for him, though he really couldn't tell how far. Up above him the tops of the trees shut out the sky, and down below the shaggy-grooved oaks and porridge-spattered buttonwoods cut off the view.

He'd never been out in the deep woods alone before. For a moment he stood there watching squirrels skittering along the tree tops, jumping from branch to branch, sometimes scampering down the long trunks to the ground and then madly up again. When he moved over to the briar patch, looking for more thimbleberries, a grouse burred up ahead of him, and what he at first took to be a dog, ran nimbly through the brush. It was a fox waiting for his prey. The picture of the snarling wolf he had met along the Turkey Creek road came back to him and the cold chills ran up and down his spine. Then he drummed up his grit, gathered what berries he could find, and made his way back up the hill. He had seen a large, hollow sycamore tree broken off the butt end, resting length-wise on its own branches two feet or so above the ground. He worked himself into the hollow, feet first, till he lay well inside, his head resting on his arms for a pillow.

He lay there for a spell before sleep came on him again. The rustle of the leaves was a quieting sound, broken now and then by a heavier crash of foliage, as if a squirrel had slipped off a limb and caught himself twenty feet below. Sometimes he heard a snapping twig or a low brushing sound as if a wild hog or a quill pig were moving along the forest duff. Then a whippoorwill began calling deeper in the woods and almost overhead a hoot owl set up its cry. Years later he could still remember how pokerish it was. There he lay, hot and tired, with a gnawing pain of hunger in his stomach. Down at his feet he could feel the cool, moist dry rot of the log and into it he wiggled and curled his toes. "Sleep on your belly and cover it with your back," Hoss once had told him.

Sometime after daybreak he woke up feeling all-overish and spit-thirsty. He couldn't move for the pain in his arms and along his back, and lower down his buttocks were swollen tight in his pants as a wedge in a railcut. It came to him then that he might die there in the hollow log. He was already buried Indian fashion. What would they say if they ever found him, though they more than likely wouldn't. Old Leazer might be sorry but the Widow wouldn't care. "I'd as lief you was dead," she had said. Nancy would cry for him, but she had left him, too, and gone off somewhere. More than likely she would never hear about it at all. Maybe a fellow might as well die, but, by god, he wasn't going to if he could help it, though he wouldn't ever go back either. Old Leazer wasn't his pap, not any more, not now or ever.

It hurt him when he moved, but he inched himself out of the log, falling on his forelegs like a young deer and then pushing himself up on his standers. He wasn't hungry now, just thirsty. He'd have to have a drink or he'd be up a gum tree for sure. He'd heard say Pretty Lake was spring-fed; better he went down there. He worked his way down the south slope, circling a marsh in the hollow, and then up the next rise. "The hills ain't higher," Hoss had said, "but the hollows are deeper." He kept on, scratching his way through the briar, dropping on all fours to crawl under logs, stumbling and falling, but always getting up again and going on.

Down in the hollows the mosquitoes swarmed about like bees

when a fellow robs a tree, and the swamp grass was choking—hard to get through until he found a place where it had been trailed down by wild hogs and deer. He might not have made it if it hadn't been for that, but the trail finally brought him out to the lake. He fell on his knees, brushed the wiggletails away, and scooped up the water in his hands. It was a Sunday-morning wonder how it felt, the cool water in a fellow's mouth after he'd been that nigh dead from thirst.

But he couldn't stay there, that he knew. It was marshy where the trail led in, with mosquitoes pudding-thick. He crawled back up the bank, wormed his way through the dogwood and shadberry tangle to the top of a small hill overlooking the lake. He lay down a long time and rested, and he was still half-dozing when it happened. He'd seen a hundred squirrels and some coon that morning, and a couple of wild hogs had left their rooting and dashed off as he'd come along. Lying there on the hill, he could see an old rotten stump chewed and clawed into fine fluffy sawdust—that would be where a bear had been feeding on ants. But a squirrel or a coon or a razorback, or maybe even a bear, would run when they saw a fellow, but not a cougar. "They'll claw your back up like a ripsaw, gouge out your throat, and drink the blood," Hoss had said.

For a whole minute after he first saw the soft lines of the cat against the green foliage and mottled bark of the sycamore branches thirty feet above the ground, he lay there breathless as a stillborn lamb. Then he breathed softly, rolled over, and looked again. There was no movement above him, but he could now see the face of the cat resting sleepily on its forepaws. For another moment he lay in frozen agony. Then he rolled over again, listened, and started crawling away on all fours. Twenty feet away he stood up, looking and listening. He saw and heard nothing. Then he ran.

He kited on and on, blindly at first, any way that would get him out of the woods. Then it came to him that maybe a fellow would never get out that way. He tried to slow down. If he went north as straight as he could, he'd come out somewhere on the Mud Corners road. That would mean keeping the sun over his left shoulder. He tried not to forget, but he had to keep his eye spotting openings. Stopping was the one thing he was afraid of. If the cougar was following him, he'd never dare fall down or stop.

He wasn't hungry any more or thirsty. Maybe there was no give-out to a fellow and he could keep on dogging along forever. But when he thought about it, he knew it wasn't so. He was all fagged out and dizzy as a tumbleweed. It was only going on that kept a fellow going. If he stopped now, he'd keel right over. There was no safe place for a fellow in the woods. He'd have to crawfish back all right. Old Leazer would beat him for running away, but he'd have the old shuck-tick to sleep on, and there would be plenty of hog jowl and greens to eat, and the old draw well never ran dry. Maybe he would have sprawl enough to make it up to the Widow Tidrick. He'd help Willie out and work harder to make a hitch of it.

It was late afternoon before he raised a hill that let him see, coming down on the far side, he was getting near the settlement. He came to a fork-and-rail fence, climbed it, and found himself in a field of wheat stubble. Forty rods further on he could see the fence on the other side. He kept on going, but he eased up some. From the second fence he could see farmyard buildings. Suddenly he felt safe and fell to the ground.

When he came to again, it was dark, but he could see the lantern light of the buildings. The road would have to be over that way. He circled the barn and climbed the post-and-bar fence into the yard next to a white clapboard story-and-a-half house. Going by he looked in at the window and saw a family sitting around the table in the kitchen. At the head of the table, facing him, sat a broad-shouldered fellow with a heavy, black beard. Children sat to his right and left. At the end of the table with her back towards the window sat an old grandmother and alongside her a younger woman.

What came over him, Perry didn't know, but all of a sudden he couldn't stop himself. He walked around to the door, lifted the latch, and stepped inside. Then he stopped dead in his tracks. The young woman sitting at the table was his half sister, Nancy.

"Why hello, boy," says the man, turning around. "Where did you come from?"

Uncle Perry just stood there and couldn't say a word.

"Are you hungry?" says the man.

Perry shook his head. There he stood, pig-wallow dirty, his clothes in shreds, his arms and face scratched from briars and mosquito bites, his long hair matted and straggly.

"What's your name?" says Nancy.

But Perry couldn't make up his mouth to it.

"Well," says the father, "let him sit down on a chair till he gets used to us. I reckon he'll talk then. Marsh, we got the chores to do."

With that he and the older boy left the room and Nancy and the girls began clearing the table.

"Come, boy, tell us your name," says Nancy.

"No," says Perry, getting up. "I got to get goin'."

"Where to?" she says.

"Back to Old Leazer's," he says.

"Leazer's!" she says. "Are you Perry Harman?"

Perry was for lying then and shook his head.

"You are too Perry Harman," she says, looking at him

hard, coming on over, and bursting into tears. "I declare, you're Perry, and I didn't even know you. You stay right here," she says. "I'm going out to tell Minot."

Before she came back, Granny Gilmore had come over and led Perry to the table. He was already sitting there eating, when Minot and Nancy came back in.

"So you're Perry Harman," says Minot. "What's Leazer been doing to you?"

"I run away," says Perry, "down to Pretty Lake."

"A fellow don't run away without a call to. Lucinda," he says, turning to one of the girls standing there, staring at Perry, "you go get him some of Marsh's castoffs. Marsh, you take him down cellar and start cleaning him up."

While Marsh was helping him wash, Minot came downstairs and looked on.

"My god," he says to Nancy, when they came back up, "that boy's all black and blue from his shoulders down to his backside. You say you were down to Pretty Lake?" he says to Perry.

Perry told them the story as well as he could.

"It's a miracle you come through alive," says Minot.

Uncle Perry stayed on at Minot's for three or four days. He was helping Marsh do chores in the barn when Old Leazer came driving into the yard. Minot saw him first, and he and Leazer went on into the house together. About an hour later Minot came out to the barn.

"Perry," he says, "Leazer's come to fetch you. He's waiting for you now."

"Do I got to go?" says Perry.

"He's your legal guardian," says Minot. "You've got to do what he says."

When they came up to the house, Perry started around the back way to the cellar door.

"Where you going?" says Minot.

"I'll just be changin' my clothes back," says Perry.

"No," says Minot, "that you ain't. You wear what we gave you. And one thing more, come any time at all, you got a bed here and a chair at the table. You keep minding that, boy."

When they got to the front of the house, Old Leazer was standing there by the buggy and when Perry got in without saying a word, Leazer followed and the two of them drove off. They were halfway home before Leazer turned on him, but later on Perry couldn't even remember what he said. What kept coming back was what Minot had told him—that, and the sight of the cougar high up in the buttonwood branches down at Pretty Lake.

Sometimes there ain't a thing in the world to teach a young feller wild-hog sense, like runnin' dog-wild.

Chapter 4

HOW UNCLE PERRY *came to know Pottawatomie Joe, and the story of the old fort cabin*

IT WAS IN the butter-bowl talk in the kitchen that Uncle Perry first heard stories about the Pottawatomies. If a fellow listened to the women, he said, all Indians were a drunken, smelly lot.

Many a time he heard Granny Grimes tell stories of the early days—how she looked up from her spinning wheel in the late afternoon, or turned away from her cooking at the fireplace early in the evening, to find an Indian in the cabin, standing there silently, watching her. He might have come to beg potatoes or *pin-e-ack*, as the Indians called them, or perhaps wheat flour, for which their word was *nap-an-ee*. Sometimes they brought a wild turkey or a squirrel in exchange, but more often they offered nothing, merely grunting and pointing to the flour barrel or to a sack of corn meal.

If you gave them something ready to eat, like corn bread or a piece of salt pork, they were more than likely to squat on the cabin floor, eat it, roll themselves in a blanket and lie down in front of the fire to sleep. They would be gone before

daylight, but it took a full morning with sand and the scrubbing brush before the smell was gone from the cabin.

And later on one time Perry heard Mrs. Alzamon Black,
sitting in the Gilmore kitchen, tell how twenty years earlier
she had been surprised one afternoon by three Pottawatomies
who came to her cabin demanding firewater. She told them
no, she said, but they had come in anyway, and one of the
bucks had thrown his arms about her and flung her down on
the bed, while the others looked for whiskey. When they had
found the jug, they had passed it around among themselves
and then began pouring the burning stuff down her own
throat. By the time Alzamon had got back that night, there
they were, all four of them, rolling on the cabin floor, drunk
as hired help in a haymow shake-down.

There were other ways of telling the story, however, as
Uncle Perry came to find out, and Minot just laughed when
Perry told him what he'd heard.

"Any fellow that knew Hattie back in those days would
know that ain't the full story," says Minot. "I reckon no Indian ever harmed Hattie unless he had a right good call to."

When the first settlers had come in, they'd found plenty of
Indians in the neighborhood, but the only one Uncle Perry
ever came to know was a fellow they used to call Pottawatomie Joe. That happened the winter he was eight and Old
Leazer sent him to live with the Kingsley's up near Lexington.
Laura was a half sister on the Harman side of the family, and
she had allowed now that she was married she might take the
boy for a spell. She and Elias lived in a single-room log cabin
with a clapboard lean-to kitchen along one end. Perry slept in
the loft of the main cabin, crawling up an outside ladder, and
more than one morning that winter his blanket was covered
with snow that had drifted in through the loose clapboards on
the roof. He had no shoes of his own and went baretoed all

winter long, except on the coldest mornings when he would get up before Laura and slip on her clumpers to do his chores in the barn across the road. Their chief food was corn dodger, boiled squirrel, and sassafras tea. The corn dodger they ate for breakfast, with more corn dodger and perhaps a baked potato at noon. In the evening there was likely to be boiled squirrel, or a piece of salt pork, or sometimes wild turkey or grouse.

The game was more than likely to have come from Pottawatomie Joe, who with a pack of yelping and barking dogs lived in the old fort cabin on the edge of the big woods, less than a mile by forest trace from the Kingsley door. Pottawatomie Joe was a straggler. Fifteen years earlier, Elias told Perry, the last encampment of the Pottawatomies near Mongoquinong had been broken up by the government.

First the army wagons had been loaded with the squaws and their children and the campsite baggage. Then the Indian braves had brought up their ponies. Before mounting, they had turned once more to shake hands with those among the white men they had come to know. For a moment they had stood there in a circle, staring silently at the abandoned camp grounds. Then in dead silence they had mounted their horses and turned to follow the train.

Two years later Pottawatomie Joe had come back again, just like a woodchuck to his burrow.

"Me come. Live Big Squaw Prairie," Joe says. "See friends."

About a week after Perry came to live with Laura and Elias, Pottawatomie Joe came over to the Kingsley cabin to barter some game for a small sack of potatoes. Perry heard the dogs barking in the yard, and when he came outside, he saw Elias talking to an elderly Indian in deerskin breeches, a ragged coat, and an old felt hat. A big black hound made a dash for Perry, stopping short and dropping his tail at a grunt from the Indian. Then the dark eyes in the square, high cheek-boned face looked at the boy and the large chin relaxed into a smile.

"Dog no hurt," he says.

The trade completed, Elias was for inviting Joe inside to sit down and share their noonday meal, but Laura met them at the door.

"You ain't bringing him inside," she says. "I can't 'bide the smell."

"Fine nose makes good dog," says Joe, laughing, as if he understood.

He took the plate of corn dodger and hominy grits that Elias gave him and sat down on a log in the yard. Perry stood there for a while watching him. Young as he was, it made him right mad. Laura had no call to be queasy as far as he could see, and when he and Elias had washed up and were ready for their victuals, he picked up his own plate.

"Where you going?" says Laura.

"I be goin' to eat with Joe," says Perry.

When he got outside, Pottawatomie Joe moved over to give him a place on the log. They ate their food without talking, and Joe handed Perry the empty plate.

"Much thanks," he says. "Sometime you come see Joe."

Then he picked up his potatoes, called to his dogs, and started away.

A few days later Perry found his way through the woods to the old *fort* cabin, and after that, whenever he could pig-twist away from chores, he'd spend the afternoon there. Bettermost he liked the days when Pottawatomie Joe took him hunting, following the dogs down through the swamp grass and aspen thickets along the river or up along the ridges into the big woods. Wild ducks and honkers were plentiful, rabbits ran everywhere, and now and then the dogs would start a fox. On other days, calling the dogs to heel, they stalked game silently in the big woods, Perry himself sometimes shouldering the big, heavy muzzleloader with which Joe taught him to bark a squirrel out of a towering oak with a single shot. On other afternoons Joe showed him how to make horsehair snares or figure-four traps for smaller, upland game birds, and how to hide them in the hedgerows and runways. Many a time Perry came home, grizzled with sticktights and cockleburs, but happy as a chip-squirrel and carrying a chance of grouse or a half-dozen quail for the family larder.

One rainy day as they sat before the old cat-and-clay fireplace where Pottawatomie Joe did his cooking, Uncle Perry drummed up his grit and asked him about the old *fort* cabin. Even then Perry had already heard about the Gage and Langdon war, for it was a story told and retold at every general store and fireside shingle-whittling in the county.

Back in 1832 when it had happened, Milford township was still a huckleberry wilderness and only the families of John Clark and Len Appleman had settled on Turkey Creek as far upstream as where the villages of Applemanberg and Mud Corners came to be. Five miles farther north, where Turkey Creek empties into the Pigeon River, Mongoquinong, however, was already a hustling village. Here Ed Brownell had built a dam across the river and put up a grist mill on the northern shore. Next to the mill he had built a distillery able to turn out thirty to forty gallons of red-eye whiskey a day. Some years before Brownell built the dam, the firm of Comparet and Cuttieaur had established an Indian trading post, which they now turned into a store for the settlers. Then Michael O'Ferrel opened a second store and established a post office, and Samuel Burnside built himself a blacksmith shop.

The distillery and the mill had brought a lot of settlers to the area, for they could take their corn to the mill, get it ground, and then take it to the distillery, where it could be sold, traded for whiskey, or brewed on shares. South of the river, across from the mill, several hundred Pottawatomies had camped each summer, and not a little of the village trade was barter with the Indians for wild game and their annual take of furs and skins. The Indians were friendly fellows—happy to trade their own goods for ear-bobs, arm bands, silver brooches, a little corn meal, or a keg of whiskey—except sometimes when they were drunk. Then the sight of two or three hundred of them, singing and dancing and shouting and fighting by the dim light of their camp fires, gave some of the early settlers the shirt-tail shivers.

Along about August one year two men, Benjamin Gage and Abraham Langdon, had been sitting in the mill late one afternoon waiting for their grinding. Seeing Ed Brownell give a group of Indians a keg of whiskey, the men had got their hackles up.

"What do you do that fer?" says Gage. "I be scared of them red devils."

"It makes good hunters out of 'em," says Brownell. "I reckon they owe me half the pelts they'll bring in this winter, and come cold weather, there'll be no more whiskey till I get the fur."

"Goddamn you, Brownell," says Langdon, "them red devils will be fer scalpin' all of us, leastways they will, if we don't take things in our own hands and burn the camp down."

Ed Brownell was always one for a jolly. Over a glass of whiskey that night he and Druryear, a Frenchman from the trading post, and Michael O'Ferrel had figured out a joke on Gage and Langdon, still waiting for their flour and sleeping on the floor of the mill. Asking Pottawatomie Joe to join them, the white men had rigged themselves out in full Indian costume with war paint, blankets, and tomahawks. About five o'clock the next morning, when Gage and Langdon had gotten up and were talking to the German mill hand in the yard in front of the mill, Pottawatomie Joe had stepped out suddenly from behind a tree, raised his rifle, and fired. As the shot rang out, the mill hand, who was in on the fun, had fallen down, crying out, "My god, I'm shot." Then the men, dressed like Indians, had come leaping forward, swinging their tomahawks, and yelling like a dozen devils beating tanbark.

Gage and Langdon had never stopped long enough to recognize any of them. At the first shot both of them had taken to their heels and scratched gravel for home. As they dashed through the village, they shouted out that everyone at the mill had been shot and scalped. An hour later the village of Mongoquinong was empty as a wheat field at stubble call. When Gage had gotten back to the little crossroad village of Lexington where he lived, the settlers there had gathered together their women and children into the blacksmith shop of George Donaldson, and while some of them had stood guard, others had begun felling trees, cutting logs, and constructing the *fort*. As soon as Langdon had brought them the news, families farther west in the township had withdrawn to an island in Cedar Lake and begun similar fortifications. On the third day nearly a hundred armed men had come together at Lexington and started a march to Mongoquinong, ready for battle.

As for Brownell and the others, they hadn't really known what was happening and still thought it just a good joke until the armed settlers came marching into the village. When they saw what was up, the white men hid for their own safety, while Pottawatomie Joe swam across the river, and persuaded his own people to hang out a white flag and ask for a parley.

Among the armed men the scare-fever gave way to anger. There was a lot of talk then about stringing up somebody if they could ever find out who had done it. But they didn't know, not for a long time. Shortly after that Druryear had left the village, O'Ferrel had moved away sometime later, and though many of them had thought Brownell must have known something about it, they hadn't at the time been able to prove that.

When Perry asked him about the old *fort* cabin, Joe sat there chuckling for a minute.

"Brownell, him friend of me," he says. "We think very funny, maybe. But no."

The old *fort* cabin had never really been finished nor ever lived in until ten years later when Joe came back from the western prairies. It was a large place, but the old building was sway-backed now and bony-ribbed as an old nag. Animal skins and strips of birchbark took the place of missing clapboards on the sagging roof. Where the mortar caulking between the logs had fallen out or had never been put in, Joe had made shift by hanging up dried skins to keep out the rain, until the whole thing inside looked rather like an Indian tepee set up within a walled-log inclosure.

"White man make one fine home for me," says Pottawatomie Joe, laughing.

Before the summer was over, however, the old *fort* cabin had been burned to the ground, and Pottawatomie Joe had left the neighborhood forever.

For that Perry felt himself blameful, and it was a long time afterwards before he could ever talk about it at all.

The year before Perry came to live with the Kingsleys, Elias had bought a small flock of sheep, which during the day they pastured in the meadowlands or in the clearings, and at night herded into an old log cabin they used for a fold. A sheep wasn't much good in the early days, for it didn't have any way of defending itself and was an easy prey for wild animals. Lots of times the ewes were bitten in the udders by rattlers, and a wolf or a fox or even a weasel or a hawk could carry off the young. There were stories, too, of wild dogs killing off a whole flock in a single night.

Every morning it was Perry's chore to let them out of the fold and drive them to the meadow. Before candle-lighting time he went out to drive them back, counting them carefully and shutting them up in the fold. Elias kept a tight rein on him, and each night at supper asked him the number and whether he had been sure to fasten the door to the fold. Whether he had counted them or not, Uncle Perry usually allowed they were all there anyway, but he always tried to shut the door tight.

Early one morning he got up, went over to take care of the sheep, and found the fold empty. The door was wide open, the wooden peg which held it having slipped out of the socket and fallen to the ground. Perry ran headlong for the meadow, hoping to find the sheep grazing as usual. He would be able to see if they were all there, he thought, and to report back to Elias as if nothing had happened.

When he raised the hill, though, he suddenly stopped. He had heard dogs yelping and barking; now he saw them driving the flock. There were about a half-dozen of them all told, and a big black hound was leading the pack. The dogs would run along snapping at the legs of a ewe. The big black fellow would dash alongside, grabbing for the wool along the throat. The ewe would stumble and go down, and then the pack would close in for the kill.

Perry ran on shouting and yelling at the dogs, throwing stones and sticks until he drove them away. Then he counted the loss. Three dead ewes lay in the meadow, two of the lambs had been torn into shreds, and a dozen others were trailing shaggy coats of wool that had been torn from their throats and backs.

Perry drove the rest of the flock back to the fold, and then he and Elias came down to the meadow with the oxen and stone-boat to bring back the dead and crippled.

"You say there was a good many dogs," says Elias. "How many?"

"Maybe six or seven," says Perry.

"You know any of 'em?" says Elias.

"There was a big black hound."

"Like Pottawatomie Joe's?"

"I ain't sure," says Perry.

He was quite sure, though he hadn't really got close to the dog, but he hated to say so because he knew what that would mean. He had heard a lot of fellows grutch about Joe's dogs running wild, though no one had ever caught them running sheep before. He had heard Hoss Martin say, too, that any sheep-killing dog could be shot dead by any fellow that saw him—that was an unwritten law in the early settlements.

By that afternoon the word had gone around the neighborhood and seven or eight men, along with Elias, all carrying loaded guns, were ready to set out for Joe's cabin. Elias called to Perry to come along.

Joe was a friendly fellow and it was fairly common for his neighbors or a group of hunters to stop at the old *fort* for a drink of red-eye or an hour's chew and banter. Now he found it hard to believe that what the men were after was no josh talk at all. He called the big black hound over to him.

"Him hunting dog," he says. "No kill sheep."

"Perry saw him leadin' the pack," says Elias.

"Step up here, boy," says Ben Ewing to Perry. "Was it that black dog or not?"

Perry hesitated.

"Come on, talk up," says Elias.

"I think it was," says Perry, afraid both to talk and not to.

That took the tuck out of Pottawatomie Joe.

"Perry no tell lie," he says. "Him friend of me."

After that Ben Ewing was for shooting the dog right then and there, and the whole goddamn pack of them, too, he said. For a while Joe just sat there, stroking the back of his dog. Then he stood up and faced the men.

"You shoot dog," he says, "but me no see."

Before he could leave, though, they had to tie up the dogs. Joe called them over one by one, and the men slipped leashes around their necks and tied them to the trees. Then Joe disappeared into the woods. When the dogs saw him go, they knew something wasn't right and set up whining and howling. Some of them crouched in the grass, others groveled on their bellies beating the ground with their tails, and the big black hound kept jumping into his leash and baying like he was on fire inside.

When Perry saw what was happening, he burst out crying and Elias told him to go on home. He started through the woods and before he had gone very far, he heard some shots ring out.

Elias didn't say a word when he came home later on, and it wasn't until a week or so later that the men found out they had treed the wrong coon. Ben Ewing came riding by one afternoon and told Elias how he and Dave Manning had caught some dogs running Dave's sheep the night before, and he and Dave had lain out for them and shot two of them dead right in their tracks.

"One of 'em was a big black hound," says Ben. "By god, I'd of swore he was Pottawatomie Joe's."

"I reckon we got somethin' to make right with Joe," says Elias.

"Oh hell," says Ben, "he's only a goddamned Indian, but I reckon we'd better look out for him. He's likely to make trouble if it gets around."

For a whole week after that Uncle Perry was trying to get up enough grit to go down to see Joe. The least a fellow could have done was to tell him what had happened and how sorry he was for the whole thing. Before he ever came to that, however, Elias told him and Laura one morning that the old *fort* cabin had been burned to the ground. There was some talk that Ben Ewing and some of the other neighbors had set fire to the place, but Elias said he didn't think so. As for Uncle Perry, he was right sure that Pottawatomie Joe had done it himself.

What a feller's born or the way he smells ain't got a goddamn thing to do with the way his heart beats.

Chapter 5

How Orin Danks *lost his job teaching school, and Minot married Nancy*

Late in october of the year Uncle Perry was nine, he started his first term of school down at the little village of Mud Corners.

The call to books come late then—always a full belly before a head full of learnin'.

A few days earlier his half sister, Nancy, still keeping house for Minot and his family, had come over to see Old Leazer.

"Why not let Perry come down and stay with me this winter?" she says. "He ought to be getting some schooling and besides I get lonesome now and then for my own kin. Minot is good to me, always helping out where he can and making the children mind, but just the same a body gets lonesome."

"Well," says Leazer, "I reckon he could. We got our corn all shucked."

That was after Perry had come back from staying with Laura and Elias, and Leazer and the whole family had moved back to the farm. As for the store at Applemanberg, Old Leazer had never made a go of it, and anyway after Esther and Lissa had gotten married, Charley had come of age and gone off on his own and there was no one left on the old place.

"I promised Diadamie before she died I'd look after him, but if Minot says it's all right—"

"I've been talking it over with Minot," she says.

"Oh," says he, "you have. You ain't been a-talkin' anything else over with him, have you?"

"No," she says, her cheeks coming to a glow like a Northern Spy apple on a frosty morning in November.

"Well," says Leazer, "if you and Minot want him, it's all right with me, but I ain't payin' nothin', mind you. The boy's got to earn his keep. I ain't even got the money fer a slate."

"I was thinking he could use an old one of Lucinda's," she says.

Perry was happy as a young chip-squirrel to go along home with Nancy. Among his own kin it was Nancy who was the real miracle. She had a lot of pitch and hustle for a Harman, a sight more sense than a Tucker, and she was the only one of Old Leazer's stepchildren that ever talked up to him. It was three years earlier that Ellen Gilmore being sick, Nancy had gone to work for them, and later on, when Ellen died, she had stayed on keeping house for Minot and Granny Gilmore and the children, because that was the likely thing to do, she said. As for Minot, he was a tall fellow and broad, too, with shoulders like an ox-yoke, black hair, and a fine beard. He was just coming thirty-six the year his wife died, and many a tongue in the neighborhood busy-wagged that he and Nancy would make a fine pair.

The day after Perry moved down, Nancy washed and mended his clothes, Minot cut his hair, and the next day after that he and Minot's children trudged the mile and a quarter down to the village school.

Mud Corners wasn't much to look at in the early days but even so, Uncle Perry said, it was a mighty fine place to be from. The whole village wasn't more than a half-dozen log cabins and two or three straight-fronts, like Abar Cain's store and Captain Barry's saloon, and farther on down the street Jim Ball's blacksmith shop and the little white clapboard Baptist meeting house, and right across the street from it the new school and the red brick building Minot and the others had built to house the general store the year the *Phalanx* had flatted out.

The new schoolhouse had just been built that summer, right on the site where the older one had stood. The old one had been made of logs. Now, figuring this one would last them a spell, they had built of stone and mortar, or niggerheads and mud, as Tom Eccles put it. He was right, too. It wasn't more than a year or so afterwards that some of the older boys sitting in the back of the room began carving away at the wall with their jackknives, and before the schoolmaster came wise, they had cut a hole all the way through, big enough so they could slip out when he wasn't watching.

The old log building hadn't had a window or a chimney. To take the freeze out of a fellow's pants, Marsh told Perry, there hadn't been but an open hearth in the middle of the room. The only light, except for the hole in the roof where the smoke went out, came from a greased paper nailed to a frame which replaced the wooden door on cloudy days. The new building was twice the size of the old one and had a hearth and chimney at one end and several glass windows. Deep double desks of sawn oak, arranged in rows, took the place of the crude, hand-hewn slabs laid across wooden pegs driven in between the logs of the old building. What hadn't changed at all was the row of wooden pegs along the wall for the children's wraps, and the big one at the head of the room where the teacher hung his gad.

Lickin' and learnin' come along together; leastways they did, if the lickin' didn't come first.

They had a large school that year, though Uncle Perry couldn't remember just how many of them there were. He and Lucinda and Pete Martin, Hoss' boy, and Emery Klingerman were among the younger children. And there were a good many older boys, too, young men of fifteen and sixteen, almost fully grown, like Marsh and Buck Latta and Welt Francis and Harry Martin, Pete's older brother. The teacher that year was a fellow by the name of Orin Danks, a tall, slab-sided Yankee with legs as springy as an ash sapling and a head hot enough to use them. Many a time Uncle Perry saw him lift a fellow clean off his feet with a hefty kick in the butt.

That didn't settle well with the older boys. Their handy name for him was Ornery Danks when he wasn't hearing what they said, and sometimes when he did. They disliked Orin for slicking down his hair and polishing his boots and being courty with the womenfolks.

Orin boarded around and when he came to Minot's that winter for his spell of keep, right off there was trouble. For one thing he hadn't been there two days until anyone could see he had a shine on Nancy. He was always saying, "Yes, Miss Nancy," or "No, Miss Nancy," or "How are you this morning, Miss Nancy?" Uncle Perry said, until a fellow was wanting to kick him in the backside, only he was afraid to, and anyway it was pretty high up for a little fellow. And Nancy was nice enough to Orin, too, smiling when he spoke to her, and thanking him kindly every time he set a chair to the table or lifted up a dish.

Orin was riding a big black horse that he called Dick, and he had as fine a saddle and a pair of saddlebags as a man ever saw. It used to make Marsh right mad—he was fifteen then and willful as an unbroken gelding—to have Orin ride by him morning after morning, him sloshing along in the mud, and Orin's boots high and dry in the stirrups.

It wasn't long after Orin had come to stay at Minot's that Marsh and Buck Latta figured out a plan to make him walk to school. Orin had been staying over at Latta's on the Lima road just before he came to Minot's so the boys calculated that if they let Dick out of the barn some night, he would go back to Latta's, and they could make it look as if blacklegs had jay-hawked him.

The very next night Marsh did it. First he swore Perry to a Bible oath never to tell; then he crawled out of the window and shinnied down over the kitchen roof to the ground. When Marsh came back Perry was asleep, but the first thing he heard the next morning was Marsh himself telling Orin that the blacklegs had been there and stolen Dick.

Orin was all put out when he heard it and went around looking for him everywhere in the barn, just as if he hadn't been told Dick was gone. Then Minot saddled a couple of horses and he and Orin rode down the road to see if they could find any tracks. But they couldn't, it was too muddy being November, so they rode on down to Mud Corners, and Minot and Orin and Captain Barry and Lafe Klingerman spent all that day riding around without finding a trace of Dick at all—hide, hair, or hoof print. Come that night, they were thinking the horse was gone for sure.

"I'm sorry, Mr. Danks," says Nancy, as the men came in to wash up for supper.

"That's real kind of you, Miss Nancy," says Orin, smiling at her and helping her by setting chairs to the table and carrying over a hot kettle of corn meal mush.

"Well," says Minot, sitting down, "maybe, Mr. Danks, you'd like to stay down in the village till you get yourself another horse?"

"No, I guess I'll stay right here," says Orin.

"Just as you're a mind to," says Minot, serving up the plates.

"I like it here," says Orin, smiling at Nancy.

That was pickery and wormwood for Marsh.

"Well, Mr. Danks," he says, "I reckon tomorrow you got to walk to school like the rest of us. It's too bad to get them nice boots dirty."

When Marsh said that, Uncle Perry saw Minot look hard at him. After supper was over, he says, "Marsh, I want to talk to you."

"All right," says Marsh with a quick look at Perry.

"Marsh," Minot says, when the others had gone, "you got a hand in here somewhere. Where's Orin's horse?"

"I don't know," says Marsh. "Let him get his boots dirty; it'll do him good."

"I'm talking about Dick, Marsh," says Minot. "Where is he?"

"I reckon he might be over to Latta's," says Marsh.

"How'd he get there?" says Minot.

"I reckon he might of got loose in the barn and gone over there by himself," says Marsh.

"Did he?"

"He might of."

"Did you take him?"

"No."

"Did Buck come over and get him?"

"No."

"Are you sure he's there?" says Minot.

"No," says Marsh.

"Well," says Minot, "you find out if he's there, and if he ain't, you and Buck better find out where he is, right off, and don't set foot in the house till you bring him back here. There's a good hiding in it before you go or when you get back. What have you fellows got against Orin anyway? He's a clean young fellow. He could teach you something if you were decent."

"He's a-gettin' sweet on Nancy," says Marsh.

"What if he is?" says Minot. "We've got to use him right. He's staying here, and if he's getting fond of Nancy, that's his sorghum and hers."

"It's mine, too," says Marsh, looking hard at his father.

"Is that so?" says Minot. "Are you getting sweet on her too? Well, you'd better tend to your books and leave Nancy—"

"To you, eh?" says Marsh.

"You get going," says Minot, "and mind what I tell you. You don't come back without Dick. I said plenty and I meant what I said."

The boys had a devil's own time of it before they found him. When Marsh got to Latta's, Dick hadn't come there at all, and he and Buck spent two days riding around the country before they came across a fellow over at South Milford who told them how he had heard that a black horse had been found wandering along by himself down near La Otto. Buck and Marsh rode down there and got him, and when they brought him back to Mud Corners, the village turned out to see what was going to happen. Old Judge Carnahan made a speech, telling the boys they were liable before the law for what they had done, and Orin Danks spoke up for horsewhipping them, right then and there. The Judge and Captain Barry told him not to, for it would just make for more trouble, but Minot told him to go ahead if he was a mind to, for he couldn't be schoolmaster unless the boys respected him. Since Minot was the school director, Orin had his way. He and Lafe Klingerman tied the boys up to a sycamore tree near the schoolhouse, and Orin laid on with a horsewhip he'd brought over from the blacksmith shop.

"I'll teach you young whippersnappers a thing or two," says Orin.

But it didn't do any good, not then nor later on, ever.

That night Nancy was rubbing salve on Marsh's back where he was raw from the whipping.

"I'm sorry Mr. Danks did this to you," she says.

"Would you be sorry if I done it to him?" says Marsh.

"Certainly," she says.

"By god, I'm a-goin' to," he says. "From now on it's Marsh Gilmore agin Orin Danks."

"Don't be getting any foolish notions in your head," says Nancy. "You're too young for that."

Minot was coming into the room and heard what they said, but he didn't say a word about it, not then.

After the horsewhipping Orin moved down to Lafe's on the other side of the village, and for a spell after that when he came calling on Nancy, he got a mighty cold welcome, but he kept on coming, cockyolly as ever.

Three weeks later around Christmas time, the older boys began badgering Orin after the noon recess about a treat.

"I'm not treating anybody," says Orin. "You keep your mind on your books."

"Charley Faulk give us a treat last year," says Welt Francis.

"What he did, he did," says Orin.

"You mean you ain't treatin'?" says Buck Latta.

"Only thing I'm buying for you two fellows," says Orin, looking at Marsh and Buck, "is a bull-whip."

The next morning Marsh got up early, did his chores, and lit out for school before breakfast. When Perry and Lucinda got there, Marsh and Buck and some of the older boys were already busy boarding up the windows on the inside. Then they brought in a big pole to brace the door and sent the younger boys out to fetch wood for the fire.

"Make yourselves to home if you're a mind to," says Buck to the younger children, "but there ain't goin' to be no school today, lessen Ornery is a-treatin' us."

It wasn't long after that Orin came riding into the village and, stabling his horse over at Captain Barry's just as always, he came walking up to the schoolhouse. The boys could see he wasn't thinking about what was up till he tried the door.

"Hold on there, Mr. Danks," says Marsh. "You ain't comin' in here lessen you're a-goin' to treat us."

"Open the door," says Orin. "I'm the schoolmaster here."

"The schoolmaster says fer to open up the door," says Buck, laughing. "Why don't you stove it in with your head, Ornery? Here's what we want, and you ain't a-gettin' in without fetchin' it along, come a whole week of Sundays."

With that he shoved a paper through the crack under the door on which Marsh had written down: 1 pk. apples, 1 pk. candy, 1 gal. whiskey.

"Not while I'm teaching here," says Orin.

"All right, Ornery," says Marsh, "then you ain't."

One or two of the fellows were for opening the door then, because they were afraid of Orin, but Marsh and Buck kept them from doing it. Orin himself kept kicking and banging at the door, now threatening to horsewhip them all, and then again begging them to open up, saying he wouldn't do anything to any of them. But the boys had their dander up. They just sat there all day. Along in the afternoon the older boys began to slip the younger ones out, one or two at a time, and send them home. As for every fellow over twelve, he had to help, Marsh and Buck said, for they were staying there till they died, lessen they got what was written on the paper.

When Perry and Lucinda got home and Minot wanted to know what was keeping Marsh, they told him. He'd see about it in the morning, he said, and the next day he came down to the schoolhouse with them. Orin was there trying to stove in the door with a long pole.

"What are they asking for?" say Minot.

Orin showed him the paper.

"Buy 'em the candy and apples," says Minot, "but no whiskey."

"I'm not buying anything," says Orin. "I'm running this school."

"All right," says Minot, "you run it."

Then he called out to Marsh.

"Marsh," he says, "I want to talk to you."

"What d'you want?" says Marsh, calling back through the door.

"Are you hungry?" says Minot.

"No," says Marsh, "the boys slipped out last night and brung us enough to last a week."

"You got firewood?" says Minot.

"Plenty," says Marsh.

"Well," says Minot, turning to Orin, "I hear say there's a way to get a coon out of a hollow tree, but seeing as how you're running things, I reckon it's your coon."

And with that he walked across the road to Abar Cain's store, where a lot of fellows had gathered to see the fun.

That whole morning Orin kept trying to get them to open

up, or to break in through the door or windows when they weren't watching, but it didn't do any good except to amuse the fellows over at the store who were laughing at him. Along about noon he came across the road and bought a peck of apples and a big bag of candy.

"Here you are," he says. "Open up."

"What d'you got?" says Marsh, taking a board from the window and peering out.

"What you asked for," says Orin.

"Where's the whiskey?" says Marsh.

"That I'm not buying," says Orin.

"Then you ain't a-gettin' in," shouts Marsh, putting back the board.

"They want the whiskey, too," says Orin to Minot, coming across the road again.

"You won't buy them whiskey," says Minot, "not while you're teaching for me."

"What did you mean this morning when you said there was one way to get them out?"

"Well," says Minot, "if I was running the school like you say you are, I'd put a board over the top of the chimney and smoke 'em out."

As soon as it came dark, that's what Orin tried to do, but while he was still on the roof, the boys caught on, stole outside, and Marsh caught him by the legs as he was sliding back down. Before Orin knew what it was all about, a dozen other fellows had grabbed hold of him, pulled him down, and were sitting on top of him.

"What'll we do with him now?" says Buck.

"Duck him in Judge Carnahan's pond," says Marsh.

And that's what they did. They had quite a battle getting him down to the pond, Orin kicking and swearing every step of the way, but they finally got there and while the others held him, Marsh chopped a hole in the ice.

"All right, fellers, give us a hand," says Marsh, and with that they threw him in.

They pulled him back out in a minute, but he was that cold there was no fight left in him, and he lit out for Lafe Klingerman's. Then the boys went home themselves.

Minot himself didn't find out what had really happened until the next day when Lizzie Klingerman came up to see Nancy. On her way out through the kitchen, she told Minot the whole story. Orin was sick in bed with a cold, she said, but he had sent a message to Nancy that would turn any young girl's head squirrel-dizzy.

Minot was right sore when he heard what the boys had done, but even then he wasn't sure who was to blame. Any fellow ought to know that was no way to handle boys.

"Marsh," he says, "you're going right down to Klingerman's and apologize to Orin. When you get back, I'll go down and tell Orin Danks he ain't teaching any more. I'll get Charley Faulk to finish out the term."

"Goddamn me," says Marsh, "that'll be the hardest day's work I ever done."

When Marsh got down to Lafe's, Lafe showed him into the bedroom where Orin was sitting up in bed getting over his cold.

"I reckon I'm sorry," says Marsh.

"It's too damn late to be sorry," says Orin. "The day I get out of here, I'm giving you the best double-twisted thrashing you ever had in your life."

"I figger not," says Marsh, standing his ground.

"Oh, you don't," says Orin.

"No," says Marsh. "Pap says you ain't teachin' our school no more."

"Your father says that?" says Orin. "Well, by god, I won't be missing any of you except Nancy, and you can tell your pap I've asked her to come along with me."

"She'll be givin' you the mitten, I reckon," says Marsh.

"Is that so?" says Orin.

"Yep," says Marsh. "She's a-marryin' Pap."

"That's a goddamn lie," says Orin.

"Is that so?" says Marsh. "By god, she and him's been sleepin' together fer over a month already."

He knew it was a lie all right, Marsh said, and that it wasn't the thing to say, but he was that mad he didn't care. When Minot came to find out about it, though, Marsh got the best hiding his father ever gave him. But it came to be true in less than a month after that, for Minot and Nancy got married late in January. Minot laughed about the whole thing many a time when he came to tell it afterwards, Uncle Perry said.

About a week later Charley Faulk came down from Mongoquinong and school took up again.

"I hear say you got a new stepmother," says Charley to Marsh. "She's a fine woman, Nancy."

"That she is," says Marsh, "but the thing I don't fancy is that after I got shut of Ornery, she took Pap instead of waitin' fer me."

"From now on, Marsh Gilmore," says Charley, "you got a call to book learning. I figure you're just a mite too big for your own britches."

And that was so, all right.

But it's a scraggly colt that don't now and then break his halter.

[54]

Chapter 6

HOW UNCLE PERRY *stayed with Minot and Nancy,*

and the story of the two bear cubs

THE WAY-UP best time he ever had in his life, Uncle Perry said, was the summer he was ten and got to stay on with Minot and Nancy.

Livin' at Leazer's was like the ague—all chills and fever and a back full of blisters.

At first, though, Old Leazer had been a hard one to dicker with.

"Perry's a mean little devil," he says on the day the school term ended at Mud Corners and he had come down to fetch him, "but he's old enough, I figger, to help pick stone."

"He's old enough all right," says Minot, "but he's a small-made fellow and light for his age."

"He could help Adelia out a lot around the house iffen he was a mind to," says Leazer, "but last summer he was gettin' that mean she couldn't do a thing with him."

That was true enough, Uncle Perry said. After he had come back to Leazer's farm from staying with Laura and Elias up at

Lexington, the Widow Tidrick had ridden tail on him day and night. If it wasn't one thing, it was a fistful of others. All day long he had worked in the fields alongside the older boy, John, and Old Leazer, and when he'd come up to the house that tired he'd have kinkles in his legs, he still had to fetch and carry for the old lady. If it hadn't been an armful of wood or a bucket of water, it had been eggs from the hen house, or a crock of apple butter from the basement, or the kitchen ashes had to be carried out to the hopper, or a ham brought in from the smokehouse—so that sometimes he'd never even got to sit down to eat until the others were all done and he was too tired. He had got to paying no attention to her at all except when Old Leazer was around, and then he had been afraid not to, and when she had taken to shouting at him, he had shouted right back. A fellow couldn't win in the end, though, for either Old Leazer heard him—or heard about it—as soon as he set foot in the house.

"There he sets eatin' off his own head when we ain't got enough fer our own children," Perry could remember her saying. "Ask him to do a lick of work around here and he'll hightail it outside, or likely as not tell you to shut your clapper right to your face."

"By god, I'll tend to him, Adelia," Old Leazer would reply, going over and lifting the stove lid to spit into the fire and then picking up the hickory poker.

But Minot wasn't for giving up easily.

"Better let the boy stay on with us for a while," he says.

"You got a houseful now," says Old Leazer.

"That we have," says Minot, "but I reckon Nancy can manage and she's his own sister."

"Well," says Old Leazer, getting down to bottom facts, "I figger the little bugger's old enough now to earn more 'n his keep."

"No," says Minot, roused up, "that he ain't. And if he stays with me, I ain't figuring on what he can earn but what he needs."

And that settled it.

What a fellow really needs is something he can't earn at all, as Uncle Perry came to find out. Minot could be right stern when he had a call to be and mighty gruff sometimes, but nothing on two legs and human was a stranger to him. How come a pretty piece of calico like Nancy ever took a shine to an old plow-jogger like him, Minot always said he couldn't figure out, but he was knee-bending thankful that she did. There was room enough for all of them in the little white clapboard house, and even for the likely more to come. Lucinda could help out Nancy with the housework, while Lydia could give Granny Gilmore a hand with the younger children, Albert and Jenny and Frederick. There would be Marsh and Perry to do the chores and help out with the farming. A day's work was the way to keep them happy, Minot said, and if they boned to it, it would all come to a mighty big count—five fingers to a hand.

As for Uncle Perry, every morning that summer he got up at sunrise and he rarely got to bed before dark. His first chore in the morning, while the sun was still low on the horizon and the earth was cool and quiet, was to bring in the cows for the morning milking. Many a time that spring he ran all the way to the meadow to rouse up the sleeping cows, so that he could warm his feet by standing on the spot where they had lain. Minot and Nancy had bought him a pair of shoes the winter before, but they were the first ones he'd ever had and he was that proud he never wore them except on Sunday. The winter he had stayed at the Kingsleys, Laura had taught him to milk a cow and milking was the second of his daily chores. After the milking he and Lucinda fed the calves. Minot had shown him how you taught a newborn calf to drink from a pail by holding its head down with one hand while you gave it two fingers of the other hand to suck, until it caught on that milk would run up the throat as well as down. Sometimes the little fellows were stubborn, and one morning when a little Durham bull butted the pail and slopped him with the milk, Perry got his mad up, beating and kicking him until the bellowing of the calf brought Minot running into the barn.

"What's going on here?" says Minot.

"He's a devil," says Perry.

"Maybe he is," says Minot, grabbing Perry by the arm and setting him down hard, "but he's got a call to be, and you ain't. You won't learn him none by beating him, and I won't stand for a fellow abusing an animal. You'd better mind that."

That was a Monday morning new thing, and Minot was that sharp Perry didn't forget, not for a long time.

Learning to drive oxen was another thing. Minot had five yoke then, each one in his own pair and all five yoke in a team, pulling the bar-share plow. Perry's job would be running alongside, carrying the big whip. But you used the butt end a lot more than you did the lash. The butt end, held up lengthwise alongside the nose, would gee or haw the lead yoke a lot better than shouting and lashing.

"That's a lazy fellow's way of doing it," says Minot. "You take it right easy and they'll all pull together."

That spring Perry and Lucinda dibble-dropped corn, a full twenty acres, while Marsh drove the oxen in the marker to lay out the checkrows and Minot came along behind with another yoke, pulling the leveler and covering up the seeds. It was fun working with Lucinda. She was a rosy-cheeked, bright-eyed little sunbonnet, chirk and chipper as a wren, and, though a full year younger than Perry, she made a mighty good yoke-fellow. Later on in haying, Nancy and Perry and Lucinda raked-after and cocked, while Marsh and Minot swung the scythes, and in the wheat harvest they were all busy from sunup to sundown raking cradle-swaths into bundles for the binders and setting the sheaves into stooks.

When Perry wasn't out in the field, he was busy helping Nancy and Lucinda around the house, chopping wood for a fire in the bakehouse, carrying water for the family washing, fetching in the kindling, feeding chickens and gathering eggs, carrying out swill for slopping the pigs—all an endless routine of family chores, though there were times, too, for games and play and a half hour's rest in the shade with Minot laughing and joking with them or spinning a yarn maybe of life in the early days.

Bettermost were the days when all the family worked together like at berry picking or at boiling Indian sugar in the spring. Cooking Indian sugar came early when the nights were still cold and frosty, but the day sun warm enough to melt the snow and thaw out the ground till it got muddy underfoot. The first time Perry came to know about that was when Minot and Marsh went out to cut the elders. They brought home a big bundle of them, and then at night after supper, Minot and the boys, sitting on the deacon bench in front of the fire, cut them into four-inch pieces and cleaned out the pith. The next day they took the auger to the woods, drilled holes in the sugar maples, and plugged in the elder pipes. Then Marsh yoked the oxen to the drag-sled, and Perry and Lucinda went along to hang the buckets. After that came the work for everybody, day after day, and many a time all night, too.

Perry and Marsh drove the oxen, emptying the sap from the buckets into hogsheads on the drag-sled. Minot cut the logs and rustled up the wood for the fire, while Nancy and

Lucinda watched the boiling sap in the arch-kettles, adding more when it was called for, and brought out the food for the hungry menfolks.

Once the whole thing started, the sap dripped and the kettles boiled all night long. Marsh and Minot took turns watching, while Perry and Lucinda went home to do the chores and hurried back the first chance they got. The warm sun was as good a tonic as molasses in the spring. When it came time for sugaring off, all the family would stay out. It was a real party then. For a while the grownups would be busy, stirring and testing the kettles, setting them off the fire and sometimes back on again, pouring the heavy syrup out to cool, while the rest of them were busy watching—and what was a lot harder—keeping out of the way. There would come a time, though, when all was ready. Then the children, each of them with a half-dozen newly gathered woodchips from the choppings, would take their turns dipping them into the warm syrup and laying them out on stumps or stones to cool.

While the chips cooled, Marsh and Perry would build up the fire and they'd all sit down to eat buttered corn bread and cold, sliced turkey or fried ham, and Granny Gilmore, holding the youngest boy, Frederick, in her arms, would tell them a story. After that the chips would be ready and each one would take his own, licking off the hardened taffy or biting into the sweet brown sugar, still warm. Each one from his store of half a dozen would have plenty left for morning, or for the hoard he'd save, all his own, and store away down in the cool cellar for later on. Then Minot would send Marsh with the oxen and the stone-boat to carry home the children, tired and sleepy, but happy as a family of woodchucks and glad to be alive.

There was time, too, for hunting and fishing when a friendly thundershower broke off the field work. Squirrels were so thick in the woodlands and grainfields that you shot them all summer and by autumn long strings of smoked squirrel hams hung in the chimney corner. Quail and partridge were plentiful, too. For fishing there was Turkey Creek a mile and a half away, where Perry and Lucinda sometimes whiled away summer afternoons luring pan fish for the kitchen spider. Minot was a good provider. "What the Lord sends, a fellow takes—" he would tell them, "the year has a wide mouth and a mighty big belly."

One day after Perry and Lucinda had been picking up field corn all week, Minot took them along with him on a hunting trip to the hilly region north of Pretty Lake. For a while that afternoon they stayed close to Minot—Perry minding he'd been there once before—running to pick up the wild turkey or grouse as it fell, or occasionally when Minot permitted it, Perry shouldering the heavy muzzleloader and pulling the trigger himself. Soon they had more game than they could carry, and Minot cached it at the edge of a fire-scald, asking them to stay there and keep an eye on the game.

The fire-scald was a tangled mass of logs and brush, overgrown with blackberry briars, grapevines, whipsedge, and morning glory. They played hide and seek, chased squirrels around the logs, and, sticks in hand, still-hunted. Across the fire-scald near the southern edge, they came upon two furry black little fellows tumbling like a couple of puppies in an open space among the fallen tree trunks. Neither of them had ever really seen a bear, but that made it no more than even, for the cubs, likely enough, had never seen a child.

Perry and Lucinda watched them for a minute or two before they figured out to grab them. They worked up slowly, stopping dead still when the cubs seemed to notice, until they got within reach length. Perry got a firm hold on his, he said, grabbing him around the throat, and though he got scratched some, he had no trouble hanging on. Lucinda caught hers by one of its rear legs, and the little fellow put up a scrap, biting and scratching, and finally squealing like a stuck pig. When that happened, they heard a deep grunt over in the windfall, and quicker than a fellow could tell it afterwards, they saw the mother bear come rumbling and tumbling up over the logs, snapping and snarling.

Lucinda made for the nearest tree and shinnied up the slender trunk like a wildcat, but Perry held on a minute too long. Before he could move, he felt the first rush of the mother as she came against him, knocking him down. Then he scrambled away on all fours and dove headfirst into a big hollow log, pushing and wiggling himself along till he got his feet well inside.

When Lucinda got up the tree and looked around, she couldn't see Perry at all and figured the bear had eaten him for sure. The bear was still snapping and snarling at the open end of the log and crawling over and around it, grunting and growling. She let out a call for help loud enough so a fellow could have heard it halfway to Mud Corners, and in a minute or two Minot came up running. When he saw the bear, he stopped short, raised his gun and fired, and the bear fell dead. Then he found Lucinda and got her down out of the tree.

"Where's Perry?" he shouts.

"He's inside," says Lucinda.

"Inside!" says Minot. "Inside where?"

"Inside the bear," she says. "She et him up."

"Oh God! No!" says Minot, running over to the bear again.

When he couldn't find anything of Perry at all, not even a piece of his breeches or a shoe, he knew the bear couldn't have got him, and he and Lucinda began to look around. Perry heard them call and tried to wiggle back out, but he was stuck fast. He called out then and in a minute Minot found him.

"God Almighty," says Minot, "here he is."

He reached in and got hold of his feet, but it took him ten minutes to work Perry back out. He hadn't been hurt at all except where he'd bruised himself crawling in, but he was covered from head to foot with log rot and dirt.

After that they caught the cubs once more—there was no use letting them starve to death, Minot said—and no hunting party in history ever came home in greater glory. There they were with thirteen wild turkeys, more than two-dozen grouse, a three-hundred-pound bear, and two live cubs.

It was funny the way it all happened, and many a time afterwards, like at the apple-paring down at Luke Babcock's or in at Abar's store or over at Jim Ball's blacksmith shop, people talked and laughed about it, just the way they did when they told about Lafe Klingerman and Minot and how Hoss won the first election, or about the time Hiram Brooks got them to build the big house. That was part of the fun, too, the way the whole neighborhood loved to hear and tell a good story.

About a week after the hunt Luke Babcock held the big apple-paring bee and Minot and Hoss and Seth Talbot and Abar and a dozen other fellows were sitting around the kitchen, peeling apples with their pocket knives, letting the long curling rinds dangle down between their knees till they fell in a heap on the floor, having give-and-take talk, and stopping now and then for another drink of cider as Mattie Babcock and Marsh and Perry and Lucinda refilled the cups. As fast as they peeled the apples, the men passed them on to the children, who carried them over to the kitchen table where the womenfolks sat coring and quartering them before

[*63*]

they sulphured them down in the big crocks, ready for pies and applesauce and boiling apple butter later on. That night there was a lot of talking and laughing about the two bear cubs.

" 'Inside.' 'Inside where?' 'Inside the bear. She et him up!' " says Minot, telling them the whole thing once more. "And then I found him there in the hollow log, stuck tight as a glut in a railcut."

"How did it feel in there, young feller?" says Lizzie Klingerman, wiping her eyes with her apron, she had been laughing that hard.

"Well," says Perry, not seeing why it was that funny at the time, "I reckon a feller could have choked to death in there."

"That he could of," says Minot, reaching over and giving him a playful cobb on the arm.

"Then I'd of been dead," says Perry.

"Well," says Minot, still laughing, "maybe you were and you're born again. By golly, this time you came feet first."

Minot was only joking, Perry knew, but it came to him a long time later that what he said was right. Staying at Minot's he had been born again. A yoke of oxen couldn't have dragged him away from there if Old Leazer hadn't come down to fetch him and hired him out to his stepbrother, Isaac, for pay.

It all comes to a lot more 'n a mess of victuals, when a feller's feet feel at home under the kitchen table.

Chapter 7

How Minot *killed three deer with one shot, and they held the first election in Milford township*

Minot always pulled his trigger on a good eye, but nobody likely would have sworn him to be the best shot in the early neighborhood.

Late in the spring of 1858 Lafe Klingerman killed a bear and that put him in the running, but everybody knew that Hoss Martin could outshoot any of them if he was sober or had a mind to.

Late in the spring of 1858 Lafe Klingerman killed a bear and Perry could remember seeing as many as thirteen wild turkeys hanging in the smokehouse, each one with the skin on its back split open like a ripe pod from falling out of a high tree—they were that fat. As for Hoss, he never squinted over the sights of his gun if he was sober lessen something dropped. But when he was drunk, he always said, he saw double and shot between them.

Drunk or sober, though, it was Hoss who won the first election ever held in Milford township—at least that's the way Uncle Perry remembered it. Just when Perry first came to know the full story, he couldn't rightly say, and more than likely it had all been patchwork, some from here and some from there, just the way it is for any fellow growing up.

Part and parcel of what a feller is, is the story of his neighborhood—even what came to happen before he was ever born.

There were only three offices in a township then, and that of roadmaster was the most important. The other two were justice of the peace and constable. The office of justice would be more apt to go to an older man, like Ephraim Carnahan, who knew the law and could read the Bible well enough for a man to take an oath on it. It was up to him to settle a dispute over a line fence, or figure out the law and equity when a fellow's pigs broke into a neighbor's corn patch and got themselves locked up in the barnyard keep, or the amount of legal and personal damage involved in a black eye or a broken tooth.

It was the constable who would serve the warrant or make the arrest, and keep the peace while the justice was holding court in his farmhouse kitchen or in Captain Barry's saloon or in the Mud Corners schoolhouse.

It was the roadmaster's job to look after the township roads, lay out the tax money for their upkeep, or call out township labor for rebuilding a stretch of corduroy after a spring thaw, and perhaps even to lay out a new road, where he would have the final say-so in shutting out or taking over a winding trail through the woods as a public thoroughfare. Being roadmaster was no job for a plow-jogger. It took a lot of pitch and hustle to do right, and see right done, by everyone in the neighborhood.

The first election in any township was a mighty big thing.

Up in Springfield township, where the land had been settled longer and they'd been holding elections for six or seven years already, the job of roadmaster was likely to go to a well-to-do farmer or perhaps a village storekeeper. In the township of Milford, just being organized, it was still odds even whether it might not be the best hunter or the heaviest drinker, for they were the fellows most talked about. Minot was no drinker, but he would have been a likely choice if it hadn't been for Lafe and his bear.

At the time Lafe was living on Judge Carnahan's place just north of the village of Mud Corners on the Turkey Creek road. Early that spring he had gone out hunting along the ridge down by Wirt's mill. As he was coming up to a fallen log about two foot through, he saw what he took to be a wild hog standing alongside just behind it with his head down, rooting in the ground.

Just as Lafe was swinging the old muzzleloader to his shoulder, his right foot cracked a twig. Quicker than a man could say Blackball Schemerhorn, what Lafe had taken to be a wild hog rose on its hind legs and looked him in the face—a full-grown bear. Lafe was pretty scared, but he came to about as soon as the bear did, and seeing he had his gun pointing right at him, he fired broadside.

For a moment Lafe thought he had hit him, for the bear dropped to his feet; then he saw he hadn't, or, if he had, it didn't faze the bear any, for he started lumbering right up over the log towards him. Lafe dropped his gun and began to scratch gravel out of there. He had a couple of rods start on the bear and going downhill it was slipshuck easy. When he got to the bottom, the bear was still coming on, and Lafe started up the next rise. It tuckered him out going uphill, and halfway up he looked back and saw the bear was gaining on him. Then he remembered he had heard Stiles Gilmore say that a bear could run uphill as fast as he could down, and Lafe got scared clear down to his backside.

He made a long turn going downhill again and up on the other side, back towards the place they had started from, thinking with all his might, what could a man do. Halfway up the ridge he thought he was done for, but he looked back once again like a fellow will even when he knows it's all over with him. Then he stopped dead still, for the bear wasn't following him at all any more. Back down in the hollow the bear was turning round and round all by himself, and in a minute or two he just lay down as if he was all tired out. Keeping a weather-eye out, Lafe worked around to where he had dropped his gun, reloaded it, and started down the hill. When he got near enough, he aimed carefully and pulled the trigger. The bear didn't move at all, and so Lafe knew he was dead.

From that time on Lafe thought he was the whole team and the dog under the wagon, leastways he did till he ran into Hoss one day down in Captain Barry's saloon at Mud Corners.

"I hear say you killed a bear," says Hoss.

"That I done," says Lafe. "Shot him down by Wirt's mill."

"Shot him?" says Hoss.

"Sure thing," says Lafe.

"That's not the way I heard it," says Hoss.

"It ain't?" says Lafe.

"No," says Hoss, "the way I heard it, a fellow couldn't figure out whether you shot him or just run him to death."

Even then Lafe felt pretty good about it, till Minot shot his three deer with one shot come that November. It was a god's fact, all right, though no one might have believed it, if it had been anyone but Minot.

Minot's word was as good as countin' a mare's teeth, come any time a-tall.

The night before he did it there had been a heavy spit-snow, and Minot must have left his house before daylight, for it wasn't more than ten o'clock when he came back by Captain Barry's saloon with the three deer lying on the bob-sled behind him. He had been driving along the road down south of Alzamon Black's when all of a sudden two does and a buck came out of the brush and crossed the road in front of him. It took him a minute to bring his gun around, but he got a fair shot at the buck, though he missed him. Minot turned the team into the woods and followed, but it was difficult to find lane enough between the trees to drive through. Finally he came to a clearing back of Alzamon's place and was tying up his team to see if he could find their tracks again, when the three deer came walking into the open as unconcerned as a bee in a privy. He grabbed his gun and fired, just as the buck, throwing back his head, made a leap that shot him out of the clearing.

After tying his horses, he began following the deer on foot, the tracks leading off towards the east as if they were heading for the thick tamarack swamp east of Pretty Lake. Minot followed for quite a spell and was about ready to give up, since he was getting too far away from his team, when he saw he was coming to another clearing he hadn't known was there at all. He worked his way carefully from tree to tree without making any noise in the deep snow, and when he got near enough, he could make out the head and shoulders of a buck standing behind a high ridge of snow-covered logs well towards the other side of the clearing.

This time he calculated not to miss. He took his time, crawling in on his hands and knees behind a big log, bigger by a foot and a half of soft snow on top of it, no more than twenty yards away from the buck, still standing there dead still. Minot couldn't see more of him than his head and the

[69]

ridge of brown hair between his shoulders, but he figured about where the heart would have to be, and fired.

The buck jumped high into the air and crashed into the brush.

"By golly," says Minot, "by that time I thought there was a hex on me."

Reloading his gun, he started across the clearing. When he came to the place where the buck had disappeared, he saw blood on the snow and the tracks of three deer. Ten yards farther on, he found the buck down on his forelegs and when he listened, he could hear the others crashing through the brush on ahead. He waited his time till he could slip in with his knife and stick the buck, pig-fashion. Then he started tracking the others. Before he had gone very far, he could see one of them was bleeding, and less than a quarter of a mile farther on he found a doe lying down in the snow. He bled her and went on. Then he saw a third one was bleeding, too, and in less than thirty minutes he came upon her where she had stumbled into a thicket, dead.

"I was plumb weak," says Minot, "I was that dumbfounded. I never even saw those two doe when I fired."

"Three deer," says Lafe, letting go half a pint of tobacco juice against the red-hot stove in Captain Barry's saloon, "a buck and two doe, all with one load of buckshot? Not even old Nick hisself could of done that lessen the angels come ridin' in on the horns."

It was less than two weeks later that the election for Milford township was held over at Cochran's Corners in Colonel Cochran's inn. About noon Lafe came riding by Minot's place on the way over.

"You goin' to the votin'?" says Lafe.

"I am," says Minot.

"Come along then," says Lafe. "I reckon it's you or me fer roadmaster."

"I don't figure it that way," says Minot.

"Why not?" says Lafe. "It's my bear agin your deer."

"That's no call for a fellow to be elected roadmaster," says Minot. "I'm voting for Luke Babcock myself."

When they arrived at Cochran's Corners, there were about a dozen men in the yard shooting mark and a dozen or so more inside drinking whiskey. Old Judge Carnahan was inspector for the election and he was inside getting things ready for the voting. Lafe got himself a good drink of red-eye to warm up and then he came outside.

"What you fellers shootin' at?" he says.

"Nail head," says Captain Barry, pointing to the corner of the old log cabin that had been built for his first house by Colonel Cochran when he came to the township in '32, "fourth log from the bottom, and, by gum, it ain't no bear."

"By god," says Lafe, "I can see it iffen you can. And I'll lay you a keg of whiskey I can outshoot you six-ways-fer-Sunday."

"Or anybody here?" asks Abar Cain.

"Man or jackass," says Lafe.

"It's a bet," says Captain Barry.

"Shoot up," says Abar.

There never come a time Abar Cain wasn't spit-thirsty, leastways not when he wasn't payin' fer it.

Lafe swung his gun to his shoulder; then he stopped and looked at the crowd.

"I say," he says, "how about you fellers electin' me roadmaster when I done it?"

"He's a-weanin' his colt before the old mare's bred," laughs Tom Eccles.

"I'm voting for Minot myself," says Captain Barry, solemn-like and slow.

"What fer?" says Joe Foos, spitting on the ground hard. He didn't like Captain Barry. "It was an accident if he done it a-tall."

"I'm voting for Minot," says Luke Babcock. "What he says he done, he done, and I'll take his word against Lafe's come rain or pitchforks, tines down."

"Hold on," says Hezekiah Butterfield, getting riley.

For a minute it looked like a fight sure enough, and many a right arm was aching to let go, but Captain Barry was a quick thinker when he had a call to be.

"Easy there," he says, "Lafe and I got a bet on here."

"Say," says Luke, "I got the trigger. Let's get Minot out here and let the best feller win."

With that he went inside and brought Minot out by the arm.

"Here's the feller that killed three deer with one shot," says Luke, "and, by god, I'll take his word fer it. I see them deer myself."

"By god," says Lafe, "when I kill a bear I shoot him myself. Ain't no angels a-workin' fer me."

Minot didn't hold with gaming or swearing and was for turning away from the whole crowd, when Hezekiah Butterfield calls out, "Good thing Minot got up too early that mornin' fer to take anybody along."

That made Minot mad. "Well," he says, "you fellows are pretty smart. I can shoot with any man here if there's a call to."

"I got a keg of red-eye on it," says Lafe.

"You fellows know I don't drink," says Minot.

"Well," says Luke, "I'll tell you what. If you win, we'll elect you roadmaster of Milford township, won't we, fellers?"

"Sure we will," yells a dozen of them, waiting to see the fun.

"That's fair enough, Minot," says Luke, "you can't woosh out now."

When Minot saw there was nothing else for him to do, he took his stand, raised the muzzleloading rifle to his shoulder and fired. His shot came a bullet width nearer to the nail than Captain Barry's.

"You got to be shootin' some, Lafe, to beat that," says Joe Foos.

But Lafe was just drunk enough to be lucky. His shot was on the other side and a little high, but it came nearer than Minot's by a knife blade.

"By god," says Luke, when they looked at the target, "he done it all right."

Lafe felt mighty numerous. "You can buy me that red-eye right now, Captain Barry," he says. "And don't forget, fellers, I'm a-countin' on your votes inside."

For a minute it looked as if the shindy was all over. Many a fellow there was against Lafe and didn't think he was the fellow for the job, but a bet was a bet, and it was made fair and square. Captain Barry himself was pretty sober as if he were sorry about the whole thing. Then he says, "All right, Lafe." And with that the crowd began to follow them inside.

When they came around the corner of the house and up onto the porch who should they see, standing at the bar drinking, but Hoss Martin himself.

"Hold on, Lafe!" says Captain Barry. "We ain't done shooting yet!"

[73]

"What's up, Captain?" says Hoss, coming out to meet the men.

"We've been shooting a little," says Captain Barry, "and Lafe was betting he was a better shot 'n you be."

"What are you doin' down here?" says Lafe. "You ain't a voter in Milford township."

It was a fact, too. Hoss lived over on the Turkey Creek road a mile and a half north of Mud Corners, and the new township line came through right this side of his house.

"Oh," says Hoss, catching on quick-like and winking at the crowd. "I was thinkin' of turnin' circuit preacher and I'm out gettin' used to the saddle. I saw you fellows here and I thought I'd rest a spell and have a drink or two."

"Right this way for the shootin'," says Captain Barry, taking Hoss by the arm.

"Hold on," says Lafe, "I wasn't bettin' agin Hoss."

"Hoss is here, ain't he?" says Captain Barry. "You said anybody here."

"That's what he said," says Luke. "Now let him prove it."

When Lafe saw he couldn't pig-twist out of it, he did some trigger-thinking for himself.

"Well, Hoss," he says, "just to show there's no hard feelin', let's grease the wheels before we go."

"Sure," says Hoss.

And before Captain Barry could stop them, they were back inside at the bar.

"Have another," says Lafe, when the glasses were empty.

"Sure thing," says Hoss, drinking up again. "Now you have one on me."

"Fair pitchin'," says Lafe, laughing to see how easy it was.

But it was worrying Captain Barry. "Hold on, Hoss," he says. "Let's get the shootin' done. You can drink afterwards."

"No," says Hoss. "Goddamn me, a drink for a drink. Here Lafe, have another one."

When they had emptied their glasses once more, they moved out into the yard with everyone crowding around them.

"All right," says Hoss. "Now what you shooting at?"

"Nail head, fourth log from the bottom," says Captain Barry, pointing careful-like.

"Iffen you can't see it, you can't shoot at it," says Lafe, so drunk the whole cabin was moving up and down before his eyes.

"I can see it," says Hoss, taking his stand, rubbing his chin with his palm, and wiping his hand on his trousers. "I can see it."

Then he raised his gun, easy-like and slow, and laughing a little he says, "Look out!"

When they found out what he had done, they broke loose, shouting and whooping as the Indians had done at Len Appleman's store-raising when he gave them a keg of whiskey for their work. Hoss' bullet had driven the old square nail head in a quarter of an inch and split off on both sides of it.

"Godalmighty!" yells Luke. "He done it! He done it! Let's elect Hoss here for roadmaster. Huzza!"

"Huzza!" yells Captain Barry. "Huzza!"

Then a lot of fellows began joining in. "Huzza! Huzza! Huzza for Hoss Martin! Hoss Martin for roadmaster!"

"Goddamn me," says Hoss, "that's better 'n I was trying to!"

It didn't make any difference then whether Hoss was living in Milford township or not. Many a man was that drunk and befuddled what with all the shouting and the slapping of backs, he couldn't mind where Hoss was living. All they knew was that he'd won the shooting.

"Come on in, men," calls out Judge Carnahan from the porch. "Come on in and do your voting."

"Come on," says Captain Barry. "Vote for Hoss!"

When Minot saw what was happening, he knew it wouldn't be right that way.

"Hold on, fellows!" he says. "Hold on a minute! I didn't come here to be elected. But you can't elect Hoss. He ain't living in this township. Let's forget the shooting now and vote for some fellow that can do the job. Let's elect Luke Babcock."

"Huzza for Hoss Martin," says Captain Barry, brushing Minot aside.

"Huzza," says Lafe. "Minot's a-saltin' the cow to catch the calf. I'll tell you what, fellers; there's a drink of red-eye fer every feller votin' for Hoss Martin."

After that there was no way of stopping them at all. When they came to counting the tally afterwards, sure enough, Hoss was elected twenty-six to two.

"Sure it's an election," says old Judge Carnahan, when he found out what they had done. He was mad from his side-bar whiskers clear down to his boot tops. "Sure it's an election. An election is an election. What the men of this township vote in, let no man put asunder."

But it wasn't so bad, as it worked out in the end.

"Goddamn me," says Hoss, when he'd sobered up, "I'm the roadmaster of Springfield township. I'm that now. Goddamn me," he says to old Judge Carnahan, "I reckon I'd better put in Minot for my deputy."

And that's how it came to be.

Chapter 8

How THEY BUILT *the big house, and Maggie Cooper came to take off her breeches*

W<small>HEN</small> MINOT and Hoss and Hiram Brooks and the others came to organize the *La Grange County Phalanx,* Maggie Cooper had been wearing breeches for more than ten years then already—that is, every day except Sunday. On the Lord's own day Maggie pulled off her breeches, slipped on a long, black horsehair skirt and came walking down to the Mud Corners meeting house, a front-pew, hard-shell Baptist.

A dozen years earlier, on the way to Indiana with a yoke of oxen in a fore-and-aft, Bill Cooper had died. Maggie had carried the body to the bury-hole, pulled on his boots and breeches, and picked up the bull-whip. She hadn't laid the whip down since, not as far as some fellows could see, and that's why some of the men were against asking her to join the *Phalanx.*

It was a hardpan, rock-bottom question. In between the farm of Lew Shingle, where they were figuring on building the big *Phalanx* house, and the land belonging to Seth Talbot, lay the hundred and sixty acres owned by Maggie. If the *Association* could have that land, it would give them a solid domain of over a section, as well as some outlying farms, and the water rights up and down Turkey Creek. Minot himself was for asking Maggie to come in, but Lew and Hoss were dead set against it.

"It's a right good piece of land," says Lew, "but I don't relish that snapper on her tongue any."

"She's been wearing the britches for a long time," says Hoss, "and I reckon she ain't likely to take 'em off."

"Well," says Dr. Hiram Brooks, "the way I see it, the men have been driving a long time now and the linch pins still keep dropping out."

Uncle Perry never came to know Hiram, he said, but from what he heard say, Hiram must have been as smart a man as ever read a book; though the minute he'd started talking about equal rights for women, Lew figured he'd read one too many. Hiram was a tall, scraggly-looking fellow with a face plain as your fist except for his beard, which he never trimmed at all, and a deep, lantern-like light in his eyes. Back in 1841 he had come out to Mud Corners from the Sylvanian Domain, carrying a doctor's kit in his right hand and a whole boodle of new ideas in his head, and it wasn't long till he'd turned the whole village upside down.

Hiram was a mighty fine doctor for all that, though he was that queer he didn't believe in using money at all. Whenever he needed something, like a pair of boots or a new coat, he'd walk right up to someone who had what he wanted and ask him for it. Many a fellow got right ashy about it, until he saw how it was and that the doctor would take care of anybody any time at all and not even charge him for the medicines and drugs. Before long there were a good many of them ready to pay up in hard cash whatever the doctor owed Selina Cain for his keep.

About six months after he first came, Hiram said he could use a little shop for an office, away from Abar's store, where it was quiet, and the very next day Minot and Luke and Hoss and one or two others began to lay the foundation. In a little over a month just working in the evenings and on holidays they had the building finished, and Lafe fitted it up inside with a bed, some tables, and benches, and a cupboard for the medicines and drugs.

By the time the new place was ready, Hiram needed some supplies and Minot and the others said they would take up a collection to pay for them, but Hiram wouldn't allow that. He wrote a letter to a drug house in Cincinnati, telling them what he needed. He had given up the use of money, he wrote, and gave his own services free of cost to anyone who needed them, and for any necessities he required he applied to those whom he thought able to give. He sent off the letter and, sure enough, after a while he had a reply. The goods were being sent by common carrier to Fort Wayne, and he could pick them up there without cost, they said, and they hoped God would bless him in his work.

"That ought to be a lesson for every one of us," says Minot.

"On how to be a doughhead?" says Abar.

"I wasn't meaning it that way," says Minot.

"The way I figure," says Lew, "it don't cost us nothing."

But whatever some of them thought of it, Hiram had become a power in the neighborhood. After he had talked to Minot and the others about how they ought to organize an *Association*, a good many of them were ready to join in, and in the fall of 1843 that's what they did. The *La Grange County Phalanx* was a joint-stock company with a legal char-

[79]

ter from the state, the stock having been issued in ten-dollar shares for hard cash or in ready exchange for the title to the land already owned by the members. Minot and Hoss and Luke Babcock and Seth Talbot and Lew Shingle were the first members with Lafe Klingerman and some of the others coming in later on when they were asked. With Maggie, though, it took them a long time to make up their minds.

"I'm for an *Association* all right," says Lew, "but I'll be dang-busted if I give in to equal rights for women." And for a long time that was final.

In the summer of 1844 they began building the big house. It was to be a hundred and ninety-six feet long, two stories high, and twenty-six feet deep. In the center of the first floor would be the dining room where well over a hundred could sit down to have their meals. To the right of that would be the big kitchen, the bakeries, and laundry rooms; to the left a ballroom, a library, and a thirty by twenty-six schoolroom. Upstairs the house was to be divided into living quarters for the families, each one with a living room and one or two bedrooms. A double veranda, upstairs and down, would run along the whole front of the building. Across the way they were already busy building barns and shops.

By the fall of that year they had over nine hundred acres —two hundred acres of farming land, a hundred acres of meadow, and the rest forest and woodland. Up on Lew's land they had planted a fine orchard of peach and apple trees, and on the neighboring farms they had put out and harvested sixty acres of wheat, fifty-two acres of oats, and thirty of corn. They owned over fifty cattle by that time and more than two hundred sheep, and the women had raised a big flock of turkeys. They only had one small sawmill, though, and the big flour mills and limekilns and brick ovens they had dreamed of were still waiting to be built. The trouble there was the water power. For the big house they were hauling the lime and brick all the way from Kendallville and Mongoquinong. Turkey Creek had fall a-plenty and could have been dammed up a lot higher, but a millrace would have flooded the west forty on Maggie's place, and hearing about it, she had threatened to sue them in court if they ever so much as dropped a stone into the creek. They came to see then that the only thing to do was to ask her to join.

"It'd give us over a thousand acres lying side by side," says Seth.

"And we could build us a fifteen-foot dam," says Lew, "with enough water for two or three big mills."

But by the time they came to ask her, Maggie had made up her own thinking-mind.

"I come in here and I cleared my land and I reckon I'll just keep what I got," she says.

Maggie had done a man's work from the day she had picked up the bull-whip, git-upped the oxen, and come on, her little pod of stepchildren asleep inside the wagon. She was a big woman and swung an axe like a man, and it was she and her own boys who had cleared her land, rolled and burned the logs, and built their barns and cabins. She wasn't afraid of catamount or titmouse, Tom Eccles once told Perry. Tom used to tell the story of how one of the Mongoquinong Indians came to her cabin one day and stepped inside to find Maggie busy at the loom. He watched for a spell and then reached in with his arms to stop it. When he did that, Maggie came down with her two hundred pounds on the treadle and held him fast.

"I'll learn you, you long-nosed, yeller-skinned buck," she says, "to keep your reachers out of my things."

But that was small scratchings alongside of what Maggie had done to the sheriff. She hadn't much more than located in the township and entered her farm in the land office at Fort Wayne until he came by, all the way from Ohio, looking for Bill Cooper, he said. Bill had never paid Luke Harper for the oxen he'd set out with, and the court had given Luke a judgment against Bill for fifty dollars.

"Bill's dead," says Maggie.

"Dead or no," says the sheriff, "he was owin' Luke Harper fer that yoke. It's the judge's orders."

"By gum, I ain't a dang thing to pay it with," says Maggie.

"I reckon I can find somethin' or other," he says, getting off his horse. "I've come a long way and I'm fer executin' the judgment."

"Well," she says, "I reckon the Lord'll provide fer us someway. I traded that yoke fer a horse and I need him bad, but if you got to have somethin'—"

"Where is he?" says the sheriff.

"In the barn," says she, leading the way.

When they got to the barn, she says, "There he be, sheriff. Iffen you want him, you lead him out."

As soon as the sheriff stepped inside, she closed the heavy oak door and slipped in the wooden pin on the outside that held it shut. It was a solid log building without a single window and overhead the loft was piled full of hay. Then she went back to work. The next morning she got up early and came out to the barn.

"How be you, sheriff?" she says.

"Let me out of here," he bellows.

"Be you fer collectin'?" says Maggie.

"I be," he says.

"Well, then," she says. "I'll be askin' you agin tomorrow."

"Hold on!" he says, "I'm fer compromisin'."

"All right, then," says Maggie. "Swear by God Almighty that you won't be fer collectin'."

"But what'll I tell the judge?" says he.

"Tell him it was a long ways out here and you couldn't find Bill," she says.

"And what if I don't?" he says.

"It *is* a long ways out here," she says, "and I reckon they won't be a-findin' you—ever."

That took the feather-edge off the sheriff.

"I'll do it, by god," he says.

She let him out then and he rode off back to Ohio, like a comb-cut rooster. Maybe Seth was minding that story the day he asked Maggie to join.

"You could take it easy in the *Phalanx*," says Seth.

"Easy?" she says.

"We got a good life for our women here," says Seth. "They ain't slaves to the kitchen no more."

"Spittlefish," she says. "I cleared forty acres with my own hands; I figger kitchen work is jest restin' on the haft fer a spell."

"So you ain't coming in?" says Lew.

"I'll be thinkin' it over," she says.

In another year or so everyone figured the *Phalanx* was a sure-go thing. They had the big house all finished then and ten or twelve more families had come in. There were some twenty families and over a hundred and fifty men, women, and children, all told. It was a sight that would do a man's heart good, Minot said, to see them all come trooping in to the fat of the land when the dinner horn called. There would be long tables loaded down with soup, potatoes, roast beef, brown bread and apple butter, and all kinds of melons and fruits. It was just like a big family reunion every day. Sometimes families would eat together at one end of a table, and sometimes all the children would eat by themselves with their nurses and teachers, while the younger people and the older folk held to themselves. There would be a lot of fun and laughing then. After dinner there would be a short rest and then they'd all go back to work. All day long, a fellow could hear the hammers ringing in the blacksmith shop and the joiners singing at their benches in the shade of the orchard trees.

After an early supper there would be games for the children out in the yard, and the young folks would hold a scamper-down in the ballroom or out on the veranda. On Sunday they'd have a big family meeting under the trees, where they'd sing hymns and one of them would read from the Bible, and Hiram or Minot or Seth would likely make a speech. One Sunday they invited Maggie and her boys over for a visit, and Hiram was minding them afterwards what a blessed thing it was, every fellow loving his neighbor and helping out. "Take it out in the world now," he says, "every fellow's for himself—"

"And it's the devil for 'em all," says Hoss.

"The only deviling in the world is what men make for themselves," says Hiram. "God didn't plan it that way. He planned for us all to live together in one big family, and that's what we're doing here. Take any fellow now, he isn't really responsible for what he is."

"Who is?" says Maggie.

"The world he's living in," says Hiram. "He's born all right till the world gets to bedeviling him. That makes a devil out of him."

"And the more devil, the better he gets along, I figger," says Maggie.

"That's right enough out in the world," says Hiram.

"I thought Lew said the good thing about this would be that everybody'd be makin' more money," says Maggie.

"That stands to reason," says Lew. "Look what we're doing now. Here every fellow ain't grubbing away at his own patch. We got two hundred acres of wheat and fifty men to do the cradling and threshing; that saves a lot of time. And someday," he says, firing an eye-shot at Maggie, "maybe we can have our own sawmills and flour mills right here on the ground, and our own brick ovens, just like we got our smithies and cabinet shops now."

"And what's to come of all this?" says Maggie.

"A better world," says Minot, "for a man to live in. Enough for everyone to eat and wear and a decent place for him to sleep, and time to do what a fellow's a mind to. We'll have schools for everybody, rich and poor, and time for reading and games. A man'll come to see it's a good world, and what it means for him to be free, and love his neighbor, and do unto others as he would be done by."

"That mouths all right," says Maggie.

"All right?" says Hoss. "That's a lot more 'n all right. By god, that's Christian."

After a Sunday meeting like that they would all go back to work on Monday morning feeling mighty good, each fellow doing what he was a mind to. The way they managed that, Minot told Perry, was by dividing the work up into what was necessary, what was useful, and what was agreeable. The first one, like swilling pigs and doing the mean chores, was paid most, and the last one, doing things that a fellow had a special itch for, was paid least—that was easy enough to figure. As for the women, those who wanted to could work in the kitchen and those who didn't, could work out in the fields, or card wool and make soap, or take care of the children in the nursery, but they got paid the same way as the men.

And when there was a call to, they'd all work together. It was a miracle thing that could happen then, like laying up a big barn or chopping a couple hundred cords of firewood

[*85*]

for the ovens and bakery or clearing a twenty-acre wood lot for planting. In a busy season like haying, all the women and the young girls would come out with rakes and pitchforks in hand, rolling the hay into windrows and pitching it into cocks, while the men loaded it into the wagons and mowed it away in the barn. In the fall all the families would go out together with buckets and baskets to pick wild berries. They'd bring in nearly a hundred bushels that way.

When they came to foot up the accounts at the end of the third year, every man and woman had sixty-one cents a day for every day he'd worked and everyone got five per cent interest on his stock. That was very near what they'd set out to do. When a fellow gets seventy-five cents a day for useful labor, then let the stock bring in six per cent, Minot had told them, and so on. A hundred dollars in a year's time, then, would earn just about what a man could in eight days. Lew had always said that was too low for the capital, but Minot held them to it as long as he was a trustee.

Against what they earned, they had to debit off what they'd eaten and the clothes they'd got from the dry goods store. Meals came to about fifty-six cents a week, and how much a fellow owed at the store depended on whether his wife was too proud to wear an old dress or he was, to go around with a patch on his pants. But they were doing all right then, and about that time Maggie made up her mind to it. Ever since the Sunday meeting they'd been over to, her boys had been hanging around the big house some and they were hankering to join up.

"I reckon I'm ready," she says, "but I got my own figgers."

"What might they be?" says Minot.

"Twelve dollars an acre fer the farm land," she says, "but I'm willin' to throw in the crops."

"That's no fair whack," says Lew. "We only got ten dollars for our land."

"Fair or no fair," she says, "it's twelve dollars. It's my land you got to have fer the millrace and that's the way you got to figger it."

They had it heads and tails then for a long time but they couldn't gee or haw Maggie Cooper, and they needed the water power.

"When we can grind our own wheat, card our own wool, and saw ten thousand board feet of lumber a day, we'll be making real money," says Lew.

But when they gave in on that there was more.

"I want a piece of writin' with your own names pot-hooked down at the bottom, that when the *Phalanx* breaks up, I'll get my own land back and every dang thing that's on it then," she says.

"We don't aim to break up," says Lew.

"You don't," says Maggie, "but I ain't chancin' it. I got a paper here from Judge Carnahan and you're a-signin' it or I won't come in."

"Well," says Lew, "I reckon we might as well. If we get the mills, we won't be breaking up, ever."

They signed up then and gave her back the paper.

"All right," she says, "and now that I'm a member, I aim to be elected trustee."

"Dadgum it no," says Lew. "Hiram and me and Minot are trustees; we're wearing the britches here."

"I reckon I know somethin' about wearin' 'em myself," says she.

"Well, you're still a woman under 'em," says Lew.

"Maybe I am," she says, looking crab apples at him. "But that's one thing Lew Shingle'll never know."

[87]

"We don't aim to have a woman run this shebang," says Lew.

"I thought you fellers was all fer equal rights," says Maggie.

"That we are," says Hiram, "in house or field or before any court of law in the land."

"Well, then," says Maggie, "I figger on bein' a mighty good bellwether."

Maggie Cooper could talk her way around a five-cornered stump come any time at all, and they had to have the water power. So in the end they gave in. Hiram resigned as a trustee and the *Phalanx* elected Maggie to take his place. The next day they sent ten ox teams and twenty men down to start the millrace on Turkey Creek.

What dumbflustered everyone, though, was that on the day Maggie and the boys moved into the big house, she took off her breeches and put on the long black horsehair skirt.

"I figger restin' on the haft fer a spell," she says.

And that's what she did. She kept her word all right—in a big horn.

The good Lord must have laughed some when He made man; or leastways it must have come to Him when He was a-workin' on the rib.

Chapter 9

How Tom Eccles *carved an emblem, and the*
La Grange County Phalanx came to break up

The *La Grange County Phalanx* was a Fourier *Association*, but in the end it was the associating that came mighty hard.

Lovin' your neighbors is a whole lot easier 'n livin'
with 'em.

For a spell in 1847 Tom Eccles came to live at the *Phalanx*. He fiddled his way through the winter, playing for their scamper-downs, but in the spring, feeling the whir and stir come on in the hive, he figured he'd best get out. When he wasn't busy fiddling that winter, he had been carving out a weather vane for the big house. Before he left he gave it to the three trustees, Maggie, Lew, and Minot. They had asked him for a cock-rooster, but it looked a lot more like an old hen with her tail feathers dragging in the rain.

"Our emblem," says Tom, handing it over, "is the barnyard fowl. We scratch fer a livin'."

"Hen or rooster?" says Lew.

"You figger it out," says Tom. "Iffen it cackles, it's a hen."

For a moment Lew got right ashy. "That don't look like a weathercock at all," he says.

"No," says Tom, "but it looks a little like Maggie. It's fitten enough, I reckon, seein' as how you got a woman fer a trustee."

"You got a long tongue, Tom Eccles," says Maggie, "but it don't clapper good."

"No?" says Tom. "Well, I was a-figgerin' on hittin' the gravel. I'm a free man and fodder where I like."

It had cost Tom ten dollars for a share of stock when he joined and he left that with them to settle his account. He was what they called a floater, a fellow who joined in the winter just for the hoecakes and honey and to keep his backside warm at the fire. There were others, too, who came in, but it wasn't the floaters who were to blame when the *Association* flatted out, not excepting maybe for Lottie Haskins. She might have been faulting some.

Lottie was a maiden lady of about twenty-six or so, and as it turned out later, head-high and bull-strong for equal rights. She had been living over in New York state somewhere and the minute she had heard a fellow say that the *La Grange County Phalanx* had a woman for a trustee, she had set out full-split for the land of promise. For a while, too, it had worked out all right. She was a fine-appearing, full-bosomed woman with a lot of grit and hustle and she had pitched right in. As for Lottie, Hoss said later, her heart was all right, though that was a lot more than a fellow could say for her head. What broke up Eden in the end was just the same old problem, women—women and sin.

The first real trouble they ever had came from drinking. Two years earlier, at the time Maggie Cooper came in, the

Phalanx had passed a rule against the use of intoxicating liquor. Maggie was hardspun strict with her own boys and dead set against drinking, and anyway ever since the big election rally over at Mongoquinong there was quite a temperance movement in the township. Seth and Minot felt the same way.

It used to nettle Hoss some, who liked his liquor, but he got along all right. It wasn't more than a mile or so to Applemanberg and only three to Mongoquinong, and they were always needing a fellow ready to ride off on an errand. Hoss wouldn't swear he was always stone sober when he came back, but he never drank on the grounds before Lafe Klingerman brought in a full keg one night and hid it in the haymow of one of the cow barns.

Lafe liked his liquor all right, but it wasn't that that made him do it. He got the keg, he said later on, because a fellow owed him some money, and what else could he do with it. At first he'd just sneak out at night sometimes to take a short drag, but one night when Hoss saw him do it, he gave Hoss a drink, too, and then he had an idea.

All day long he'd talk about liquor to the fellows he worked alongside of, and if the other fellow drooled any, he'd cut him in on the keg. He sold the first keg out at six cents a snort and when that was all gone, he went over to Mongoquinong and got some more. He was doing a right smart business before long.

Then his wife, Lizzie, began to wonder about Lafe. He'd dig out after supper every night, he had a cow coming fresh in the barn, he said, and he'd not come back till well after midnight. She was beginning to feel like a widow and one night after he came in, she roused him up, and when she did she could smell the liquor on his breath. He said he'd had a nip just to keep warm, and she said the cow had been a mighty long time a-coming. The first one was fresh, Lafe said; he was waiting on another one now. The next day Lizzie got to talking to Nell Babcock and some other women working in the kitchen and come to find out, there were a whole lot of cow-freshing widows. Maggie came by just then and overheard them, and that night she got up about midnight and went out to see for herself what was going on.

Maggie broke up a mighty fine gander party. Lafe was the only fellow with a cup in his hand, and that, he told her, was a tincture of *nux vomica*, some medicine for the cow. As for the rest, they were just sitting there chinning, Lafe said.

"Cow medicine?" says Maggie.

"That's what it be," says Lafe.

She reached for the cup and he tried to spill it handing it to her, but she caught it before the liquor spilled out. She took a good sniff, sipped a little with her lips, and tossed what was left in Lafe's face.

"It might kill the cow," she says, stramming off to rouse out the other trustees.

When Minot and Lew got to looking around, they found the keg, and the next day after dinner the whole *Phalanx* held a hearing. The full story came out then.

"The way I figger," says Lafe, "whether a feller drinks or not is his own gum tree."

"You knew it was a rule," says Minot.

"That we did," says Hoss. "And we're sorry for it."

"Sorry talk don't put it back in the keg," says Maggie.

After they'd talked a while, some of the words came to have bark on them. Now that it had happened, every woman was for sticking by her own man. Lafe couldn't have gone to the cow barn more than once or twice, Lizzie said, and he wasn't a drinking man a-tall, and they'd better be minding that.

Then Minot, seeing how it was, told them a rule was a rule, but all of them together could change the rule if they were a mind to.

That didn't set with Maggie. She got up and told them if they changed the rule any, she and her boys would get out. The men would be drinking up a ton of profit that way, and anyway it wasn't just a rule, it was a sin, the devil's own sin, she said.

It was the talk about sin that nettled Lottie Haskins. As for her, she said, she would never touch a man if he was anyways given to drink, but she figured Minot was right—it was only a rule. And it was a mighty hard thing to sit there and listen to a member of an enlightened group like a phalanx, deacon out such pious flumdiddle about sin.

"Hold on there, Lottie," says Maggie, biting in.

"Hold on yourself," says Lottie. "I'm talking. No member of a phalanx believes in sin."

"Spittlefish," says Maggie, pepper-hot. "Maybe you don't, but I do. I ain't no free-thinker. Call me a freewill, pine-shingle Baptist if you're a mind to. What I believe is pure quill and no water," she says.

When the storm was over, they didn't any more than vote a fine on Lafe, and then they all went back to work. But from that day on they were coursing straight into trouble. Lottie could see by that time that Maggie Cooper was no enlightened woman, trustee or no trustee, and she had been counting chickens on that. If the whole thing was going to be her fight, well, she was ready to gird up her loins, and from that time on she talked blue-streak steady. The real trouble in the world was that women needed equal rights, and the first thing for a woman to do, Lottie told them in the kitchen, was to get rid of the dust-catching, wrap-around, saddle-blanket called a skirt, or the next best thing was to shorten it. She kept up her ding-dong for a week or two, and then one Saturday night came down to the ballroom for a scamper-down in a skirt cut off about level with her knees, and under that two trouser legs that came down all the way to her shoes with draw strings at the bottom. For a moment it was that quiet you could have heard a death tick in the walls when she walked in.

"I never see the beat of it," says Maggie, "fer downright sinful."

"Oh, I don't know," says Lew, laughing. "It sure looks mighty pretty."

"Pretty?" says Maggie. "It's plumb indecent, that's what it is."

"I recollect I've seen you wear britches," says Lew.

"A man's britches," says Maggie, "because I done a man's work. It ain't the same thing. She's doin' it just to show she's got benders."

"Well, she has that," says Lew, laughing away.

"Lew Shingle," says Maggie, "you ain't fitten to be a trustee. You got a mighty carnal eye fer women."

The next day Maggie sailed into Lottie in the kitchen.

"Just like they done in Sodom and Gomorrah," says Maggie. "I figger it'll be free love next."

"And why not?" says Lottie, lifting up the ladle and letting the batter run off real slow-like. She could smell out an issue for a fight like a cold-nosed hound can a polecat. The real trouble with Maggie, Hoss told Perry, was that Maggie figured she could save the world in just six days if people listened to her, plumb forgetting that it took God Almighty that long just to make it, and even then He had to rest.

Maggie went ramping out of the kitchen and got hold of Minot.

"We're a-goin' to settle this right now," she says. "As a Baptist I ain't a-stayin' in, iffen that woman does."

They had another big meeting then.

"I don't care what a woman wears so long as her heart's all right," says Minot.

"It's a shameless thing," says Maggie. "It's a sin."

"It's a sign of equal rights," says Lottie, her eyes blazing.

"When you've got the rights, you don't need a sign," says Hiram. "The women here lead happy lives, doing what they're a mind to. What they wear doesn't make any difference."

"It's a lot more handy," says Lottie.

"Handy fer what?" says Maggie.

"For work," says Lottie.

"Fer other things, too, I reckon," says Maggie. "Who knows what goes on when we ain't a-lookin'."

"You wore 'em," says Lew. "I figure you'd better be minding that."

"It ain't the same thing a-tall," says Maggie. "I'm no fancy woman. Come right down to bottom facts, Lew Shingle, I figger you got a shine on Lottie."

"Better bridle that tongue of yours," says Lew. "You're tying knots with it now that you can't untie with your teeth."

"I've taken a mighty lot of sass offen you, Lew," says Maggie. "I'm a-standin' by what I said. Iffen that woman stays in—"

"Well, that's too bad," says Lottie. "I figured being a woman you were on my side."

"The only side I'm on is my own," says Maggie.

By that time a lot of others felt the same way about Lottie. It was a brand new thing, and it did look mighty sinful. Minot took a vote, and when they counted up the tally, the members had voted with Maggie against Lottie. There would be no more wearing of bloomers, and if Lottie Haskins didn't like that she was free to leave, which she did the very next day.

Lew Shingle stormed out of the meeting angry as a ring-nosed bull. It didn't help any what Maggie had said about him and Lottie. The next day he figured out a plan to get even with her, though to do that he had to win some members over on his side. Human nature being what it is and greenback-hungry, that came mighty easy in the end.

Lew was still secretary and treasurer of the *Phalanx*, and the annual meeting was less than four days away. When he got to work footing up the accounts, he found they had done right well. On the twelve hundred acres of the domain they had harvested three hundred acres of wheat, over a hundred acres of corn and oats, and gardens of potatoes and melons, stretching across fifteen acres. And by that time they owned over three hundred sheep, seventy head of cattle, twenty span of horses, thirty-two yoke of oxen, well over a hundred pigs and big flocks of turkeys and geese. They had finished the millrace on Turkey Creek and erected a sawmill, sunk a tannery, and fitted out a dry goods store.

"I figure on paying seventy-five cents a day for useful labor," Lew says, after Minot had called the meeting to order, "and six per cent on ten-dollar shares of stock, but only five per cent on the twelve-dollar shares."

"What coon you treein' now, Lew?" says Maggie. "All our stock is in ten-dollar shares."

"It's all in ten-dollar shares," says Lew. "But you were allowed twelve dollars an acre for your land and we only got ten—that's the difference."

"Lew Shingle," says Maggie, "you can't come the yankee over me."

"By gum, I'm secretary and treasurer," says Lew.

"You agreed to the price when I come in," says Maggie.

"But not to the same rate of interest," says Lew.

"Hold on a minute," says Minot. "I figure this is no more 'n a kettle-pot, saucepan squabble. Why the whole thing would only come to a few dollars' difference."

"It ain't the money," says Lew. "Share an' share alike, that's what we agreed to."

"What we agreed to," says Minot, "is for all of us to work together like a family."

"Spittlefish and big talk," says Maggie. "Money talk is a whole lot bigger 'n big talk."

When Minot saw Maggie and Lew couldn't come to terms, he broke up the meeting. They had better think it over for a few weeks, he said, and then he would call another special meeting for them to settle it.

But that time Maggie really set up her ebenezer. She left the *Phalanx* the next day without saying anything to anybody at all and rode over to La Grange. When she came back, she told them she'd filed a suit in circuit court against the *Phalanx* and Lew and Minot for the recovery of her land.

Sometimes, Hoss said, it was between jackass and mare-mule figuring out which one could be more notionate and meaner, Lew Shingle or Maggie Cooper, when they got to pulling uneven on the doubletree.

Before they came to have the suit, though, Minot called another meeting. It was a mortal sad thing, he said, that just when the cattle and crops were coming along fine, humans couldn't make a hitch of it. He figured they'd forgotten something all right. Luke and Seth and Hiram stood up then and said what they could to keep them together, but it just wasn't any use. Half of them stood by Maggie and the other half went over to Lew's side, and after that you couldn't gee or haw any of them. When Lafe moved that they break up, the tally stood thirty-six to ten.

Then Minot told them they had come together of their own free will, and he hoped if they were going to break up, they could part that way. All they had to do was to ask the state legislature to dissolve the earlier act of incorporation and to appoint two commissioners to distribute the property and to make the deeds and transfers. And that's what they did.

But Maggie got the last chip. She still had the paper they'd signed before she came in, saying they agreed to give her land back and anything that was on it. On the day before the commissioners arrived to begin their appraisal, she got her boys together. That night with four yoke of oxen they pulled down a cabin and a log barn and slip-dragged the logs across the line. Then they rounded up a dozen milking cows, two or three heifers, a big flock of sheep, and a team of horses, drove them over on her land, and laid the zigzag fence back up.

The next morning she defied the commissioners or anyone else to set foot on her land.

"I plain told 'em when I come in, they wasn't a-goin' to honeyfuggle me," she says, pulling on her breeches once more.

She had, too, but many of them figured it wasn't quite straight furrow. In the end Lew bought the big house for a quarter of what it had cost, and most of the others got their own land back. Then the commissioners evened up what was left. There wasn't enough to go around, of course, not after they'd paid off the mortgage on the big house, and all of them except Maggie were poorer than they'd been five years before in livestock and produce.

"What we got for our money, I reckon," says Hoss, "was a lifetime of human nature in just five short years."

But that wasn't quite the full story.

[98]

*Bustin' up ain't the big failin', not lessen the dream
dies in a feller's heart.*

It had all taken place before he was born, Uncle Perry said,
but you could always tell a *Phalanx* man in the early neighborhood, fellows like Minot and Seth and Hoss, and Hiram,
too, who after the *Association* broke up, moved on. And
afterwards Minot and the others moved the general store
down to Mud Corners, where it stood owned by the neighbors and supplying their needs for nigh onto a hundred years.

As for Maggie Cooper and Lew Shingle, they never again
passed the time of day when they met. A year or so later
when Lew came to tear down part of the big house, he gave
the weathercock back to Tom Eccles.

"You can give that to Maggie Cooper sometime when you
go by," he says. "It's a hen all right; I heard it cackle."

Chapter 10

How Hoss Martin *killed a man in Sawyer's marsh,*
and they built the plank road from Fort Wayne
to Lima

For all his heavy drinking, Hoss Martin was as fine a
man as ever pulled a pair of breeches over his backside, Uncle
Perry said, though he had his own way of doing it. He was
quick-spoken, and hot-tempered as a quill-pig once he got his
dander up, but a fair-minded fellow for all that, ready to do
right by every man, woman, and stranger in the neighborhood. He killed a man one time, down in Sawyer's marsh, but
it was a long time before he ever got over it.

What a man is and what he ain't, lies a lot deeper 'n
his hide.

That was back in the summer of '51, back in the days when
long trains of wagons, loaded with wheat, would gather over
at Cochran's Corners on the plank road, ready to set out the
next morning on the five-day trip to market at Fort Wayne.
Sometimes there would be only eight or ten farmers and
sometimes as many as twenty-five or thirty, each with his

own load, but all of them waiting to make the trip together.

That would take them two full days going, a day or so for the marketing, and two more full days for the return to Cochran's Corners and home. At night the whole train would pull up alongside of the road, and, unhitching the teams and tethering the horses to the wagon wheels, the men would roll up in their blankets under the wagons or more likely around a campfire if the night was airish. But it wasn't so much that the men liked each other's company, though they did that, nor that traveling together they could double up the teams in hard-going stretches of the road. It was the fear of blacklegs that made them do it—the horse thieves and highwaymen that had come in with the building of the plank road.

Before that, that is, before the summer of 1848 when a group of eastern capitalists organized the *Post Road Company* and laid the planking, the old road from Fort Wayne to Lima had been little more than a slow-crawling wagon trail through the forest mud, winding its way among the hills and around the numerous swamps and peatbogs. Down below South Milford the road crossed the Little Elkhart and cut its way diagonally across three miles of Sawyer's marsh, a low-lying area of swamp grass and tamarack. Here the early settlers had cut the heavier tamarack poles and laid them crosswise for a roadbed, and long after the later planking had broken up and given way, the corduroy still lay there, and more than once Uncle Perry said, he himself bore home a blistered bottom from the jolting and rumble-tumble of the wagon.

But that had all been changed by the summer of '48. Erecting dozens of sawmills and employing a hundred men, the *Post Road Company* had laid a solid roadbed of three-inch oak planking on ten-inch sills the full fifty-six miles from Fort Wayne to Lima. Sawing out the planks, laying the roadbed, and building the tollgates had taken three years, but now wagonloads of wheat made a trip in five days that had earlier taken a fortnight. Twice a week, too, the huge stagecoach came thundering out of the south or down from Lima, bringing mail, immigrants and land speculators. Then the horse dealers came, buying and selling among the settlers, leading and riding their mounts the length of the thoroughfare.

With the stagecoach and the horse dealers had come the horse thieves and highwaymen, and the dense tamarack growth of Sawyer's marsh became an easy hide-away for goods and horses stolen from the countryside. Little side trails, breaking off from the main road, led through the tall grass to clearings deep in the tamarack, so hearsay had it, where the goods were hidden and the horses herded by blacklegs of such desperate character that no one ever dared for a long time to investigate the truth of the stories. On the north side of the marsh and a mile to the west of the main road lay the little village of Tamarack, a half-dozen log houses, a village smithy, an old abandoned tannery, and the famous Tamarack House, itself a gathering place for swindlers, robbers, and highwaymen bold enough to do the devil in if he ever turned up.

There were a dozen fellows who had gotten beaten and robbed down in Sawyer's marsh, one of them an old-world peddler whose pack had been taken and he himself left bruised and half-dying by the roadside. And only the summer before Phil Beisel had lost a spanking team of big bays right out on the plank road, coming home from Kendallville. Coming out of Dan Hawk's saloon that afternoon, he had found two strangers admiring his team.

"Mighty fine bays there," says one of them.

"That they be," says Phil.

"You figger on sellin' 'em?" says the other fellow.

"No, I reckon not," says Phil.

"No harm in askin'," says the first one.

"No," says Phil, untying his team and climbing up on the wagon.

For a moment it left him a little uneasy in his mind; then he figured they were just ordinary horse buyers; so he thought no more about it and started out for home. It got pretty dark before he got through Sawyer's marsh and about a half mile this side of the road leading off to the Tamarack House, he heard a couple of horsemen coming up from behind. He still didn't think anything about it till they came up close and he saw their kerchief-covered faces and the pistols they were carrying.

"Hold on!" says one of them.

"I ben't stopping," says Phil.

"All right, Jim," says the other fellow. "Grab that team. I'll take care of him." And with that he rode up close and held his pistol to Phil's face.

Phil started to shout to his horses, or leastways he said he did, but the fellow called Jim was too quick for him. He grabbed the team by the bridles, unhitched them from the wagon, threw the harness down on the highway, and then remounting his own horse, led the trotting bays off into the night.

"We'll just set here a spell," says the other blackleg, still holding the pistol up to Phil's face.

Phil said he was hoping someone might come along then, but nobody did, and in about twenty minutes the second blackleg rode off in the opposite direction from that taken by the fellow called Jim and the bays. When Phil thawed out of his scare, he ran back to the Tamarack House and told them his story. But they never found hide nor hair of the horses, though a dozen men helped him to cover the countryside that night and the next day.

[*103*]

And that's the way things were when Hoss Martin killed a man down in Sawyer's marsh.

They were on their way back when it happened. They had been gone five full days then and had gotten back as far as Kendallville, when Hoss, whom the men had elected boss for the trip, pulled up his team at the hitching post in front of Dan Hawk's saloon.

"Boys," he says, "I've got a little stop to make. I promised Aus Carney I'd fetch him home a keg of whiskey from old Dan's."

It was getting on towards four o'clock and they still had sixteen miles to Cochran's Corners and home, so some of the men were for going right on. Besides that they knew how Hoss was. Like as not if he got to drinking, they wouldn't be leaving there before midnight.

But when they tried to hurry him along, he was stubborn as an off-ox.

"Tie 'em up and come on in!" he says. "I'm setting up a round of drinks. Goddamn me, it's cold and I reckon a little whiskey'll just set the fire going."

And then he went on inside.

Some of the men still wanted to go on, but others began to agree with Hoss. It wouldn't be right, displeasuring him that way, they said, and anyway a good many of them liked their whiskey just as well as Hoss, leastways when it was likely to come free.

As soon as they got inside, Hoss set up drinks for the crowd. Then they had a round or two more. After that a good many of the men were for going on home, but Hoss swore he was drinking his belly full.

The summer before the *Mayflower Lodge of Good Templars* had closed every saloon in Applemanberg and Mud Corners, and there wasn't a place left where a man could buy a drink in the whole of Milford or Springfield townships.

"Come on. Let's go on home," says Lafe Klingerman.

"What for?" says Hoss.

"By god, I'm aimin' to sleep in my own bed tonight," says Lafe.

"Well, the old lady'll like you all the better for a drop of whiskey in your belly," says Hoss.

But some of the men were downright worried. They had been five full days away from their families, away from a warm bed and a good meal. Their wagons were loaded with victuals and winter clothing, they had money in their pockets, and their way home lay through Sawyer's marsh.

"Suppose," says Lafe, "there's a whole gang of blacklegs layin' fer us, enough to take everythin' we got?"

But Hoss kept right on drinking. When the men saw it wasn't any use to talk to him, they got their hackles up. Banging out of the saloon, they untied their teams and got ready to go. When they had the wagons all lined up, Lafe called out to Hoss, who came to the door with a bottle in his hand. When he saw what was up, Hoss was right mad.

"Well, I'll be goddamned," he says.

"It's time to go," says Lafe. "And we're a-goin'. If you don't come now, we'll be leavin' you behind."

"Oh, you will, will you?" says Hoss. "By god, don't figure on me sneaking along behind. Go on home, Lafe!" he says. "Go on home and change your britches! I'm coming when I'm goddamn good and ready."

"But you can't come through Sawyer's marsh alone," says Lafe.

"Oh, I can't?" says Hoss. "I'd as lief come through there with the devil riding my wagon as I would with any of you fellows." And with that he went inside and slammed the door.

Some of the men were for waiting, but most of them were for going on. It'd teach him a lesson, they said. And those who were for staying were afraid to, and so by and by they all drove off.

It was about eight o'clock when Hoss came to enough to make up his mind to go home. He had been drinking heavily, but he was that angry it kind of held him up, and when he staggered out of the saloon and over to his team, there wasn't anyone who dared to stop him. He had quite a time untying the horses—so onlookers said afterwards—but he finally got himself up on the wagon and, muttering and swearing to himself, he drove off.

No one knew afterwards exactly what had happened. The next morning Hoss himself could hardly mind. He said he didn't know whether he was more scared than he was angry or more angry than he was scared. He knew, though, that he was pretty well bent from the drink, that he was goddamn mad at somebody, and that the blacklegs would likely be for robbing him. When he came to the marsh, he took his whip —it had a long lash and a handle with a pound and a half of lead in it—and wrapping the lash around his wrist he grasped the stock in his right hand like a club.

As the wagon lumbered on over the planks, halfway through the swamp he caught on there was a fellow crawling out from under some empty sacks on the back of the wagon, where he had been hiding. Drunk as he was, Hoss sat still until the fellow crept up and reached for him. Then he turned, he said, halfway in his seat and struck the fellow one blow with the handle of the whip.

What he had done to the blackleg, Hoss was too drunk to know. When the man fell, he just chucked to his horses and the wagon went on rumbling over the planks. It was after one o'clock when he got home and the grays turned into their own yard, Hoss still sitting high up on the wagon, but dead to the world for all that. His son, Harry, heard him drive in, and he and his mother got Hoss off the wagon and into bed, where he dropped off into a deep sleep. Then Harry went out to the barn, unhitched the horses, and fed them. By that time Aus Carney, who lived about a quarter of a mile across the fields, had arrived. Aus had been sitting up waiting for his red-eye, seeing as how he had been out of liquor for nigh onto two weeks and dying for a drink, and when he saw the light in the barn, he got himself a lantern and came right over.

"Did Hoss fetch me somethin'?" says Aus.

"I don't know," says Harry. "He's drunk. We put him to bed."

"Likely there's none left," says Aus.

"We can see," says Harry. "It'll be in the wagon."

When they came to look for it, they found the blackleg lying dead on top of the sacks where he had fallen, his head bashed in from the base of his nose to the middle of his skull. Aus and Harry were that scared they forgot all about the liquor. After a hard tussle with Hoss they woke him up.

"Where'd that dead feller in your wagon come from?" says Aus.

"What feller?" says Hoss, raising himself on his arm.

"Don't you know you got a feller in your wagon with his head bashed in?" says Aus.

"By god, no," says Hoss. "I hit one that was trying to rob me back in the marsh. Goddamn him, I must of knocked him right off the wagon."

"You didn't knock him off the wagon," says Aus. "He's a-layin' in the back of the wagon now, and he's dead."

"Dead?" says Hoss.

"His head's bashed in," says Aus.

"Well," says Hoss, "if he's dead, I killed him. Harry, you

[*107*]

get on Dick and ride over to La Grange and fetch the sheriff. Aus, you and me'd better lay him out somewhere, out in the barn if Hattie don't want him in here."

By afternoon Harry was back, the sheriff coming along to look at the blackleg. He was a young fellow, you could see that all right, no more than eighteen or twenty, and he didn't have a thing on him to let you know who he was. The sheriff rode down to the Tamarack House and then on to Kendall-ville to make inquiries, but no one seemed to know the young fellow or had ever laid eyes on him before. So the sheriff told Hoss to go ahead and bury him.

Hoss came over to ask Minot to help him, and Minot and Marsh went along back. The men dug a grave for him out in the apple orchard, and Minot and Hoss carried the body out of the barn. Before they began to fill in the grave, Minot said a prayer. Then Hoss picked up the shovel, but he had tears in his eyes.

"Well," says Hoss, standing there for a spell, "I reckon I had a call to kill you, but I'm goddamn sorry just the same. It's a mortal sad thing, a fellow dying like that and being buried without a friend around—save his own enemy."

Chapter 11

HOW UNCLE PERRY *worked for Isaac Grimes, and*

Big John Leaper got struck by a rattler

BY AUTUMN of the year Uncle Perry was eleven, he could make a fair hand on a farm. He was a little light in the poop, as Isaac put it, but he got along all right.

It ain't the weight of a feller's backside as much as sheer grit 'n hustle that gets things done.

Before that he had always worked for his keep, but now Isaac paid him a full shilling a week besides, and even Old Leazer had to agree that the little shirttail was earning his salt. He could plow five acres of corn a day with the double-shovel plow, swing a scythe or a cradle alongside of older men, and hold his own binding and stooking, pitching hay, or mowing it away in the barn. That fall he carried his axe to the woods, took one end of the crosscut saw, or swung his turn at the maul, riving a white oak log into puncheons and fence rails. Before the year was out he had tried his hand at shearing sheep, shoeing a horse, and even stringing up a hog with a gambrel between its hocks at butchering time.

All that came from working alongside of a fellow by the name of Big John Leaper. Big John was the regular hired man at Isaac's, an old batch of thirty-five or so, who always bragged that he pulled more ganders, stripped more rattlers, broke up more camp meetings, raised jack with more women, and drank more whiskey than any other fellow in the country. Most of it was true enough, Uncle Perry said, though it took him some time before he found out about the women.

Big John could swing a broadaxe easy as a blacksmith's hammer, felling a good-sized tree with a dozen blows, and turning out twenty to thirty hewn logs a day. He was a corner man at cabin raisings, with a right good eye for the notch and saddle, able to do a handstand on the ridgepole when the building was completed to the huzzas of the log raisers and the admiring womenfolk below. All day long from sunup to sundown he could swing a scythe, singing in the grass, and he was the only man Uncle Perry ever knew who could cradle three acres of wheat, bind, and stook it in a single day.

He began slowly, though, on Monday morning and didn't come to his real pitch and hustle until the middle of the week. Come Wednesday and Thursday there was no give-out to him and he could do a week's work in two days, but by Friday he was thinking of another gander-pulling, camp meeting, and whiskey.

Gander-pulling came easy for Big John. He could mount a running horse at a single bound, rein him in and hold on, or bring him back to the starting line. He had a big claw-like hand and when he once got hold of the goose's head, grease or no grease, something was bound to give way. More often it was the webfoot of the gander where he'd been nailed to the crossbeam, sometimes broken off clean and sometimes the flesh torn through by the spike. Other fellows missed the goose, or their hands failed to hold onto the greased heads, or they tried too hard and fell off their horses. But not John Leaper. After the run he and a couple of other fellows would ride over to the nearest woodlot for a roast, washing down the fat meat with a jug of red-eye.

After that they'd more than likely ride off to camp meeting. Not that Big John or any of the others ever gave a dried apple damn for what the exhorter might be saying to them, though they liked the hymn singing well enough. They'd prowl the outer edges of the crowd, like a tomcat might a hen roost, just a-looking, as Big John put it, for a stray piece of calico that was easy on her benders. Many a time he rolled a woman in the grass, he said, before the last amen was over and near enough to camp to hear the singing, too. "Give 'em a little hell-fire and brimstone to warm 'em up, a drink of red-eye to cool 'em down, and they come easy," he would say. Sometimes Big John wouldn't come riding back till nigh sunup on Monday morning.

The first time Big John saw Perry he let out a snort.

"Why he's no more 'n a half-pint bushnipple," he says to Esther. "He needs a lot more corn meal mush and sowbelly before we can use him in the fields. But come along, young feller."

Then he took Perry out to plow corn. The double-shovel plow was clumsy-heavy and apt to woggle sideways, uprooting or covering up the corn. Once headed in between the rows, Perry got along all right, but turning around at the end of the field was a hard thing to do. The plow would slew around, Perry hanging onto the handles, the horse nervous and brigaty at Perry's gee and haw. Before Big John came over to see how he was getting on, he'd plowed out or covered up close to a half acre.

"Goddamn you, you little shavetail," he says, "you're out here to plow corn, not to bury it."

"I couldn't help it," says Perry.

"Help it, hell!" says Big John. "Unhitch Nellie and go get the hoe."

"By god," says Perry, "that I ain't."

"Ain't what?" says Big John, coming on over.

"Ain't a-goin'," says Perry. "A hoe is fer a woman."

Big John burst out laughing.

"All right, then," he says, "you mind when I show you how to do it."

With that they started up again. But when Isaac came to see what had happened, he was angry.

"Oh, leave the little shavetail alone," says Big John. "By god, he can't learn it any younger."

After that he showed Perry how to do things all summer, Perry standing by and watching wide-eyed how easy it was to hammer a clevis or a horseshoe out of bar iron or to swing a scythe and cradle when you knew how. Then Perry would have a go at it. If he caught on and did it right, Big John would slap him on the backside, or maybe give him a drink of red-eye when Isaac wasn't looking, or haul out his plug and let Perry bite off a chew. If he didn't Big John would rip out a foul oath, spit tobacco juice in a steady stream, and swear at him for being a goddamned, muddleheaded, tumble-turd. Then he would work Perry like a horse, forcing him to take the first swath and keep ahead out of the way, making him take his turn with the axe or hammer, or pitching the newly-raked hay in a frenzy and hustle that left Perry sweating and breathless trying to stay on top of the load.

The handiest tools Big John had on the farm were the tip of his boot, a stout stick, or a rawhide. He couldn't walk past a dog or cat without kicking them. Swilling pigs, he'd have to hit them on the snouts with a stick. He'd bellow at the cattle, lash them with a rawhide, or kick the young bulls in their privates. The geldings he drove with whip and rein, cutting their backs with the snapper and then throwing his weight into the lines to check them, until they were that dancy and brigaty no one else could drive them at all. Ringing the old sows or altering the shoats, he seemed to like best of all.

For Big John it was all a regular shindy. He'd call Perry over to turn the grindstone to sharpen up the knife, whet the blade on his boot top, and try the bite by shaving off the black hair on the frog of his arm. Then he'd take his stance in the corner of the pigpen, while young Perry and Isaac caught the pigs. Down on one knee he'd whip the blade across, and with a quick movement of his arm and a foul word, he'd be waiting for the next one. The more the pigs squealed, the better Big John seemed to like it.

When he caught wild game in the field or the woods, he was like that, too. Coon he killed outright, for he was after the pelts, he said, but a snake he'd abuse and kill the way he felt like it. He swore he'd once killed sixteen rattlers in a single day, and he kept all the rattles strung on a belt like an Indian did his scalps. He'd never taken a rattle off a dead snake in his life.

"Any goddamn plow-jogger can do that," he says.

It was in the dog-day whim-whams that Perry first ran afoul of Big John. Come harvest time and threshing there was a lot of work on the farm for a woman, and seeing as how Esther was carrying a baby, Isaac rode over to Luke Babcock's and got his girl, Mattie, to help out in the kitchen. Mattie was about fifteen, plump as an apple dumpling, and pretty in her own way. Perry had known her when he was staying at Minot's—the Babcocks were elbow neighbors—and liked her right well. She teased him some, and he her, when he was carrying water for her or fetching in wood, and once she slapped him hard in the face when he pulled her pigtails, but he didn't mind that, he said.

Right off Big John began to ogle Mattie. He'd angle up to her in the kitchen and put his arm around her, or pinch her in the arm or the backside when she went by. She'd push him away or slap at him playfully and there'd be a lot of give-and-take words between them. But it never came to more than that for a spell. She knew Big John, she said, bird and egg, and she had sense enough to lock her door at night.

Then one night after supper in the cow barn it happened. Mattie had been helping out with the milking, and when they were all through, Perry had gone off to feed the calves. Why he came back that way he didn't know, but when he came in he heard a scuffle over in the corner. When he looked he saw Big John had her down and was holding his hand over her mouth. She was kicking some and kind of giggling, too. When he saw Perry, Big John was that startled he let go his hand. Perry had picked up a pitchfork.

"By god," he says, "you let her go."

Big John looked kind of sheepish; Mattie got up and gathering up her skirts, ran out of the barn. Then he came over and got hold of Perry.

"You goddamn little muttonhead," he says.

"What did you want to do that to her fer?" says Perry.

"By god, the way I figger," says Big John, "half the world was made to field-roll the other half, and I'm fer gettin' my share. It's high time fer you to start, young feller."

"I ain't ever," says Perry.

"Shovelin' Jesus," says Big John. "You ain't got the git-up of a peckerwood nubbin."

Then he told Perry not to say a word to Isaac; if he did, he'd ring him like a shoat. He shook him up once or twice to make him mind and then lifted him out of the barn on the end of his boot.

Perry never said a word to Mattie, and she never mentioned it to him, but once or twice he made up his mind to tell Isaac the whole thing. But he never did. And he was just as glad later on that he hadn't.

About three weeks later they were cutting marsh grass for hay down on the flats near Turkey Creek. Isaac and one or two of his neighbors would get together for the cutting and divide the hay. Uncle Perry couldn't remember who was with them at the time except for Pete Martin and one or two of Seth Bulmer's boys. Big John put Perry to mowing the head swath; he came next, and the other fellows were strung out behind him. They used to mow down from the higher ground to the marshy land near the creek, and then carry the scythes back up and come down again.

They were about halfway down the first time after they'd stopped to eat their lunch at noon, when Perry heard a rattle as he swung his scythe. He jumped back quick and there she lay, the scythe having passed right over her, curled and ready to strike. Her head was up a good sixteen inches and he could see she was a big one, nigh as big around her belly as his arm.

"What's up?" says Big John.

"It's a rattler," says Perry.

"Leave me at her, shavetail," he says.

He dropped his scythe and came up on the run, giving out a low whistle when he saw her.

"By god, she's a whopper," he says.

"You'd best be careful," says Perry.

Perry was mortally afraid of rattlers. He'd heard stories about snakes that made a fellow's blood run cold. In the early days there had been a lot of massasaugas, water moccasins, and rattlers, though the rattlers were the most common, and Joe Foos had told him he never stooked a bundle of wheat in his life before kicking it with his foot and listening for the rattle. Joe knew more than one fellow that had been struck, but Abe Hansen was the only one he'd ever known who didn't die. Abe got struck one day when he and another fellow were rolling logs down on his farm near South Milford. The other fellow was driving the oxen and Abe was reaching under a log to fasten the chain when she hit him.

"Quick," he says to the other fellow, laying his arm down on the log. "Cut her off! That was a big yellow rattler." The other fellow took up the broadaxe and cut off the arm with one blow.

They way they usually did it, Joe Foos had told Perry, was to tie a string around a fellow's arm and twist it tight, slit the wound open with a knife, pour a handful of gunpowder into the wound and set a match to it. That would sear the flesh in deep, but even then the wound would likely gangrene and the fellow get sick inside.

"By god," says Big John, "I'll show you fellers a trick."

With that he called to Pete to bring him a pitchfork. He took the handle in his right hand and began circling in closer and closer. Then he struck with the fork, pinning the snake to the ground, but a good eighteen inches below the head. The snake lay there threshing about, churning and writhing, but Big John held steady and just laughed.

"I can beat a rattler six-ways-fer-Sunday," he says, as he bent over slowly, his left hand holding the fork handle, his right one steady.

Quick as lightning he reached for the rattles, but the snake was even quicker. She struck him in the left arm just below the elbow.

"By god, she got me," says Big John, jumping back, standing up, and turning ash pale. For a moment they were that scared there wasn't a one of them knew what to do. Then Perry came to, tied a handkerchief around the arm and twisted it up tight. Big John took his jackknife out of his pocket and handed it to Perry.

"All right, shavetail," he says, "slash her deep both ways."

Big John set his teeth and Perry cut away. After that Pete brought up the jug of whiskey and Big John took a long swig.

"Now fellers," he says, "get me down to the marshy ground next to the creek."

They helped him down there, and Perry took his scythe handle and jabbing up and down in the soft muck, worked it into an ooze. Big John rolled over, thrust his arm down in the hole up to the shoulder, and called for more whiskey. He drank up half the jug before he passed out. They left him there for about an hour while one of the Bulmer boys went up to the village for help, and then they hauled him dead drunk up to the saloon at Mud Corners, where Captain Barry made a poultice of blue ash leaves soaked in scalding water. By supper time his arm was as big around as a man's thigh and red as a ripe boil. The next morning the fever had set in.

Big John lay sick at Captain Barry's for almost a month. He had enough poison in his system to kill him, Doc Kimball said, even if he hadn't been struck by a rattler. It wasn't any more than right, Isaac said, that Captain Barry should have to take care of him, seeing as how Big John had been one of his best customers. It wasn't easy, though, when Big John got the fits. He'd rare up in bed, screaming and shouting, like as if he'd seen the devil coming after him. Then he'd fall back, whimpering and crying like a baby. He'd try to pray some then but his words would get all tangled up.

Then he'd rare up again, until they'd have to sit on him or tie him to his bed with a stout rope to keep him down.

Two weeks later when Perry went to see him, Big John lay there all pale and thin, the flesh wasted away until you could see the bones bugging out of the skin.

"Howdy, young feller," says Big John.

"Howdy, Big John," says Perry.

"Doc ain't sure," he says, "but I still figger on overin' it. By god, whiskey and women'll do a feller in all right. The bite's slower 'n a rattler's, but the poison's just as deadly."

Isaac always said Big John got just what he had coming to him, and maybe that was right, Uncle Perry said. He always figured, though, he had cut an eyetooth working alongside of Big John.

Sometimes a feller'll get his whole fun in doin' what he'll be sorry fer afterwards.

Chapter 12

How the farmers *of Milford township organ-*
ized the Regulators, and Malcolm Burnham
came to peach on the blacklegs

It was when the farmers of Milford township organized
the *Regulators* that they ran the blacklegs up salt creek. But
it took a mighty long time.

It's a whole lot easier—every feller fer himself and the
devil fer 'em all.

Hot money had come to be a lot more common than cold,
and every night highwaymen and horse thieves were riding
the roads. The summer Perry worked for Isaac, Phil Beisel
and Luke Babcock both lost teams, and one night some fellows broke into Abar's store, emptying the cash box and
carrying off two sets of harness and a dozen bolts of calico
along with a good many pairs of boots. But the worst thing
of all was what happened to Old Joel Bedford later on that fall,
after Perry had gone on back to Minot's for another term of
school down at Mud Corners.

Old Joel lived a mile east of the post road, about a mile

and a half this side of South Milford. He was a widower, staying alone in the old, double log cabin. His wife had been dead for some years, his son was out West, and his daughter married to a fellow by the name of Cringle over on the Haw Patch. Old Joel had some money, that everybody knew. He never spent a cent, not even buying himself a stove to cook on, and wearing his old buckskin breeches till he was eighty and maybe buried in them in the end, for all Uncle Perry knew.

Old Joel always got up early, sometimes before daycrack, and one morning, just as he was buttoning his breeches, two men came riding into the yard and tied their horses. It was still dark, but Old Joel, from where he stood on the stoop, could see them come walking up towards him between the two cabins.

"Howdy," says Old Joel.

"What we come fer ain't howdyin'," says one of the fellows.

With that he grabbed Old Joel's arm, twisted it behind his back, and pushed him inside the cabin where he slept.

"We're after the money," he says. "Where is it?"

When Old Joel wouldn't say a thing, they pushed him into a chair and tied him down. They cut a swath through the cabin, tearing the blankets off the bed, cutting up the old shuck-tick, emptying the chest upside down, and feeling around the floor puncheons to see if one was loose. When they didn't find a thing, they went across the entryway into the kitchen. There they emptied out the cupboard, ripped the hinges off the old washsink with the leaded-in top, and tore the mantel off the fireplace looking for a hidden crevice in the stone. They emptied the flour bin, ran their fingers through the flour, and even cut open an old cheese that Joel had on the shelf covered with a piece of muslin.

"Goddamn you, where's the money?" says one of them,

coming back and hitting Old Joel over the head with the leg of a bench.

But Old Joel kept shut-pan and wouldn't say a word.

"By god, you'll talk," says the second fellow.

Then they dragged Old Joel over into the kitchen cabin, where one of them raked the fireplace ash till he came down to some live coals from the night before. He took the old dutch oven off the hearth and filled it half full of live coals with the fire shovel. Then they tore off Old Joel's breeches, set him down on the dutch oven, and held him there until it nearly burned all the skin off his backside.

Finally Old Joel broke down.

"It's in the bedpost," he says. "The right one at the foot is holler."

They left him lying there, and he was that weak from the burning and beating that he couldn't move at all. It wasn't till late that evening that Jim Sollers, one of his neighbors, found him, minding that he hadn't seen Old Joel about all day, and hearing the mooley lowing in the barnyard, her bag was that full.

When the fellows in the township came to know about Old Joel and what the blacklegs had done to him, they were mighty roused up. Breaking into a store, or stealing a horse was one thing; beating and burning an old man and letting him lie there—that came nigh onto murder.

All the next day in the streets and stores of Mud Corners the story got passed along, and even over in the schoolhouse Charley Faulk gave up and sent the children all home early, for there wasn't a thing any of them wanted to talk about except what had happened to Old Joel. That night a big crowd gathered at Captain Barry's saloon.

"Goddamn me," says Hoss, "we ought to get every jack man in the township that's got a horse and gun. We could ride down and raid the Tamarack House and if we don't find 'em there, start in combing the swamp."

"I'm for it," says Luke Babcock.

"I figure the time has come all right," says Minot, "for us to get together and do something."

There was a lot of talk about forming a posse then, and more than one fellow was ready to ride, though it wouldn't have done them much good, except maybe to burn the Tamarack House to the ground. But even then they wouldn't likely get the men they were after. As for the tamarack swamp itself, it was too big and filled with bogs and quagmires for a man to venture into, and anyway the men might have been from Northport or Rome City or even Kendall-ville or Fort Wayne. But the feeling was running high.

"What about Latta's mill down to Northport?" says Abar. "I hear say there's fellers ridin' in and out of there every night. We could burn that down."

"Hold on, men," says Judge Carnahan, who had come right over when he heard what was going on. "Don't go doing anything illegal. I hear say," he says, "that some time back the state assembly passed an act making it legal for fellows to organize, if they do it right, a regular society to put down horse thieves and counterfeiters. I say you fellows ought to do that. I'll look into it."

"That's the right thing to do," said Minot.

"All right," says Hoss, "and before sundown tomorrow."

"Give me time to get the legal papers first," says Judge Carnahan. He was an off-ox at being driven.

But the very next day he rode over to La Grange to look up the legal end of it, and two days later they called a meeting at the schoolhouse over at Wright's Corners. Minot rode around the township, telling the men about the meeting, and Hoss brought along about twenty men from up around Applemanberg and Mongoquinong. There were a good many fellows from Mud Corners—Luke and Abar, Lafe and Isaac, Phil Beisel, Captain Barry—and two or three of Old Joel's elbow neighbors, like Jim Sollers and Malcolm Burnham. Malcolm was a newcomer to the neighborhood. Early that spring he had bought out the Abe Beechy place, just a mile this side of South Milford and a half mile east of the old post road.

"Well, men," says the Judge, calling the meeting to order, "we're here to organize a society to protect this community against blacklegs and counterfeiters, and I'm going to tell you how to do it. You can elect up to fifty men, that's the law, and every one of 'em has got to sign these papers. First you elect a chairman, a secretary, and a treasurer, and they make up a membership committee and pass on every man that wants to sign up. If a fellow don't qualify to be a member, they reject him and elect someone else to take his place. Then you take these papers over to La Grange and file 'em with the county commissioners. Every man has got to take an oath to abide by the decisions of the group. If anything goes wrong, or any man does what he's not supposed to do, the whole organization is liable for him down to the last man. That's the law."

"Whew," says Lafe, "what does a feller get fer all that?"

"Every man elected is just like a constable," says Judge Carnahan, "but there isn't any pay."

"What do we need all that fer?" says Abar. "We can hang a horse thief iffen we catch him without all that."

"That we can," says Isaac.

"I'm for doing it legal or not at all," says Minot.

"The way I figger," says John McNutt, "the lessen a feller's got to do with the law, the better. I don't want a dang thing to do with it iffen I got to sign any papers."

"That's right," says Malcolm Burnham. "I move we leave this to the regular officers and courts of law."

"Goddamn me," says Hoss, "we've been doing that for a mighty long time, and they ain't treed a coon yet. Luke and Phil here lost their horses, Abar got his store broke into, and every fellow here knows what happened to Old Joel. He ain't setting down for a spell yet if he'll pull through at all. I say it's high time to quit swapping knives and get into the saddle."

"Bein' a neighbor of Old Joel's," says Malcolm, "I feel mighty bad, but as I see it, there ain't a dang thing a feller can do—"

"By god," says Hoss, biting in, "he can spit on his hand and try."

"Except ridin' posse," says Malcolm, backcapping at Hoss, "and that's like tryin' to beat the devil at his own game. You get a lot of fellers in the saddle and who knows what's likely. The first thing you know they'll be fer hangin' somebody."

"I ain't asking for that," says Hoss, "lessen it's the only way to stop it."

"But it's what's likely," says Burnham, "and you heard what the Judge said. Every feller that signs his name is responsible fer what happens down to the last man. By gum, the only feller I'm a-goin' to be responsible fer is myself. You go rousin' up a lot of fellers—"

"Mr. Burnham," says Hoss, getting riley, "I figure we ain't rousing up a lot of fellows. We're just talking amongst neighbors. I trust my neighbors like I do my own right hand. I figure what we do—all of us standing together—is bound to come out all right."

"Not when you're a-takin' the law into your own hands," says Malcolm.

"The law," says Judge Carnahan, cutting in, "is the express will of the people, and contrariwise, I figure, the will of the people is the law of the land. For me, I say whenever a people or a community feel themselves thus aggrieved and imposed upon by a gang of felons, they've got a right to demand redress, and if the sheriff and the courts of this county fail to come to their rescue, they've got a right to act for themselves. I'm a judge myself, but you fellows know where I stand. I say, go ahead."

"Huzza for Judge Carnahan!" says Hoss.

"Huzza! Huzza!" says a lot of other fellows.

"I move we organize," says Isaac.

And that's what they did. Minot was elected chairman, Hoss, secretary, and Phil Beisel, treasurer. Then they voted to call themselves the *Milford Township Regulators*.

"Every man here who wants to join up, sign his name before he goes," says Minot, and a lot of fellows came right up, crowding around the table to pot-hook their names to the signing-sheet.

"By god, I ain't a-signin'," says John McNutt, walking right on out, and one or two fellows like Lew Shingle and Cellus Blodgett following him.

When it came down to the end of the line, Malcolm Burnham walked up to the table.

"Mr. Martin," he says, "no offense fer what I said in meetin'."

"No, sir," says Hoss. "I figure every fellow's got a right to his own say-so."

"Well, then," says Malcolm, "I reckon I'd kind of like to join."

For a minute Hoss gave him an eye-over from his yellow sidebar whiskers down to the bottom of his gum boots.

"I admire for a man to stand up to his lick-log, salt or no salt," says Hoss. "Besides, we don't know you."

"You'll know me soon enough," says Malcolm.

"That's likely," says Minot, "and we'll be needing every fellow that'll join."

"Before you fellers are through," says Malcolm, "I figger an extra hand may come in mighty handy."

And it did that, though it was the other end to from the way Malcolm was meaning it.

For a time, though, nothing seemed to happen, until many a fellow came to think the whole thing was a lot more bark than bite.

"What are they doing now that they're high and mighty *Regulators*," says Lew Shingle over at Captain Barry's saloon, "except setting on their butts and talking?"

Hoss and Minot were gone a lot that winter, while Perry and Marsh did the chores, though nobody really knew what was going on until later. Before long they came to see they were up against a mighty big thing. They had a line on some fellows like Gregory McDougal from over at Northport, and fellows like George Ulmer and Perry Randolph, but you couldn't be sure they were blacklegs unless you caught them red-handed. Minot and Hoss and the others had been keeping close watch of likely hide-outs, like Latta's mill, and a hawk-eye on all strangers riding in and out of Northport and the little village of Tamarack all winter long. But it was just like beating the devil around a five-cornered stump, Minot said. For one thing there were a lot of fellows handling hot money all through the township. Some might be guilty and some not, and some of them might be highwaymen and horse thieves for all a fellow knew, though he couldn't be sure, for the blacklegs were laying mighty low just then. The whole thing was just about to come dead end, when a chance shot brought down the whole covey.

The way that happened was no Sunday-morning miracle. When Abe Beechy sold his farm to Malcolm Burnham, he had moved on out west, nobody knew where. Half of the money Malcolm had paid him for the farm was in good hard cash and the rest had been in notes drawn on the Merchants' Bank of Lowell, Massachusetts. Abe had been owing Jim Sollers a debt when he left and had given him one of the bank notes to settle up. Jim had held onto it for a while and then turned it over to the bank at Kendallville. Six months later a United States marshal called on him and told him the note was counterfeit. Minot was mighty dubersome, seeing as how Malcolm was a *Regulator*, when Jim came to tell about it, but Hoss was against taking any chances and along about sundown a night or so later, he and Minot and Phil Beisel and a dozen other fellows came riding down the post road and turned off into Malcolm's.

"Howdy, fellers," says Malcolm, as the men dismounted and came walking up to the porch where he stood.

"Howdy," says Hoss. "You said one time an extra hand might come in mighty handy."

"Yes, sir, that I did," says Malcolm.

"Well, sir," says Hoss, "I reckon we can use you right now."

"How's that?" says Malcolm.

"Let's go into the kitchen and set down," says Hoss.

Malcolm led the way inside and they all sat down around the kitchen table.

"Now then," says Minot, "we got a question to ask you. The notes you paid Abe for this farm were counterfeit. Did you know they were bogus?"

"That I didn't," says Burnham, looking around at the men, "so help me God."

"You being a *Regulator*, I'll take your word for it," says Minot, "and now it'll be mighty helpful if you tell just where you got 'em."

"I reckon I can do that all right," says Malcolm, coming back easy. "From the bank at Marysville, Ohio."

"Mr. Burnham," says Hoss, biting in real slow-like, "I figure that's a goddamn lie."

"You callin' me a liar?" says Malcolm.

"That I am," says Hoss, firing a blue whistler. "I figure you got them notes off Gregory McDougal from over at Northport, twenty-five cents on the dollar."

With that Malcolm jumped up and made a lunge for Hoss, but before he could do a thing, Minot grabbed him by the shoulders and sat him back down.

"Now you just tell us where you got those notes," Minot says.

"I ain't a-sayin' a damn thing," said Burnham. "This is my farm and I paid fer it, and you fellers'd better get your butts out of here."

"We're staying right here," says Hoss. "We came to get help and we're going to get it."

"Not from me you ain't," says Burnham. "You ain't got any legal right to come bustin' into a feller's place."

"We got all the legal right we need," says Minot. "Every fellow here is a *Regulator*."

"That don't mean a thing," says Burnham. "That don't give you any right to arrest a feller without evidence or to hold a hearin', now or any time."

"Well, we're doing it," says Hoss.

"Then I ain't a-sayin' a damn thing without a lawyer," says Burnham.

He shut up pan-tight. They sat there for a spell, pleading with him, but it just wasn't any use.

"By god," says Hoss, "if you want an ox to bellow, I figure you got to twist his tail."

He went outside, got a saddle rope, brought it into the room and tied a noose in the end of it. He swung the rope over the open beam above his head; then he walked over and dropped the noose on Malcolm. Joe Foos and one or two of the other fellows grabbed onto the other end, and the rope tightened up. Then Hoss took out his stem-winder and laid it on the table.

"All right, Burnham," says Hoss. "You got five minutes to start talking or if you ain't talking, start praying."

Malcolm just sat there for a minute looking at them, but he could see it was no jolly they were after.

"You said you wouldn't hang a man," he says.

"Goddamn me," says Hoss, "I'd as lief hang you as shoot a dog for killing sheep. A dog don't know what he's doing."

Hoss kept counting off the minutes on his watch. When the time was up, he says, "All right, men," and two or three more fellows laid hold of the rope and gave a heave. Malcolm's eyes bugged out and he was breaking sweat like a bull in fly-time.

"Hold on a minute!" he says. "Hold on!"

When the rope slackened for a minute, he got to fumbling with the noose.

"Get the goddamn thing offen me," he says. "I'll talk."

But even then he drove a hard bargain.

"What I know'll hang a lot of men," he says, "but I ain't a-talkin' lessen I go free."

"We ain't making any promises," says Hoss.

"Look-a-here," says Malcolm, "I got the facts and figgers. I can tell you everything you want to know."

"That's what we came for," says Hoss.

"But I'm a-goin' free," says Malcolm.

"I don't know about that," says Minot.

"I'll turn state's evidence fer the courts," says Burnham.

"I figger that's a fair shake," says Phil, but even then some of the other fellows were against it.

"I'll tell you what we'll do," says Minot. "We'll give you our word there'll be no hanging, but a fair court trial."

"Well," says Malcolm, after he saw there was no other way, "I'll take my chances on that."

Then he told them the notes were bogus all right. He'd got them from Gregory McDougal for twenty-five cents on the dollar, just as Hoss had said. He could get all he wanted at that figure from Gregory McDougal, George Ulmer, and Perry Randolph. They were the leaders of the whole black-leg gang. Nearly every man that had cooned a horse in the county was in cahoots with them and many a fellow that had broken into a store or done robbing on the highway. He could give them every name they needed. It was Gregory himself and Sol Stout that had blistered Old Joel into telling them where his money was. As for him, well, he wouldn't deny what he had done or that he'd been a member of the gang.

It was well after midnight before Malcolm was through. Hoss kept taking down what he said and afterwards they had him sign his name to it. When it was all over, the *Regulators* had a record of the activities of nearly all the men they'd been after and a good many more they hadn't even thought of. Before they left the next morning, they were laying plans for a mighty big raid that would bring in every blackleg in the county.

What to do with Malcolm, though, was a knotty problem. To arrest him right off and take him away to jail might give away the whole show. They could let him stay there, but then he might skip out or even get word to the others more than likely. He was all soft corn and friendly now, but you couldn't be sure, not with a man like Malcolm.

"By god," he says, "I figgered I could beat the game, and maybe I did."

"Maybe you did," says Hoss, "but it don't happy me up any. Hell won't be full till you get there."

"Easy there," says Malcolm. "I figger I done the handsome thing."

"Weaseling?" says Hoss. "I smelled a polecat the first time I ever laid eyes on you, but your tail's down now, I reckon."

So they left Phil Beisel and Joe Foos there to act as guards, and along about daybreak they rode on home.

Ridin' horseback with the devil, a feller ought to figger some on gettin' his backside blistered.

Chapter 13

How the Regulators *hanged Gregory*

McDougal, and what he said before he died

Shootin' a man is trigger-quick, but a hangin' takes time and company.

Four days before the hanging of Gregory McDougal, Minot came home from Ligonier to see his family. Uncle Perry remembered being awakened by the neighing of a horse late at night. Then he heard the voice of Minot, calling out to Marsh to come stable his horse. Later on Minot and Nancy sat talking quietly in the kitchen until long after Marsh had come on upstairs.

"By god," says Marsh, "they're a-goin' to hang him."

"Who?" says Perry.

"Gregory McDougal," says Marsh. "Pap just told me."

"Hang him?" says Perry.

"With a rope around his neck till he's dead," says Marsh.

In the morning the whole family had breakfast together, Minot saying grace low and solemn-like. Then he got ready to go.

"Hoss and I figure on letting the boys come on over," he

says to Nancy. "It'll be something for them to remember."

Two days later Perry and Marsh filled the saddlebags with provisions, swung on some extra blankets for it was airish outside, and, with Harry and Pete Martin along, they set out. Uncle Perry could remember the long ride from Mud Corners to South Milford, past the Tamarack House to Northport, where Marsh pointed out the house in which Gregory lived, and then on west, winding around the lakes and over the hills, to Ligonier, where they saw Minot again, ashen gray and shaken by his own responsibility. Minot had arranged for them to sleep in the loft of the Byler Livery Stable, and there they lay on the soft hay, listening far into the night to the hubbub of voices, the neighing of horses, and the crying of buggy wheels in the street gravel.

In the morning the crowd was terrifying: oxcarts and wagons, buggies and buckboard carriages, men, women, and children, mounted and on foot, milling through the streets. Towards noon the mile-long caravan began the trek to Diamond Lake, led by fifty mounted *Regulators* riding two abreast.

On Minot's orders the boys had ridden on ahead, tethered their horses in the woods, and sat waiting for the first sight of the horsemen coming over the hill. Eighty years later Uncle Perry could still recall the cloudless spring day, the blue water of the lake, the big crowd of people, and the lone oak tree against the sky. For a few minutes he saw the figure of McDougal, a tall, pale man with dark, bushy hair and black mustache, standing on the wagon addressing the crowd. He heard the wagon rumble, saw the body fall, stop jerkily, and stiffen. Then the crowd, quiet and subdued, melted away, and Minot and Hoss came over to gather them together to start the return journey to Mud Corners and home.

"God knows whether we done the right thing or not,"

Minot says to Nancy at the breakfast table the next morning. "I was against it to the very last."

"It's done now," she says, "and you're home again. Lucinda, you'd better be getting busy with the dishes. Boys, you hump along and do your chores; it's getting late."

"Gregory McDougal is dead," says Minot, "and that's how we voted it. But he died like a man. That I got to say for him."

For Minot any man's hanging was like a neighbor's. Gregory McDougal was a horse trader, and though he lived way down at Northport, Minot had run into him more than once at South Milford and Kendallville and had even sold him a three-year-old filly. It wasn't long, though, after they had organized the *Regulators*, and Minot and Hoss and the other members of the central committee had begun to ferret out the evidence, until some of them were ready to bet a bar-share plow against a broken horseshoe that Gregory was a member of the ring.

For one thing Gregory was gone too much at night, some of his own neighbors at Northport said, and no one, not even his own wife, ever knew the next morning where he'd been or where he was going next. For another, Gregory spent a lot of time down at Latta's mill, and he was an old hand at the Tamarack House. There were some fellows down at Northport, too, who said Gregory had passed a lot of bogus and that he more than likely never paid for half the horses he rode in and out of town. But the real clincher had come the night the *Regulators* were ready to string up Malcolm Burnham. Under oath and in the fear of death he had sworn that in the case of Gregory they had the saddle on the lead horse all right.

Four nights later the *Milford Township Regulators* had held their big raid. By daylight the next morning the company had come riding into Ligonier with its prisoners roped and tied saddlefast, down Caven Street to the Haskell and Ellis Hotel, which they had taken over, quartering their blacklegs in the hotel rooms under guard. They had brought in twenty-one men that night, peacefully and otherwise, though two of the men they had been after, George Ulmer and Perry Randolph, had somehow found out about it and skipped the country the night before.

By midmorning the central committee had been ready to begin its hearings in the grand ballroom of the hotel.

"Don't try to bully-rag me," says Gregory, when they brought him in, mean as a young bull just let out to pasture. "No man ever laid a hand on me lessen he was sorry for it and no man ever will."

"We hog-tied Malcolm," says Hoss. "By god, that took the feather-edge off of him."

"Look here, Gregory," says Minot, "we know everything about you that Malcolm knew and then some."

"That's right," says Phil Beisel. "We can hang you, shut-pan or open."

"That's a lie," says Gregory. "Malcolm never talked."

"Is that so?" says Minot, holding up the record so he could see for himself where Burnham had signed his own name. "We got a sworn statement here that says you're a counter-feiter and a horse thief and a leader of the whole gang."

"That's a goddamn lie," says Gregory.

"You broke into a jail in Canada," says Minot, "and you killed an old lady there by hitting her over the head."

"Damn you, that's a lie," says Gregory. "I hit her, but I didn't kill her."

"You and Malcolm broke into Abar Cain's store at Mud Corners," says Phil.

"You can't prove that," says Gregory. "You're just firin' a pot shot."

"By god," says Hoss, "we know when we got the lead bird. How about that fellow's house you burned down over in Kosciusko county?"

"That's a lie," says Gregory. "Malcolm Burnham boggled that job himself. If you fellers want my story, I can tell it to you, but goddamn Burnham for a liar."

"We're wanting the whole story and we want it straight," says Minot, "and you're going to sign your name to it."

"What if I do?" says Gregory.

"We ain't making any promises this time," says Hoss.

"Then what if I don't?" says Gregory.

"Here's the rope that strung up Burnham," says Hoss.

"You hang him?" says Gregory.

"Not yet," says Phil. "He talked."

"I ain't afraid of hangin'," says Gregory. "But nobody else is tellin' my story."

He was born in Wallaceburg, Canada, he told them, the son of a minister. He got married when he was nineteen and set up as a tavern keeper in Wallaceburg. About six months after that his brother, Miles, got arrested for stealing a horse and was locked up in the jail at Chatham. He and another of his brothers, John, decided to get him out.

"No damn jail was ever strong enough to hold a Mc-Dougal," he says, "and, by god, this one ain't a-goin' to be."

They rode over to Chatham one night, and while John held the horses, he clambered over the stockade wall and stove in the jail door. He found the jailer's wife sleeping inside and hit her over the head with a stick, until she gave him the keys to the lockup and a bag of money from under her pillow which he hadn't even asked for. After he'd let Miles out, he'd tossed the money and the keys back to her before they made their getaway, saying, "Here, I don't want your gold."

"That ought to be proof enough I didn't hurt her," he says.

After that he couldn't stay on in Wallaceburg, he said, so they separated, he himself crossing the border over into New York state. He worked around some at one thing or another for a month or so before he met Sherman Marlott at Springwater and hired out to ride horses for him. It wasn't long before he knew what Marlott was doing all right, but by that time he'd seen some good money.

"It's on the shady side of the law that it comes easy; any feller knows that," he says.

It wasn't long, then, before he set out for himself. The first span he ever took, he said, belonged to a farmer near Havana. He drove them all the way to Michigan where he sold them to a farmer near Burr Oak. There he broke into a store, hid the stolen goods out in the woods till he'd found another likely team, and then brought it with him to Latta's mill at Northport, where he found some fellows who knew what to do with cooned stuff, just as Sherman Marlott had told him he would. He liked Northport and decided to stay there. With the money he'd made, he had gone shares with Perry Randolph and the others in getting some counterfeit dies, bought the Winthrop property, and then went back to bring his wife and child from Wallaceburg, telling her he had bought into a well-established business, which it was, as they themselves knew.

"Name me any ten men in northern Indiana," he says, "and I'll name you one that's handled hot money, and some of 'em high and mighty *Regulators* who were damn glad to get it for twenty-five cents on the dollar."

He kept on buying and selling horses, he said, sometimes paying for them in bogus and sometimes cooning them. The two fellows that took Phil Beisel's team were working for him all right. He later drove them to New York state, where he sold them for seventy-five dollars and a gold watch. It was true he helped Malcolm break into Abar Cain's store, but that was in return for a favor that Malcolm had done him. It was Malcolm who had told him and George Ulmer about Old Joel Bedford and his money, saying he was too near a neighbor to do it himself.

"It's too damn bad," he says, "that Old Joel got burned, but he's a mulish old ox. Why didn't he tell us where the money was right away?"

There was a great deal more to the full story and it took him until three o'clock that afternoon to finish. Gregory said he figured it wasn't exactly a good record, but many a man had done a lot worse. As for him, he wasn't afraid of the *Regulators*. He told them what he did because he wanted to. There wasn't a court in the land that would convict him on his own testimony, he said, for he'd go into court and swear it was all a goddamn lie, given to them under duress. Besides, he said, he never laid a hand on any man in his life, except for hitting the old lady up at Chatham and setting Old Joel on the dutch oven with the live embers in it and one other fellow in New York state, where he and Marlott tied a cloth soaked in chloroform over his face—he might have gotten sick some—but so help him, he never killed anyone.

But in the end that's why the *Regulators* came to hang him.

At the time they were questioning the men they had brought in on the night of the big raid, there was a lot of rumor and hearsay, and the news of what was going on traveled fast. A day or so after Gregory had told his story, a fellow from Michigan arrived at Ligonier and swore that the old lady at Chatham had died from the beating Gregory had given her, and that in Canada a reward was being offered for him, dead or alive.

"I move we hang him," says Hoss.

"For murder," says Phil.

"We ain't but one man's word for that," says Minot.

"We got his own word for it that he's a blackleg," says Hoss, "and that's enough. It ain't just that fellows have lost horses or the thieving that's been done. And it ain't even Old Joel or even the old lady up at Chatham, though any man's my neighbor come rattlers and blacklegs. By god, we got a bounden duty. If we let Gregory off, every jack man of 'em will go free."

"That's right," says Minot. "But it's a hard thing to hang a man."

"Not for murder, it ain't," says Phil.

"We can turn him over to the courts," says Minot.

"He'll get a year or two when they get around to it, or more 'n likely go free, just like he says," says Phil.

"We've tried all that before," says Hoss. "If we let him go now, fellows like Lew Shingle will still be saying the *Regulators* are all talk and no cider. Even the blacklegs will be laughing at us. And what about the fellows outside there in Caven Street? They're the ones whose horses were stolen, whose houses and stores were broke into, who were cheated out of their lands by bogus money, and waylaid and beaten. They'll hang ever' jack man of 'em to the nearest tree if they ever get their hands on 'em, and they got a right to, if we don't act now. I tell you, if we let Gregory go now, no man will be safe even in his own home after nightfall."

Even Minot knew that Hoss was dead right about that. From the first day the story got around about the raid, the people had been streaming in from all over the county, and even from down around Fort Wayne and over in Ohio and up into Michigan. Some of them came just to see what was going on, but others came to tell how they'd been robbed, or had their horses stolen, or their buildings burned down, or to claim the stolen goods the *Regulators* had found hidden in Latta's mill and the Tamarack swamp, or to see what justice would be done now that they had the men. There were a good five hundred people in town before the end of the week; every house in the village was overflowing and a good many were camping right out in the streets.

Many a man was swearing at the *Regulators*, wanting to know why they didn't string them up right away, and when was it all going to happen, and why not. If the *Regulators* couldn't make up their minds, let them turn over the black-legs to the crowd; they'd take care of them. But there were others, too, who were friends of the men that had been arrested, knew them for good neighbors, swore they were honest fellows, and what did the *Regulators* think they were doing. Maybe the crowd ought to get some guns and clubs and go on in and free their friends. Before the week was out, there were a lot of fist fights, black eyes, and bruised shins.

When the crowd outside found out that the committee was voting whether to hang Gregory or not, there was a brabble of voices up and down the street. Some fellows were cursing Gregory. Some were crying for him. Some were even kneeling down in the streets and praying. Some young fellows began hurling stones at the hotel. Old Judge Gower, a justice of the peace for Perry township, mounted a store box in front of the hotel and addressed the crowd.

"I'm warning you," he says, "that what the *Regulators* are doing is against the law of the land and the will of Almighty God. Gregory McDougal has got a right to a jury trial."

"We elected a jury to try him," says a *Regulator* in the crowd.

"The law belongs to the courts," says Gower. "You're taking it into your own hands."

"What's the backin' and fillin' and wrigglin' of the courts ever done fer us?" says the *Regulator*.

"Let every God-fearing man that's for giving Gregory McDougal a jury trial," says Gower, "come over here on my side of the street and stand by me."

"And let every man of you wantin' to see justice done, come over here and stand by me," says the *Regulator*, walking across the street.

For a spell, then, there was a lot of pulling and shoving, men arguing with their friends and neighbors and even women with their husbands, pushing each other this way and that, and calling back and forth across the street.

When the central committee found out what was going on, Minot and Hoss and Phil came on out to see for themselves.

"All right, fellows," says Minot, "let everybody stand still and be quiet."

Then he told them what the *Regulators* were doing and why. Gregory McDougal was a blackleg; they had his own word for that. He had owned up to taking more than forty horses, to twenty-one robberies, and to passing thousands of dollars in counterfeit money, but they had no evidence that he was a murderer—only one man's word for that, and Gregory himself swore that he had never killed a man. That he asked them to remember. Then he told them to change sides if they wished to, and after that for every man to stand still and be counted.

When they were all quiet once more, Hoss and Phil counted the votes. Two hundred and eighty-nine voted for hanging; sixty-three men and five women voted against it. Minot told them the final tally.

"What the *Regulators* do is in the name of the people," he says. "We will abide by what the people say."

He set the date then for the hanging, one week from that day, and asked every *Regulator* to be there, mounted and armed, and in good file and order. Then he told them all to go home quietly and accept their own decision.

What happened in Caven Street took the tuck out of Gregory. The next morning he begged to see his wife and child, and Minot and Phil drove over to Northport and brought Mrs. McDougal and the boy back to Ligonier. On the morning of the day set for the hanging, he asked for a minister to come and pray with them and to bless his wife and child. After that he kissed his wife tenderly and asked her to take good care of the boy. Then he came over to the door and told the men outside that he was ready. They took him down the steps to an open carriage where he sat with four members of the *Regulator* committee. With the companies falling in ahead and behind, they set out for Diamond Lake.

When they got there, Jim Black drove his wagon under the oak tree, and the men rigged a plank, one end resting on the wagon and the other on a prop near the tree. Charley Peck swung a rope over a limb up above the plank. Gregory got out of the carriage and walked over to the wagon.

"Mr. Gilmore," he says, "you're a fair-minded man. Can I say somethin' now?"

"I reckon you got that coming," says Minot.

Gregory got up on the wagon and looked at the people standing around.

"No feller is happy to die," he says, "but I'm right glad to see a large crowd here today. I hope some of you will take a warnin' from this. I confess before all of you that I have been a counterfeiter, a robber, and a horse thief. I've got no hard feelin' towards any of you. I hear say some of you think the *Regulators* are wrong in what they're doin'. I don't figger it that way. I think they're right. Some of you are just as guilty as I am, and I hope you'll all take warnin' from me. For my old mother in Canada and for my wife and child, I'm sorry. I hear fellers say that I bragged I wasn't afraid of God or the devil. But I am afraid of God. It is His will that I die for my sins, and I trust in God to have mercy on my soul."

Charley Peck tied a cloth over his eyes, dropped the noose over his head, and Jim Black drove the wagon out from under the plank. No one said a word after that, and when Minot came over to the boys, he still had tears in his eyes.

A week after the hanging, Minot and Hoss set out again, riding around the neighborhood and to all the *Regulators* until they had raised three hundred and fifty dollars which they took over to Northport and gave to Mrs. McDougal. Then the central committee turned over all the rest of the blacklegs to the regular officers and courts of law. Malcolm Burnham was tried in the United States District Court and was sentenced to two years in the pen. Ed Kessler and Sol Stout were found guilty in the circuit court at Albion and got six months. Others were involved in long legal battles, and some of them had served their sentences and were out again before the rest came up for trial. For some of them Andy Morrison from over at La Grange won an acquittal.

Two months after the hanging, the central committee placed a marker on Gregory's grave in the Northport cemetery. "Gregory McDougal," it reads, "b 1831–d 1859. 'I trust in God to have mercy on my soul.'"

Ridin' along at night, two men make fer company, but when a blackleg hangs fer what he done, he hangs alone.

Chapter 14

How Orsemus Highbargin *hanged himself, and*

the Regulators came to have their last meeting

A good neighbor makes a fine mornin', but it's a long time till sundown.

For a spell after the *Regulators* hanged Gregory Mc-Dougal, Minot was the big talk of the township.

"By god, it takes a lot of grit and courage to do that," says Luke Babcock down at Captain Barry's saloon.

"That it does," says Lafe Klingerman, drinking up. "The way I figger Minot's too big a man fer this place. He ought to be a circuit judge—"

"Or a state assemblyman," says Seth Talbot. "By gum, that's right. He'd learn 'em down there how to fish or cut bait."

" 'What we do, we are doing for the people,' he says, 'and we'll abide by what the people say.' That's what he told 'em over to Caven Street and that's what he done," says Luke. "I figger that's a mighty fine say-so."

"That it is," says Seth, "but it don't get any spring plowing done. I was talking to Marsh yesterday. Minot ain't turned a furrow all spring. Marsh and Perry got the ten acres plowed, but they ain't touched the new-ground Minot was aiming to break this spring."

"That's too bad," says Luke. "You fixing to plant?"

"Monday," says Seth. "The boys ran the marker today."

"I got mine in," says Luke. "Finished last night. How about some of us fellows getting in there and helping out Minot? That's about the least we could do. How about a couple yoke from you, Lafe?"

"Wednesday I could," says Lafe. "I'm figgerin' on finishin' up my own on Monday and Tuesday."

"Good enough," says Luke, "let's make it Wednesday. If we can get about twelve yoke and three bar-shares, we can turn that new-ground in three days."

But it didn't take that long. When they found out what was going on, nearly every man in the township joined in. Some sent two or three yoke with their drivers, others brought their plows, still others came with the oxen dragging stone-boats hanging heavy with log chains and loaded down with mattocks and pickaxes. By midmorning there were thirty-five yoke of oxen and two dozen men and boys at work on the twenty. Some of them got busy grubbing out the stumps and butts that had been left to rot three years before, when Minot and Marsh had cut over the twenty and rolled the logs for burning. Then they swung the log chains around the stumps or a tough root while the boys, Marsh and Perry and Pete Martin and Dave Talbot, lined up three or four yoke of oxen. There was a lot of heave-ho, prodding and bellowing, and then suddenly—Joe Foos letting out a war whoop—the stump would give way, uprooting and tumbling over, digging out holes and furrows and scattering dirt. The chains would fall slack and the oxen come to a stop. The boys would load the pieces onto the stone-boats or, driving the oxen, drag them to the edge of the field for burning; while the men filled up the holes with their spades and leveled off the ground. Then the huge breaking plows, each drawn by five yoke of oxen, began turning over the heavy sod.

At noon the oxen were unyoked and fed hay and grain, while the men and boys trooped down to the house, where long slit-deal tables had been rigged up in the shade of the farmyard trees. There the womenfolk—Nancy and Nell Babcock and Lizzie Klingerman and Lissa and Esther and Lily Talbot—were loading down the tables with turkey and chicken, venison and head sausage that had been salted down during the winter, egg noodles and wild rice, and boiled hominy, and big messes of spring greens. There was corn bread and wheat bread, too, and Mattie Babcock and her younger sister, Betsy, and Lucinda were carrying out steaming hot pies that had been baked in the old, brick bake-oven back of the house.

Before the men came over to eat, they washed up at the farmyard draw well. There was a deal of pushing and crowding, good-natured jibing and laughter.

"By gum, it's amazing what Joe's war whoop will do to a yoke of oxen," says Seth Talbot.

"It's the best day's work Joe ever done in his life," says Lafe, laughing, "and damn near the only one, I mind me."

"I just figgered every one of them stumps was a blackleg," says Joe, "and they come up mighty easy."

While they were eating, Captain Barry drove into the yard with three jugs of whiskey. After that had gone the rounds, there was a lot of huzzaing and some speeches.

"Neighbors," says Minot, "I'm mighty thankful."

"No need for that," says Luke Babcock.

"Sometimes a fellow don't know whether he's doing right or not," says Minot, "but if we all work together, I reckon things are bound to come out all right. No man knows right lessen he trusts his neighbors. That I know today better 'n I ever did before."

"Huzza! Huzza!" says a dozen fellows.

"I figure as long as we all stand together like we did down to Caven Street and like we're doing today, we'll be doing the right thing, all right. I hear say some fellows think we did wrong hanging Gregory—they call it murder."

"Hanging Gregory wasn't murder," says Luke. "That wasn't any more 'n a plain act of justice."

And that's what they all thought up in Milford township, Uncle Perry said, but some folks have a mighty good forgettery. With Gregory dead and in his bury-hole, it was plumb easy to forget what he had done, and before the corn on the new-ground was knee-high, some fiddle-minds were giving out a new tune.

"They took a feller's life in cold blood, that's what they done," says John McNutt one afternoon down at Jim Ball's blacksmith shop.

"You hear say what's happening down to Rome City right now?" says Lew Shingle. "I was talking the other day to a fellow that knows old Charley Peck. Well, sir, old Charley has been failing steady. They say he ain't slept a single night. Now and then he'll doze off all right, but then he'll dream that it's all happening again. There he'll be standing on the plank with Gregory, fumbling with the noose, trying to get it down over his head. Try as he will, it won't go. Then the plank wiggles and skitters out from under him and he and Gregory fall down with a big crash."

"That don't surprise me a-tall," says John. "I knowed a feller once—"

"That ain't the worst of it," says Lew. "This fellow says, when that happens, Charley wakes up and there sure as life is

Gregory himself, standing at the foot of the bed, dead as when they cut him down, his eyes bugging out, his chin dropped down, the red marks of the rope on his neck, plain as day."

"By god," says Luke Babcock, "I wouldn't want to be in Charley's boots for a thousand dollars."

"I figger that's just a story," says Seth. "I was talking to Minot the other day. Minot says Charley has been dreaming some, but then he's had bilious spells fer a good many years already. He ain't been well for a long time."

"I say it's true more 'n likely," says John. "I knowed a feller once that see the devil before he died. He hadn't even killed a man, though he'd done him some wrong. There ain't a man in the *Regulators* fitten to face Almighty God. I figger some day Minot'll be reapin' what he sowed."

And it's a downright curious thing the way the Almighty sometimes seems to be a-takin' the wrong side.

By the middle of July the corn on Minot's twenty stood shoulder-high and began to show tassel, a full week ahead of most of the fields in the neighborhood. Then, though the early summer had been givey enough, the weather turned hot and dry, burning up the meadow lands and stubble fields and curling the corn leaves just when the stalks began driving ear. A good rain right then might have made a thousand bushels of corn on the new-ground, but if the weather held, there would be nothing for it except to cut the whole field for fodder.

A morning or so later there were two or three clouds coming up slowly from the west, too light for rain though the weather looked more hopeful. Towards noon the larger one had come directly overhead. There were a few drops of rain, a jagged streak of lightning, and one long rumble of thunder. Then a burst of hail, like cherry stones at first, Uncle Perry said, then as big as hen's eggs and walnuts, came cracking down from the sky, rattling against the roofs and walls, breaking windowpanes, stripping and riddling the leaves on the farmyard trees. Afterwards the corn on the new-ground stood stripped and broken like a bed of reeds in the bottom lands in the spring. There was nothing even to cut for fodder now, nothing at all except a few days of soiling corn for the cattle.

The hailstorm hit less than a section of land, petering out later on into a pleasant sprinkle of rain. When the word got around what had happened, many another fellow began to be dubersome, and—minding the planting—came riding or driving by to see what he couldn't but figure was an act of God.

"What's Minot a-sayin' now?" says John McNutt to Luke Babcock.

"He ain't saying much," says Luke.

"By gum, it's just as plain as the writin' on that Bible feller's wall."

"I'm beginning to see it myself," says Luke.

But the worst thing of all that summer was what happened to Orsemus Highbargin. After the *Regulators* had hanged Gregory, they turned the body over to Orsemus to prepare for burial. Orsemus was an odd-job carpenter and cabinet maker who lived over at Northport, a spindly old fellow who had been suffering crazy spells for a good many years then already. Late in the summer he went crazy once more and killed himself. His neighbors found him the next day, hanging by a rope from one of the rafters of an old outhouse, his face turned blue and dried slobber over his beard and clothes. The talk that went around was that the devil himself had hanged him, for there wasn't a stool or bench around that Orsemus could have stood on to tie the rope.

"I hear say," says Lew Shingle, "that Orsemus knew Old Nick was coming for him. The night he was working on Gregory he had a sign. He was turning the body over on the table, measuring for the bury-box, when all of a sudden, sure as daylight, Gregory's arm reached out and his finger pointed right at Orsemus. Orsemus was that scared he broke out in a cold sweat and his knees gave way. But from that time on he was sure he was next. 'Old Nick put the finger on me today,' he says."

"You sure of that?" says Luke.

"It's a god's fact," says Lew. "Murder is murder, and the devil's had his hand in this whole thing."

"I'm getting out of the *Regulators* right now," says Luke.

"You should've done that long ago," says John McNutt. "Even Minot'll come to see that."

Two weeks later the *Regulators* had another call to duty. At the time of the big raid, when they caught Gregory and the others, two of the ringleaders, George Ulmer and Perry Randolph, had gotten away. After the hanging of Gregory, the *Regulators* offered a reward of three hundred dollars for their capture to a detective from Chicago by the name of Bradley. Bradley followed the men through five states, Indiana, Kentucky, Tennessee, Pennsylvania, finally making the arrest in a small tavern three miles west of Newton, Ohio. When the news came to South Milford and Mud Corners, the township was in an uproar once more.

"More blood for the hangman," says John McNutt.

"Ain't they done enough already?" says Luke. "Charley Peck is dying; Orsemus hung himself."

When Minot got word from Bradley, he and Hoss called for a meeting of the *Regulators* to take over the men. But more than one fellow by that time found that he'd mired his oxen in the ditch or had married a wife and couldn't come.

Others, like Lafe and Isaac Grimes, said openly that they were now against the whole thing, they didn't like what had happened, and they'd have nothing more to do with the *Regulators*. For a time it looked to Minot as if there would be no more than a handful of men ready to stand by him and Hoss and see the thing through to the edge of the clearing.

On the day before the meeting at South Milford, Minot rode over to La Grange to see Sheriff Cummings, and then he and Hoss rode the rounds summoning the men. The next morning the *Regulators* gathered in South Milford—such of the men as would come, about twenty all told—waiting for the arrival of Bradley and the prisoners. Before long a large crowd of spectators gathered around them, some like Marsh and Perry waiting just to see what would happen, some hoping for excitement, and others already taking sides openly against the *Regulators*.

It was almost noon before the detective's carriage, preceded and followed by six horsemen, rolled into the village. In the open carriage where the crowd could see them, with iron chains on their wrists and ankles, sat George Ulmer and Perry Randolph, their faces ash pale and a down-look in their eyes. As the procession came to a stop, the crowd became silent. Mr. Bradley alighted from the carriage and shook hands with Minot.

"Well, Mr. Gilmore," he says, "we got your men all right, but they led us a mighty wicked chase. I feel mighty proud to deliver them into your hands."

"Oh, my god," says Perry Randolph from the carriage, "he's a-turnin' us over to the *Regulators*."

"You keep your pan shut," says one of the guards, clapping his hand over Randolph's mouth.

But it was too late then. What he'd said was like a friction-match in dry tinder.

[*151*]

"You *Regulators* figgerin' on murderin' another man?" shouts John McNutt from the crowd.

"Murder's right," says Lew Shingle.

"Let's take 'em away," says another fellow.

Then the fight broke out. It began with a lot of pushing and shoving, some fellows in the crowd shouting and swearing at the *Regulators* and calling on others to help out. The *Regulators* stood their ground—though they never fired a shot—and tried to keep the crowd back with the butt-ends of their guns. Fellows kept crowding in though, butting and wrestling, some lunging out with their fists, others down on their hands and knees trying to crawl through to the blacklegs, until it was tuck and go whether the crowd wouldn't overpower the *Regulators* and let the men go. When Bradley saw what was happening, he shouted to his guards, and Sheriff Cummings of La Grange and his deputies swung in, too. There were a half-dozen shots, and then the crowd began to fall back. No one was killed, though some fellows got hurt, and Cellus Blodgett lost an arm from a bullet wound that gangrened afterwards. When the crowd was quieted down once more, Minot climbed up into the carriage.

"Hold on, neighbors," says Minot, "I want to say something."

"Ain't you said and done enough?" says Luke.

"You hung one feller," says John McNutt, "and you got his murder on your soul right now."

"God Almighty can judge that," says Minot.

"He's already done that," says John.

"Now that Gregory McDougal is dead," says Minot, "he's got a mighty lot of friends. I mind me the day over to Caven Street when you were all against him. Many a fellow in this crowd voted to hang him that day. As a *Regulator* I helped to hang Gregory McDougal and whatever guilt that puts on my soul, I'm ready to own to before God. I mind me the last thing Gregory ever said—'I trust in God to have mercy on my soul.' The way I figure that's all a man can ever ask for—that and knowing that he done his duty as he saw it."

Then he turned to the *Regulators*.

"Men," he says, "what we done, we done because we thought it was the right thing to do. We agreed to stick together till we'd laid our hands on the last horse thief and counterfeiter in the county. I figure we've done that right now. Mr. Bradley," he says, "we accept your prisoners and we're turning them over to Sheriff Cummings of La Grange and to the La Grange County Circuit Court. That's our last official act. From now on we can go back to tend to our stores and our farms. It wasn't an easy thing, and let no fellow be proud in his heart, but I figure we done exactly what we set out to do."

And Minot was right, as many a fellow came to see later on. It was the hanging of Gregory that put an end to the blacklegs. Not a man arrested by the *Regulators* and later sentenced by the courts—or even those who won an acquittal like Hank Gore and Miles Payne—ever came back to the county to live after they got out. And more than one man down at Northport and the Tamarack village left the county and moved on, even though he wasn't arrested at all. Uncle Perry couldn't recall a highway robbery or a store broken into or a horse being stolen in the township after that.

When Minot was through talking, he thanked Mr. Bradley and paid over the money for the reward. Sheriff Cummings and his deputies rode off with the men, and the crowd on the streets slowly began to break up. Not a man in South Milford said a word to Minot, as he and Hoss and the boys got on their horses and rode away.

"I know it ain't the same thing and I ain't justifying him

any," says Minot, "but sometimes I figure I know how Judas Iscariot must have felt."

"By god," says Hoss, laughing, "you ain't got thirty pieces of silver."

"The hardest thing of all," says Minot, "is a fellow like Luke Babcock. He and I've been neighbors for nigh onto twenty years. He's a notionate fellow now and then, but that don't explain it all."

"Well," says Hoss, "I got old John McNutt living next to me. He ain't said a word to me, not even to pass the time of day, since we hung Gregory, but it don't faze me any. I figure the surest way of knowing I'm right is when old John's against it."

"But it's an uneasy thing," says Minot. "The sun don't rise the same way in the morning, not with trouble between a man and his neighbors."

Sometimes, doin' his duty, it ain't the ease, it's the heartache a feller remembers.

Chapter 15

How the good Lord *drowned Jim Ballard, and Libby Dingham saw the angels before she died*

Any wag-tongue in the neighborhood could tell you how Libby Dingham saw the devil before she died. For three nights running she held him off with a poker and a pair of fire tongs. On the last morning, propped high up on the goose-down pillows, she saw two angels all in white with wings on their shoulders kneeling by the deacon bench in front of the fire. An hour later she was dead.

"Praises be," says Lizzie Klingerman, who had been a bedside sitter night and day, "she's bust home to glory."

"From a world of wickedness," says the Elder Gibson. "It was a mighty close call."

And it's a hard thing to figger, whether it was the devil or the angels the neighborhood come to find the glory in.

Poor Libby had come a long hard way. She bettered fifty when she died, but for her it had all been flax in the fire with the devil at the bellows. Five years earlier at a camp meeting in the woods near Cochran's Corners, she had found religion for the third straight time.

"Oh Jesus," she says at the big experience meeting, "Oh Jesus, I've been a vile sinner. Twice I come to the table of the Lord and both times I backslid. Oh Jesus, I was meanin' to be good, but sinnin' comes easy. 'Jim,' I says the last time, 'Jim, I ain't a-livin' with you in sin no more. The Lord has washed me clean.' But he wouldn't get out, and I couldn't get him to the preacher's, and there we went right on, and I backslid on the Lord. But I'm saved now. I'm saved. I feel the glory. Hallelujah! Hallelujah!"

But even that time the good Lord had to drown Jim Ballard to bring in the victory.

Jim had been living with Libby off and on then for ten years or more in what used to be known as the old Buckhorn Tavern on the west shore of Long Lake. He was a big, trunchy, slow-moving fellow with a deep bullfrog voice when he talked at all, which wasn't very often. He fished some in the lake when the weather held up, faulted the Lord when it didn't since he couldn't get his hoeing done, ate what victuals she set on the table, and slept with Libby.

It was the living in sin that Libby never quite came to cater to. Besides that she was right folksy, and the sight of humans on foot and horseback, ox teams and jolt wagons, all moving over to the Methodist camp meeting always brought the longings on her. Jim had forbidden her to go, and when Libby sneaked off before he ever knew what she was up to, he had gotten himself ring-tailed drunk and followed her there.

Libby arrived late, walking around in the ring of darkness outside of where the great tallow lanterns hung in the trees until she saw where Lizzie Klingerman was sitting deep in the crowd, and then she worked her way in and slipped into a seat alongside of Lizzie.

The two women sat there for a minute whispering before they joined in the singing, and then later on settled down to listen to the hour-long sermon, Libby drinking in the fire and brimstone words like a rain-thirsty corn patch come a summer shower.

After the sermon was over and the congregation began singing the coming-on hymn, the Elder walked down the aisle, shaking hands with the sinners and calling on them to come out for the Lord.

"Come to Jesus," he says. "Oh sinners, come to Jesus."

Libby had been through it all before, and when the Elder stretched out his hands, she rose uncertainly on her feet, took one step, and fell forward into his arms.

"Praises be," says the Elder, holding her up, the big brown hand stroking her shoulder. "Praises be to God. Here is a sinner come to Jesus."

It was then that Jim came moving out of the darkness into the light of the lanterns, walking heavily and stiff-legged down the center aisle. "Goddamn you, leave her be," he bellows in a voice that stopped a good many of them in their singing.

"She's got a call," says the Elder. "Praises be. She's a-coming home to the Lord."

"I says to leave her be," says Jim, coming up and grabbing Libby by the arm.

"You setting yourself between this woman and the Lord?" says the Elder.

"Come on," says Jim to Libby, pushing the Elder aside. "Come on, you prattlin' flutter-bird! We're a-goin' on home!"

Libby screamed out and clung to the Elder. "Oh Jesus, save me," she says. "I'm a-livin' in sin."

"Hold off!" says the Elder. "Hold off in the name of the Lord. You let this woman go."

Jim turned back on the Elder with his fists doubled though he never got to hit a blow. The Elder could see Jim was blind-staving drunk, and being a big fellow himself and agile as a panther, he could have downed Jim like a head-hammered ox, but he never laid a hand on him. Instead of that, he just dropped right down on his knees, there in the sawdust-covered forest aisle, and started in praying.

"Oh God," he says, "drive the devil from this fellow's heart. He's a mighty big man, mean and strong, and he's a sinner. Take the swearing from his lips, the taste of liquor from his tongue, and the desire for sin from his heart. Go on up to the altar, sister!" he says to Libby, interrupting his prayer. "Go on up! Sing on!" he calls out to the congregation. "Sing on!"

And they sang out then, loud and strong:

> Just as I am, though tossed about
> With many a conflict, many a doubt,
> Fightings and fears within, without,
> O Lamb of God, I come! I come!

while the Elder, kneeling there, went on wrestling with the devil for big Jim's soul.

"Save him, Oh Lord, save him," he says, "if that be in accord with Thy will, and if it ain't, keep him from interfering with Thy work. Oh Lord, the devil is a mighty lion, seeking whom he may devour, and he's got a mighty hold on Jim."

For a minute Jim just stood there kind of dazed as if he didn't understand what was really going on; then with a shamefaced down-look, he turned on his heel and lumbered on out of the grove, swearing and cursing in his beard. He was that drunken mad Libby was afraid to go back to the

Buckhorn alone after the meeting was over, so she went along home with Lizzie Klingerman to Mud Corners to spend the night.

The next morning she set out for Long Lake still afraid of what Jim might say or do, though it was a useless fear for she never set eyes on him again, not in the living flesh. When she got to the Buckhorn, she could see he'd been there, for he'd slammed things inside the cabin every which way, but he wasn't there any more, and she couldn't find hide nor hair of him inside the house or out in the barn. She called out once or twice and when there wasn't any answer, she got uneasy and went on down to the lake. Sure enough, the boat was gone from the landing, and when she walked along the shoreline to where she could see around the bend, there it was turned over and floating about ten yards offshore.

She let out a scream and ran for help. As soon as the news got around a good many of the neighbors came down, and Minot and Lew Shingle and Abar and Marsh and a dozen others built a raft and tying a canthook onto a hay rope began dragging for the body. Just about sundown Abar hooked into Jim's coat, but he was dead all right and it wasn't hard to tell what had happened. Still drunk more than likely when he'd gone fishing, he must have stumbled and fallen onto the side of the boat, turning it over. It had rained some that morning and Jim had been wearing his gumshoe boots which had filled and dragged him down. It was a mortal sad thing to see him all laid out there, the heavy, bloated body and the bloodshot eyes before they closed the lids, and the Elder Gibson's minding every one of them, as he did, what had happened the night before.

"O depart from me, ye workers of iniquity," he says the next day at the funeral, quoting from the Good Book. "Woe unto him that is mighty in strong drink. Let death seize upon him and take him quick into hell, where the worm dieth not and the fire is not quenched."

At the time Libby carried on something fearful. It was all her own fault, she said. God had made her a mighty temptress just like Eve, and she had led Jim into sin. And then she had disobeyed and run away from him, and Jim had followed her in drunkenness and anger. And now he was gone forever.

Gradually, though, a change seemed to come over her. She hustled around, sand-scrubbed and whitewashed the little cabin, hung some white curtains at the windows, and sorted out and polished the pearl-handled silver she had brought all the way from Vermont state. She took out her best dress, too, washed and ironed it, and after that many a summer afternoon she walked the full three miles to Mud Corners, just to see folks and to pass the time of day. All summer long she never missed a donation bee nor an apple-paring nor a quilting. But that very fall, just when everybody thought Libby had turned up a new leaf for sure, she up and joined Hugo Rogers and the Spiritualists.

A few months earlier, like a first locust heralding a swarm, Hugo Rogers had appeared at Mud Corners. He was some far-off kin to Selina Cain, a second cousin or so, and belonged to the *Order of Patriarchs* down at Cincinnati. Right off he had begun to tell Selina and her neighbors all about the rappings, and how the spirits could move tables and lift a fellow right up into the air and bring folks messages from the dead. The spirits would do it for him, too, he said, and he was ready to show them all. After the talk had gotten around and Selina had had one or two meetings with her close neighbors, it swept through the township like a plague.

Hugo wasn't but a spindly little fellow, but he burned like a white flame inside, and there was a deep, lantern-like light in his eyes that made any woman feel fainty, if she believed in him at all.

On the first night Libby went, they all gathered around in a circle, put out the candles, and held hands. Libby could feel Hugo's hand stiffen in hers as his body grew rigid and he spoke a stream of gibberish. Then the table in the middle of the room slowly rose from the floor and tapped out some answers. When they relit the candles, she was ashy-white and trembly, and when Hugo told her he had seen and talked with her dead boy, Arad, Libby fainted dead away.

It was a way-up new thing for Libby and mighty comforting, until later on when the whole neighborhood got to talking about her and Hugo. Winter had come on by that time, and when Libby had a sick spell and couldn't leave her house, Hugo took to calling on her down at Long Lake. It wasn't but a friendly bedside visit once or twice, Libby said, but it wasn't long till Abar was ready to qualify that many an afternoon Hugo never got home at all, that is, not until nigh onto daylight the next morning. And before the winter was out, it had grown into a regular fireside scandal, and even the children down at Mud Corners school had come to hear about it.

"My god, it's nigh unbelievable," Abar says, down at the store one afternoon, "after what come to pass with Big Jim."

"I hear say sometimes they never get over it," says Luke Babcock.

"Libby's just like an old wrinkle," Lew Shingle joins in. "Bend her any which way, she'll never wear out."

And to a lot of folks that's all Libby Dingham ever was— just a plain, common, village fancy woman who never in her life could stand off, or up to, a man.

But that wasn't the full story, Minot told Perry a long time afterwards. He had known Libby Dingham for twenty years, almost from the time she and her husband, John Dingham, had first come to the township, floating down the Maumee by flatboat to Fort Wayne and then by ox team and fore-and-aft up northward. Libby couldn't have been more than a young woman and mighty pretty more than likely, Minot said, when she and John had first set out with their small son, Arad, for the Indiana wilderness from way up in Vermont state.

The country had been new then. The road from Fort Wayne to Lima had been viewed a year or so before, but it had still been little more than an Indian trail winding through the forest and around the huckleberry and tamarack bogs. At the site of what later on came to be Kendallville, the viewers had built a rude cabin shelter taken over by a squatter, who, in putting up an occasional traveler or teamster along the road, had come to call it the Bundle Tavern. When the Dinghams had gotten that far north, they had bought the place from Bundle who had disappeared up the trace.

About their life there for the first year or two, Minot knew little except that during the very first winter her husband had died. Libby might have turned go-back then, but she hadn't. It would have been a long, hard journey through the wilderness with her small child, the setting-out money all spent or tied up in the tavern and the oxen already sold to a teamster. So she had stayed on, cultivating a little garden plot around the cabin and thankful for the wild game brought in and left there by those who traveled along the road.

It was there she had first fallen into sin. As it was, she never knew the fellow's real name, though he had been a tall, handsome man, Libby said, and might have married her if there had been a man of God or a justice of the peace within twenty miles of unbroken forest land or bog. He had come riding up the trace late one afternoon, travel-weary and spit-thirsty, and swung off his horse.

"Howdy," he says, opening the door and looking in. "Be this the Bundle Tavern?"

"That it be," Libby says, mighty glad to see a fellow human. "Do set down and rest your hat and coat."

He had come on in and taken off his greatcoat and sat there talking and playing with the boy while she had set out a supper for him of cold corn dodger and rabbit pie.

"Mighty fine," he says, looking up when he had finished. "I heard say I'd find a right comely widow, but the victuals I wasn't even figgerin' on."

It had all been a wonder what a fine man he was, Libby said, and for a time she figured the Lord had heard her prayers. But He hadn't. He had only sent the stranger to tempt her into sin.

"But it wasn't any real sin," Minot says to Libby on the afternoon before she died. "It was a common law marriage."

"No," says Libby, "it was livin' in sin. But it was mighty human. I figgered maybe the good Lord'd be a-mindin' that."

A month later the land on which the Bundle Tavern stood had been entered for in the land office at Fort Wayne by a speculator, and Libby had been served a trespasser's writ. And a morning or so after that the fine stranger had gone. Whether the young widow seemed less attractive now or simply that the wanderlust had once more overcome him, Libby never knew. Grimly she had taken her child and once more set off into the wilderness.

By that time there had been further immigration from the north. From the settlements at Lima and Mongoquinong, land-hungry settlers and squatters had pushed steadily southward along the Fort Wayne-Lima road. On the west shore of Long Lake, Libby had met the families of two squatters who lent a neighborly hand to her and her child, ax-marking a small claim and erecting a cabin. In a year or so, traffic in-

creasing on the road, Libby had begun once more to accom-
modate travelers, this time her cabin becoming known as the
Buckhorn Tavern.

For a while Libby had done a middling business at the
Buckhorn, that is, until the day the post road had come to be
laid out and cut through a mile and a half farther to the west.
Then business had fallen off except for occasional fellows,
land speculators, gamblers and blacklegs, who heard of a
young widow and her boy keeping a public house on the west
shore of Long Lake. They'd stop in for a drink or two, many
times stay the night, and then move on. It wasn't long before
there had been some mighty big stories in the neighborhood
about the gambling and drinking going on, and many a fellow
saying that it came to a lot more than that.

But what really happened no one ever knew for sure. What
they did know was that one night when the boy was sixteen,
he had been killed in a fight at the Buckhorn Tavern. The next
morning Abar Cain had found him there, stabbed to the heart
with a bowie knife and lying in a pool of blood on the floor,
Libby crouched down sobbing and gibbering beside him.
Abar had picked her up and brought her back with him to the
Corners, but all she had been able to tell them afterwards was
that they had been drinking with a tall, slab-sided fellow, a
blackleg or land speculator likely, who had dropped in. The
story that got around, though, was that the boy himself had
stepped in to keep the fellow from bedding with his mother
when it happened.

For a while the murder itself had brought some business
back to the Buckhorn—some folks coming to see the blood-
stains on the floor, others just to say they had seen them, and
some fellows riding by to see a woman that much worth fighting for—but trade had begun to dwindle by the time Big Jim
Ballard had come to stay there and he and Libby had taken

[*164*]

the tavern sign down from the door. No one ever really knew much about Jim or where he'd come from, but there was some talk at the time that he already had a wife and family over in Ohio, and that was why he would never marry Libby.

"A weddin' is a beddin'," Jim says to her. "What's more is all fee-fum and trumpery."

And for some folks after all the trouble she'd been through, Minot said, it might have worked out all right, but not for Libby. Living in sin never cut down her thinking-mind, and now and then she'd remember way back to Vermont state. She'd get lonely for the village store, or the pews of a little New England church and the sight of humans, and when it came camp-meeting time the longings would sweep over her like a brook-driving freshet in the spring, and that's how it happened that Big Jim drowned and Libby came to join up with the Spiritualists.

But even that brought her no comfort in the end—though it did come mighty near to breaking up the Spiritualists. When Abar and Lew Shingle and one or two of the others heard about Hugo's going down to see Libby, they were that mad they were all for riding Hugo out of town on a rail, though before they came to do it, Hugo skipped out. Then a very curious thing happened. Libby herself came to have a call, and spirit-rappings broke out down at the Buckhorn Tavern on Long Lake.

The whole thing was a seven-day Sunday wonder. Almost every afternoon along about sundown the bed in the corner of the cabin would begin to shake and have the jerks, Libby said. It would come on and off for an hour or more, gentle-like sometimes or even with a good deal of rattle and bang, and stop or start up again when she got near or far away. She held off as long as she could, and then one day she threw herself right onto the bed to hold it still and right away the thing had stopped, though she could hear water dripping down, and later on there was a big pool under the bed. When she mopped it up by daylight, it was water all right, but one night she did it by candlelight and the whole pool turned to blood. She knew then that it was her dead boy talking to her, and the spirit-rappings brought her peace.

Sometimes it happened nearly every day and sometimes not for a spell, but the little cabin came to have more folks in it than it did when it was the Buckhorn Tavern and the main trace came right by the door.

Perry himself could remember how that fall at butchering time, he and Lucinda went along with Nancy to take Libby some fresh pork and hog lard, and how the two of them spent the afternoon shying around, half-hoping and half-fearing the whole thing would come on, though it didn't. For weeks afterwards they talked about it, and at school all the younger children played spirit-rapping during big-noon, till Charley Faulk put a stop to it.

Later on Libby took sick again and Doc Kimball said she was like to die for sure because she had a big lump in her breast. When she got so low she couldn't leave her bed, Lizzie and Lafe Klingerman went down and brought her home with them in the dearborn to spend her last days. They sent for the Elder Gibson and he came down to Lafe's to pray for Libby.

"Oh God," he says, "for a long time now the devil's been after Libby's soul. Time and again You sent the blessing on her, but she backslid and fell into sin. But she's a sick woman now, Oh God, and needing of your help. Save her, Oh Lord, save her from the devil and the everlasting fires of hell."

He prayed on and on, nearly every day and sometimes all night long, but Libby kept failing more and more. One night

[*166*]

she sat right up in bed, her eyes on fire. She could see the devil, she said, standing at the foot of the bed with two sharp horns coming out of his head, laughing and grinning at her. She screamed and called for the fire tongs and beat and flayed them around till she'd broken the footboard into splinters. Lizzie called for Lafe and together they tried to hold her down, but they couldn't do a thing with her till daylight. Then she fell back, white and exhausted, and lay like dead.

The next night it came on worse. The Elder Gibson was down on his knees by the bedside praying. Minot had gone on down to help, and it was more than he and Lafe could do to hold her in bed, she screaming and crying and threshing about till they gave her the tongs once more and she started hitting at the bottom of the bed. On the third night the spell came on late, but she fought back fiercely like a wildcat cornered by a dog. Suddenly, though, just before daylight, she threw the fire tongs away, fell back, and rested her hand on the Elder's head. "I'm saved," she calls out, "glory, glory, hallelujah!"

Then she dozed off again and slept till daylight. When she woke up that time, she saw the angels kneeling by the deacon bench and she knew then that she was going home to glory. She lay back quietly and slept again, and an hour or so later with Minot and the Elder and Lafe and Lizzie standing by her bedside, she slipped away.

When they had the funeral up at Brushy Chapel, half of them couldn't get inside at all, Uncle Perry said, but sitting there outside the open window, they could hear the Elder's voice, clear and strong. He told them the full story to the end. *Glory, glory, hallelujah,* he would say, and the folks inside would say *glory, glory, hallelujah,* and you could hear the womenfolk crying and weeping and shouting *glory, glory, hallelujah* in their tears.

It was a wonderful thing and for a long time everybody talked about how the Lord Himself had won a victory against the devil. Over and over they told the story, and the sins they kept laying to Libby grew and grew—fornication, adultery, drunkenness, murder, and witchcraft, until it was the sinning that got to be a kind of miracle.

"God will forgive her, I reckon," says Minot, on the way home, "a long time before the people will."

"Let 'em talk," says Hoss, "even the saints get tired of saying hallelujah!"

"It's a mighty human thing, all right," says Minot. "God forgive us all."

"I reckon He'll have to," says Hoss. "Anyway, I hear say that's His line of business."

Chapter 16

HOW THE ELDER GIBSON *was a power for the Lord, and the free-thinkers built Union Hall*

ALL DEACONED out in a shadbelly coat and heavy mutton-chop whiskers, the Elder Gibson was a power for the Lord in the early neighborhood. He first came to the township as a circuit rider back in the early thirties and he kept right on coming until in 1845, when the Methodists built Brushy Chapel two miles west of Mud Corners. Then he settled down and stayed on regular, a pine-shingle gospelizer for nigh onto forty years.

Sometimes, though, a feller long on God is just a little short on humans.

Minot was a free-thinker and no Methodist at all, but he and the Elder were right good friends. Minot was a God-fearing man all right, but he didn't hold with any split-hoof devil or the brimstone fires of hell. That was all in a man's thinking-mind, he said, like a hoop snake or a towel-milking witch. God made us all more than likely just as he did everything else, for it all had to come from somewhere, but there was no sense in bragging about what a fellow didn't know. And how come a man was a man and where he was going when he died—that a fellow couldn't know for sure. To do what a man came to see was right, that was the big thing, Minot said, that and believing that it all came to good.

There were a good many other free-thinkers in the neighborhood, men like Hoss and Seth Talbot and Phil Beisel, or free-inquirers, as they called them then. And there were the Universalists, too, men like Captain Barry and Jake Avery, who believed that all men would be saved in the end. The very first time Minot himself ever laid eyes on the Elder was down at Jake's blacksmith shop back in '36. Many a time Uncle Perry heard Minot tell that story.

The township hadn't even been organized then, and the Turkey Creek road was no more than a wilderness trace. Some of the early settlers, like the Beisels and the Gilmores and the Butterfields, had already come in, though, and taken up their land. Jake Avery had been one of the very first fellows to set up shop, a full two years before Captain Barry came in and rolled the logs for his first general store and tavern.

Jake was an ornery fellow and stout as a shorthorn bull. He'd met up with plenty of hell-fire and damnation Methodism before, he said, over in Lorain, Ohio, and after he came to Mud Corners he swore he'd lick the boots off of the first circuit rider that ever set foot in his shop or came riding up the trace. He did, too. After a dozen or so families had come in to settle, an Ohio conference sent in a pindling little fellow by name of Philander Pringle, and Jake stopped him in his tracks when he turned up at the Corners.

"Go on back," he says, catching hold of his horse as he came by and seeing who he was all right from his round-breasted coat and his gray, broad-brimmed felt hat. "Go on back. We ain't a-hankerin' after no milksop, lickspittle piety, and no hell-roarin' calamity howler is ever goin' to scare us into it."

With that he turned the fellow's horse around, picked up a rawhide, gave him a cut across the hocks, and Philander Pringle cut a shirttail on horseback for Ohio. It might be a lot easier if God called a bigger fellow to go into the wilderness, Pringle told them when he got there, and that's how they came to send the Elder Gibson. He wasn't an elder then yet, but he was big. He stood six feet two in his stocking feet and weighed upwards of two hundred, though he wasn't much more than twenty-one or two. Jake was working away out in front of his shop the day he heard young Gibson come singing along the trail.

Am I a soldier of the Cross,
A follower of the Lamb,
And shall I fear to own His cause,
Or blush to speak His name?

"Howdy," he says to Jake, when he came up even.

"Howdy," says Jake, walking out to where he could lay his hand on the bridle reins.

"I'm a minister," says the Elder, "looking for a fellow by name of Hezekiah Butterfield. He lives up this way, they tell me."

"He ain't a-lookin' fer you," says Jake, "you slab-sided hypocrite. You turn your horse around and go on back. I'm Jake Avery and I'm fer lickin' the tar out of every Methodist minister I lay my hands on."

"Jake Avery?" says the Elder. "I mind hearing of that name. You be for interfering with a servant of the Lord?"

"I be," says Jake. "We ain't a-needin' any hell-fire and damnation around here."

"I reckon a little of it comes free," says the young fellow, swinging off his horse. "But do me a favor first. Give me time to draw my greatcoat. I ben't for soiling it."

"Off with it then," says Jake.

As he was pulling his arm out of the last sleeve, the Elder stopped in the doing of it and came up mighty hard with his fist right in under Jake's ear, knocking him to the ground. Jumping on top of him like a panther, he held Jake down, sitting astraddle and pinning his arms down with his knees. He went on with his singing then, keeping time with the music by slapping Jake in the face, right and left, as he sang.

> Sure I must fight if I would reign;
> Increase my courage, Lord—

He was well along in the second or third stanza when Minot came riding up.

"What's going on here?" he says.

"I'm giving him a little hell-fire and damnation," says the Elder, going right on with the beating.

Minot knew how Jake was and he figured the young fellow likely had a call to do it, so he just sat down on a bench and looked on for a spell.

"Hold on," says Jake, when he had had enough. "Get offen me. I give you leave to pass."

"You're doing a lot more 'n that; you're coming to hear me preach," says the young fellow.

"In a big horn," says Jake. "You wait till I get up."

"I'll wait," says the Elder. "You think it over."

And with that he went on with his singing. He finished the whole hymn and then he started another one. Jake was taking the blows, turning his face this way and that. He was stubborn as an off-ox, but he began to be mighty weary. Minot could see his face was red as a boil and swollen like a goosedown pillow, and when he figured Jake had had enough, he told the Elder to let him up.

"I'm against interfering in a fair fight," says Minot, "but it's getting on late. Jake gave you leave to go and that's fair enough, I reckon. The trace is free. It's late, though, and you'll never find Hezekiah's before dark. You'd better come up to my place for the night."

With that they shook hands all around, Jake, shamefaced and worse for the pummeling he had taken, and Minot and the Elder went up to the Gilmores for supper. And from that time on the Elder Gibson came riding the circuit every month or so and many a time he stopped off at Minot's for the night, and even when he didn't do that, he'd come by just to pass the time of day. He was a fearless man and a mighty fire-scald in the pulpit, and folks used to come from all over the township just to hear him preach.

All through the late forties and the fifties the Methodists held their camp meetings over in the woods near Cochran's Corners, and many a time when Perry was staying at Isaac's or later on working for the Cooneys or the Wash Butterfields—all of them members—he got to go along. Long before sundown the post road would be heavy with horsemen, single and double riders; the wagons rumbling along; men, women, and children laughing and talking as they came. At the head of the grove near the Corners stood the pine-board pulpit and below it the altar for the mourners, and stretching away from that, row after row of puncheon benches. Hanging around on the trees were the great tallow lanterns, ready to light up that part of the forest as the darkness came on. As the crowd got bigger and bigger, the Elder would walk over to the pulpit, pick up a hymnal, and start the singing, and the babble of talking and laughter would give way as the people filed into the benches, the old folks and the children first, and the young fellows more than likely still hanging on the outer edges, talking and laughing in low voices. Then the Elder would pray and the whole congregation sing some more, and then would come the preaching.

"Are you in the highway of holiness?" the Elder would cry out. "Oh hear the voice of Jesus, lest your names be blotted from the Book of Life and your souls lie in ruins forever. Oh my people, God has set you in slippery places and you have become an offense to the Almighty. Oh ye abandoned of God, repent lest the Lord rain snares upon you, fire and brimstone, and a horrible tempest. Hear the voice of God crying, depart ye accursed into everlasting fire, prepared for the devil and his angels."

The preaching would go on and on, circling around and eddying like a river, from the love of Jesus to the fear of God and the terrors of damnation, and then from the fires of hell back again to the love of Jesus.

"Are you saved? Are you saved?" the Elder would cry. "Oh sinners, are you saved? Are you washed in the blood of the Lamb? Come to Jesus; He will save you. Oh sinners, why not tonight?"

Then the congregation would break out into the coming-on hymn,

> Just as I am, without one plea,
> But that Thy blood was shed for me,
> And that Thou bidd'st me come to Thee,
> O Lamb of God, I come! I come!

the Elder walking up and down the aisles, calling upon the sinners to come forth, the people shouting *amen* and *hallelu-*

jah when one of them would move forward to the mourners'
bench. Song would follow song as long as the trickle from
the audience forward continued, the *hallelujahs* and *glorys*
ringing out louder and louder, mingling with the cries for
mercy and the piercing screams of *glory, glory,* as the blessing came on someone, or so he thought. It was a thing to see,
all right, big men and women crying like children: some of
them shaking with the holy jerks; others rolling on the
forest floor; and sometimes a whole two hundred of them,
lifting up their hands, waving and shouting for the glory.

The revival fever would spread over the whole township
then, and men would come for miles and miles to be saved.
Strong men, too, like Jim Ball or Abar, or even Captain
Barry himself, and dozens of women and young girls, some
housewives and mothers, like Lizzie Klingerman, some way-
ward and backslidden and living in sin, like Libby Dingham,
and some of them young girls just about to be married. Sometimes the conversions would run upwards of a hundred in a
camp-meeting period, and the Elder would seem to have the
whole township cleansed and renewed like in a spring freshet,
until six months later when the whole thing was waiting to be
done over again.

That was the mortal sad thing about it. A month after the
holy rousement was over and the last experience meeting had
been held, there was Jim Ball down at Captain Barry's saloon,
drinking and swearing like before, and Abar just as mean and
stingy, or Libby Dingham gone back to living in sin, and
the young girls and men field-bedding like before.

"Up today and down tomorrow, just like a ripsaw," says
Hoss to Minot one time. "The fun ain't in the repenting; it's
in the sinning, I figure."

"No," says Minot, "sinning comes easy but so does being
sorry for it. I figure that's the thing that makes man human."

*Give humans the right to work out their own salva-
tion, though, and it's a funny thing what they'll get into
sometimes.*

What came to break up the Elder's yearly harvest in the
end was Hugo Rogers and the Spiritualists. That was like a
fever, too, infecting the whole township in the fall of '57.

After the first couple of sessions the Spiritualists began to
meet in the Mud Corners schoolhouse, and Perry could remember one night when Minot allowed he was going on
down to see what it was all about and told him and Marsh
they could go along if they felt for it. There was a big
crowd there and the little schoolhouse was cram-jamb, seam-
busting full. Hugo stood there on a table in front of the
room, his face pale, and his long yellow hair roached back
from his forehead like a halo. He talked on for a while about
what a wonderful thing Spiritualism was, and then he asked
them to put out all the lights except one candle in the back
of the room. He stood there quiet-like and stiff while everyone was holding his breath so that you could have heard a
death tick in the wall, and pretty soon he began to have the
jerks and foam came to his mouth and he threw his head back
and held his hands out straight and started talking, though
nobody could understand a word he said. Then those in
front said they saw his feet raise right up off the table till
they didn't touch at all, and there he was, hanging in the air
between the ceiling and the table, though afterwards some
said it didn't happen, and as for Perry, he said he was that
scared he couldn't really tell at all.

After a while Hugo came to and they lit the candles again,
and there he was, sitting down on the table swinging his legs.
He had messages for a good many people that night, so he

said, and seeing Minot in the audience, he told him that he had a message from his father, Stiles.

"Well, what might it be?" says Minot, speaking right up.

"He was a big strong fellow like you," says Hugo, "only with a white beard and thinnish white hair. He says to tell Minot not to do it till next year."

Minot thanked him for it, but he said it didn't mean a thing unless Hugo could tell him what he was to put off, and putting off wasn't like his father anyway. But Hugo couldn't tell him, not just then, he said, though some other night he'd try again.

Minot kept on being mighty skeptical, but it took the township like the ague, and before long nearly everybody could feel the spirits coming on, even fellows like Abar and Lew Shingle. That summer hardly anyone came to the Methodist camp meeting and the Elder Gibson didn't convert but his oldest and regularest standbys, like Jim Ball and Lizzie Klingerman. Even Libby Dingham gave him the go-by for the new fellow, Hugo Rogers. It was then that the Elder Gibson and the Methodists got mighty roused up, and the Elder and Wash Butterfield and Eliphalet Waterhouse came to see Minot. Minot was school trustee for Milford township, and what they asked him to do was to keep the Spiritualists from using the schoolhouse. The schoolhouse was a township building, they said, built on tax money, and they wouldn't stand for it being used, not by a lot of spirit-rapping infidels.

Minot countered back. He was no Spiritualist, but he believed in free speech, and everybody's right to say what he was a mind to and to be heard. The schoolhouse belonged to the township and nobody had ever been turned down as far as he knew.

When the Spiritualists found out what was going on, they got their dander up, too. They didn't have any other place to go, big enough to hold the crowds, Abar and Lew came to tell Minot, not unless the Elder might let them have Brushy Chapel, which they knew very well he wouldn't do. By god, they were standing up for their rights; it was a free country, that's what it was, and if they couldn't use the schoolhouse, let them raze it to the ground.

When it got that far and Minot saw the township was being split right in two, he decided to call a meeting and talk the whole thing over.

"I'm aiming to be fair," he says, "but things have come to that pass, it's a pretty hard thing to be."

"We got a right to the schoolhouse, I figger," says Abar. "We're a-payin' taxes, too."

"That's the way I figger," says Lew.

"No," says Eliphalet. "A school building's fer the education of our children. Spirit-rappin'——"

"Hold on there," says Abar.

"What belongs to one, belongs to all of us in the neighborhood," says Minot, "and it's just a question of doing the fair thing. I mind me you Methodists used it for a spell back in the forties before you built Brushy Chapel."

"It's not the same thing," says the Elder.

"And why not, I'd like to know?" says Abar.

"I'll tell you why," says the Elder. "Spirit-rapping comes straight from the devil."

"By gum," says Abar, "I'll take a differ with you there. There's a good many spirits it tells about in the Bible."

"Evil spirits," says the Elder, "or else fellows possessed by the devil."

"The Holy Ghost come Pentecost Day wasn't but a spirit," says Abar, "and that's the truth."

"The truth," says Minot, biting in, "is a mighty hard thing to find. I say, let every fellow go at it in his own way."

"There's not but the Lord's way," says the Elder, "and He told us plain out there'd be false prophets and deceivers."

"Yes, by gum, and it's always the other feller," says Abar.

"Well," says Minot, "I mind me the Bible says the devil can quote Scripture for his own purpose, but so, I figure, can the Universalists and the Spiritualists and so can the Baptists and you Methodists."

"Mr. Gilmore," says the Elder, "that comes mighty nigh to blasphemy."

"No, sir," says Minot, "the Bible is a good book all right, but it's too full of contradictions for a fellow to take stock in every word it says."

"The Bible is the Holy Word of God," says the Elder.

"All of it?" says Minot. "And the full and whole word? I figure not. Man's been coming along a mighty long time and he's got a long ways to go. Any fellow that figures he knows all the answers is cutting himself off from a whole lot, from a million people that are dead and never heard of the Bible and from millions more not even born yet."

"That's enough," says the Elder, getting to his feet. "I didn't come here to listen to an infidel. I take my stand by the word of Almighty God."

They hadn't settled a thing, of course, and after the Methodists and the Spiritualists had gone on home, the free-thinkers like Seth Talbot and Hoss Martin and Phil Beisel kept on talking. Before they left that night, they had agreed on a plan. They had all stood together once in the *Phalanx*, and they still believed in the free and untrammeled discussion of human rights, as Seth put it. Minot could close the school-house to the Spiritualists, but they would put up a building in the township where anybody at all could speak his mind.

That very summer they got busy and laid out and built a free hall down on the Turkey Creek road. It was a white, feather-edge clapboard building, fifty-six by forty, and looked something like a New England church. *Erected by those who believe in the freedom of thought,* the old sign used to read, *and dedicated to religious, scientific, and benevolent purposes, open for lectures on any subject, without fear or favour, to any class or sect.* Before the Spiritualists ever got to use it, Hugo himself had skipped out and the whole movement spent itself. It was a mighty fine building, though, convenient and useful for many a lecture and a meeting or a musicale, and a symbol of the early neighborhood for many years to come.

At the time the Elder Gibson found it a hard thing to forgive Minot. The free-thinkers, he kept thundering away up at his pulpit in Brushy Chapel, were a group of outspoken, argufying, atheistical, iconoclastic, blasphemous infidels. They were doing a lot more than giving the devil his due. They were providing him a pulpit and had even built him a church. God would strike them down in His own good time, he said.

That hurt Minot some, but it didn't bother Hoss any. He was just for laughing it off. Jake Avery told him once, he said, that even the devil would be saved in the end. By god, he wouldn't go that far, but he was willing just once—if that's the way the Elder felt about it—to hear what the devil had to say for his own side. He'd been listening to the Methodists for a long time now, and they had never said a good thing about Old Nick yet.

As for Minot, it was quite a spell before he and the Elder got to talking kindly again. At the time Libby Dingham died, though, they were both bedside sitters the full three days and talk came easier then.

"Minot," says the Elder, "you're an old friend and a mighty good neighbor, but you're still an unbeliever and a sinner in the sight of Almighty God."

"Maybe I am," says Minot. "I ain't the one to gainsay you. I figure all a fellow's got is to stand on his own two feet and do what he thinks is right."

"Even the devil came to think that once," says the Elder. "That's the mighty sin of human pride."

"As for the devil," says Minot, "I take no stock in him. And as for pride, well, I trust you ain't laying that to me. All I ever said was that nobody could be sure he was the only one talking for God."

"Come a long time ago now," says the Elder, "I had a call. I felt the Lord himself touch a coal of fire to my lips. From that day on I saw the wickedness—"

"But not the glory," says Minot. "It was knowing his own sin that gave man an image of Almighty God. The way I figure, man himself is the salt and the savor, and the leaven for the whole loaf."

Chapter 17

HOW THEY HAD *a big belling for Wash Butterfield,*
and sister Hattie came to leave home

THE BIGGEST, bang-up belling ever held in the neighborhood was on the night Wash Butterfield married Anna Elliot.
It was a thing to call to mind all right, Uncle Perry said. He
and Wash carried up bucketfuls of red currant wine from
the cellar and set them down on the front porch, where the
boys crowded around and everybody dipped in with whatever thing handy he could find. That was in 1860, and Perry
had been working for Wash all summer and knew his way
around the house. He got himself a noggin from the kitchen,
but it didn't hold very much and anyway he had only gotten
to dip it full once, when Ted Coplin came around with the
old washbasin from the pump and scooped right in before
anybody could stop him. Perry waited until Wash brought
up the next bucketful, but by that time the boys crowded in
so, he never got another drink.

There was a lot of wring-jaw in that red currant wine. It
slipped down easily and got a toe-hold on a fellow. He
never knew that he had enough until it was a whole lot too

much. By one o'clock there wasn't one of them, Ted Coplin or Welt Francis or Asa Blackman, sober enough to stay on his standers, and fellows from Mud Corners and Appleman-berg were lying around the yard like a drove of ridgebacks in a hog wallow. It was a mighty good thing the wine was there, too, Uncle Perry said.

Anna had been kind of free and easy with the boys. She was trim as a daisy and mighty good to look at, with blue eyes full of fire-play and a smile that melted a fellow's heart like a sugar-crusted piece of apple pie. She was just eighteen when her family moved up on Wash's place, and it wasn't long till every unmarried fellow in the neighborhood was coming to church on a Sunday morning, boots polished and hair slicked down, and sat there to listen, just so he might chance to be walking home that way or maybe lean over the garden fence for a word or two before Anna went on into the house.

It wasn't much of a life for her and her younger sister what with the old folks both bedridden and the girls kept busy waiting on them and taking care of the garden and truck and never going out at all or seeing anyone, save for the fellows that came calicoing around, and you couldn't blame Anna if she liked to talk to them or let them come on in and sit on the porch some. She just wasn't born to be a dropt-stitch.

Marsh himself was mighty fond of her and he told Perry he was for beating every fellow's time in the neighborhood and marrying her himself if she'd give him a tumble, and a lot of other fellows, like Ted Coplin and Asa Blackman, felt the same way. There wasn't one of them that didn't like to give out now and then down at Captain Barry's saloon that he had been playing highjinks with her up in the barnloft or under a garden hedgerow. But Marsh always figured she was

cutting a straight furrow; she never let him cut the traces any
—nor anyone else, he figured, not that they didn't all try it
now and then. And that was why some of the boys felt they
had their combs cut the day it came out that Wash was
marrying Anna. You could have dropped him dead with a
hoecake on his chin, Marsh said.

But that was only one side of the story. The other side was
Wash's sister, Hattie.

*God Almighty must of figgered on it happenin' some:
He made 'em male and female, leastways that's what the
Good Book says.*

The trouble was that Hattie could never see that. She and
Wash had been living together then, brother and sister, ever
since old Hezekiah had died in '48. The old homestead was a
fine place, a full three hundred and twenty acres, which
Hezekiah had entered for when he first brought his family to
the township from New York state. It wasn't more than a
year or so after they'd come that the mother died and Hattie,
just fourteen then, set up keeping house for her father and
later on, when he died, for Wash. The place had been pretty
well cleared by that time and just two years before he died,
Hezekiah had built himself a fine clapboard house along the
Fort Wayne-Lima road. Wash himself was no rain-gully
farmer and had kept the place up well, and Hattie swept
broom-clean in the house. Year after year they'd gone on living there, mighty good yoke-fellows, everybody said, and
nothing to wonder at at all, except maybe now and then why
one or both of them didn't get married.

But they were too busy doing good for that. When the
Elder Gibson came in to organize the first Methodist church
in the township, Hezekiah and his family were among the

first members. It was Hezekiah who gave them the land for the church when they built Brushy Chapel in '45 and later on an acre alongside of it for a burying ground and some money besides, and soon after he died, Hattie asked them to make Wash a deacon in the church. Folks used to say without the Butterfields there wouldn't have been any church at all and wasn't it a fine thing for a brother and sister to carry on like that. Religion was pure quill and no water when it came that way.

Hattie was the nigh-wheeler. All summer long the year Perry worked there she kept up her ding-dong. Had Eliphalet Waterhouse paid his church tax yet, she wanted to know. And if not, why hadn't he? Goodness knows, Elph could afford it a lot better than some others she could name. What was the world coming to, she'd like to know, with the young folks carrying on like that up to Hoss' cornhusking-bee, drinking hard cider and dancing all night, and likely field-bedding, too? And when was Wash going to cut thistles? The oats in the south forty were feathering out, and the thistles were waist high and looked ready to bloom. And what were the deacons ever going to do about the Elliot family? How long was the church to carry them, she'd like to know? She had a mind-set on that.

The Elliots lived three miles down the road to the west of the church then, in the woody hill section stretching off towards Bloomfield township. Jim Elliot had the rheumatism and his joints were that dry he couldn't do a day's work at all. His wife, Jenny, was sickly, too, and bedfast a good deal of the time, and the two girls hardly old enough to work out, and by the time they were, they were needed right there to take care of the old folks most of the time. They were grass-hopper poor, but they were Methodists, and why did the Good Lord make them, Wash said, except to incite a fellow's charity. He was always after Hattie to hold a donation-bee, and afterwards she and Wash would drive down through the woods with a buckboard load of wornouts and castoffs and a half-dozen stone crocks of salt pork and head cheese, chitterlings and hog lard, or maybe a sack of corn meal or wheat flour or a piggin of maple sugar.

Earlier in the winter that year Hattie had been under the weather for a spell, and Wash had gone down and brought back the older girl, Anna, to help out Hattie in the house. She was gone again before Perry got there but that Perry reckoned was what gave Wash the idea.

"I've been thinkin'," he says one day early in the summer.

"Well I declare," says Hattie. She could be short as pie crust when she felt like it. "What about?"

"Hold on," says Wash. "If you weren't so sharp I'd of told you by now."

"Go on," says Hattie.

"Well, I was thinkin' as how we might be doin' somethin' more fer some of our neighbors," says Wash.

"The buryin' ground needs a fence," says Hattie.

"Don't be bitin' in that way," says Wash.

"Go on," says Hattie.

"I was thinkin'," says Wash, "that it ain't enough fer us just to be settin' here and makin' money fer ourselves and livin' off the fat of the land."

"Whatever you gettin' at?" says Hattie. "It takes you the longest time to empty out of any man I ever see. Go on, go on and finish!"

"And some people pretty nigh starvin' to death," says Wash. "That's all I was goin' to say."

"You mean the Elliots?" says Hattie.

"I do," says Wash.

"Ain't the church takin' care of them?" says Hattie.

"It comes to the same thing in the end," says Wash.

"Well, what is it you was plannin' to do?" says Hattie.

Wash just sat there a minute. Then he says, "Well, I was figgerin' on givin' 'em two acres east of the buryin' ground and buildin' 'em a house on it. They could keep a cow and a few chickens and a garden—just what the girls could take care of easy, and Anna could come up and help you out with your work when you're a mind to."

"I can do my own housework," she says. "I ain't figgerin' on runnin' no *Phalanx*."

"I wasn't plannin' on that," says Wash. "It'd be their own house."

"With us payin' fer it," says Hattie.

"Now don't come bitin' in with that," says Wash.

"I don't like to picture it," says Hattie, "them girls that close. Lydia may be all right—she's young yet—but that girl, Anna, she's a wild one. I can see it in her eyes."

"Well, that's what I was thinkin'," says Wash. "You know you could do the girls a lot of good if they was near enough so you could keep an eye on 'em. You could see they come to church regular-like and all that."

"I could that," says Hattie, letting up for a minute. "I ain't sayin' as I like it, but you do as you're a mind to. You're the deacon, I reckon."

And for one time Wash had his way. As soon as the spring planting was done, he got Eliphalet Waterhouse and one or two neighbors and they built the house. It was a big log cabin with a lean-to all along one side, a loft with an inside ladder, and a clapboard shed for the cow and chickens. When it was all laid up and daubed, Wash and Perry took one of the heifers over and tied her in the barn and Sam Cooney came along with a dozen hens. The next day Wash and Elph took the oxen and the big farmwagon and moved the Elliot family, the whole kit and boodle, into the new house. It was a mighty fine thing, everybody said, Wash and Hattie taking care of the Elliots that way.

Hattie came to take a real interest in the girls. On the day they moved, she came down and helped them straighten up the house and told them where everything ought to go. After that she saw to it Anna combed her hair down plain and didn't wear any fancy fixings on her dress, leastways not when she came to church. A decent young woman comes walking down the aisle with a down-look, Hattie said, carries her prayer book proper-like, and never crosses her benders in the pew.

It seemed to work out all right until the crowd of Sunday fellows began to sorghum around and set tongues wagging. That brought some worriment to Hattie. She'd go down now and then and give the girl jessie, but it just didn't seem to do much good. By late fall Hattie was suspicioning a lot more than she could know for sure, until one day when she went down to fetch Jenny Elliot some chokecherry jelly she'd been making. She was dead certain then.

"Why Anna," she says, looking at her sharp-like, "I can't believe my eyes. Are you that way?"

"What way?" says Anna, her cheeks pinking up, her hands busy fussing with her apron.

"You are too," says Hattie. "Stand up and hold still. You are, you know you are."

"I'm not," says Anna.

"Don't backcap me," says Hattie. "You're gettin' big. Anybody can see that."

Anna must have figured it wasn't any use arguing for she just sat there without saying a thing. Then the tears came, but she still smiled.

"I'm happy," she says.

That was like dry tinder in the fire.

"Anna Elliot, you're a wicked woman," says Hattie. "You'll have to confess it to the whole church. It's a wicked sin."

"I won't ever," says Anna.

"You will," says Hattie, "and the feller too. Now you tell me who done it."

"Never," says Anna.

"Oh, yes, you will," she says. "Wait till I get hold of Wash, you—you fancy woman."

She felt better for having said it, picked up her skirts, and strammed out of the house right across the fields to the meadow where Wash was mending the fork-and-rail fence.

"Now you can see what comes of your charity," she says. "I knew Anna was a bad one the first time she stepped into the kitchen. Now we got this thing on our hands. She's havin' a baby, Wash."

"No," says Wash.

"She is," says Hattie. "She's big now and she's that callous she won't tell who it was."

"She won't?" says Wash.

"She will before I'm through," says Hattie. "We'll turn her out of house and home. We'll throw her out of church."

For three days the whole thing was the fireside gossip in the neighborhood. Anna Elliot was going to have a baby, and she wouldn't tell who the fellow was.

By god, if it was him, Marsh said, he would be more than ready to step right up and say so and marry her, and he couldn't figure out whoever it was, why he didn't. Ted Coplin and Welt Francis and Asa Blackman and most of the other fellows felt the same way about it, though now that it had happened, they all allowed they didn't give a dried apple damn. As for Hattie, she kept saying, if Anna wasn't just that wicked she didn't know, she was a smart one all right, for with all those young fellows hanging around, she could take her own pick and choice. Likely as not she'd put it on some rich fellow's son and get to marry acres or at least a good cash settlement.

But Hattie was a lot madder when Anna did talk. On the fourth day she and Helen Cooney and Lizzie Klingerman were down there scolding Anna and pleading with her, telling her that the church would throw her out and she'd go to hell forever, until she finally broke down.

"It was Wash," says Anna, all choked up with tears.

"Wash?" says Hattie, turning ash-pale, then red again with anger. "Anna Elliot, you're lyin'. Wash Butterfield would never touch a woman."

"Well, why don't you ask him," says Lizzie.

"Come on," says Hattie to the women. "We're goin' right up and find out. If it was Wash, may the Lord strike him dead."

When Wash saw them coming up the road, he could see that something was up all right. He sat down on the porch with his feet hanging over, and waited for them.

"Wash Butterfield," says Hattie, "are you the one? Are you that unclean?"

"I am that," says Wash, seeing as how she couldn't go on, she was all choked up. "I was just aimin' to wash up."

"Don't you jolly me," says Hattie. "Anna says you done it."

"Done what?" says Wash.

"Done the carnal act with her," says Hattie. "Oh, how could you, Wash?"

"Does Anna say that?" says Wash.

"She does," says Hattie.

For a minute Wash didn't answer but just sat there. Then he says, "Well, what do you want me to do about it?"

"There's only one thing to do about it," says Hattie. "Confess you're a sinner before Almighty God, you whited sepulchre."

"Yes, Hattie," says Wash.

"And then you'll marry Anna," says Hattie. "I'll see to that."

"Well," says Wash, "iffen that's the way you want it."

The day Wash and Anna were married the little church was like to burst its seams. Folks came a long way to see Wash get himself undeaconed and married all in one ceremony. He stood there stiff and tall, kind of like a schoolboy, ashamed of being up front, but mighty proud of the licking he was taking. Anna was prettier than ever, calm about the whole thing, but with a down-look in her eyes.

"I knew she'd pick a rich one," says Lizzie Klingerman on the way home.

"I don't know whether it was him or not," says Lafe, "but I figger it's a good thing. It'll go far to make a man out of Wash."

"Iffen it was him," says Marsh, "Wash told one whopper of a lie, when he said he was sorry fer his sins."

That was the night they held the big belling. Marsh and Ted Coplin and Welt Francis were for getting it up, and they asked every fellow in the neighborhood that could play a fiddle or blow a horn or ring a cowbell to bring along his fixings and make noise. After he had done his chores, Uncle Perry went down to Minot's and he and Marsh rounded up every cowbell on the farm.

Then Marsh loaded the shotgun, and Jim Wirt and Welt Francis came by with a big circle saw on an iron bar they'd taken off the Wirt mill. When a fellow swung the maul against that, you could hear the boom a mile away. It was along about ten o'clock when the fellows from Mud Corners met the Latta boys and the fellows from up north and east to Applemanberg. They all lined up around the house in the shadows quiet-like, and Marsh and Ted Coplin fixed up a pound of gunpowder in a bag on a flat stone. Then they rigged up another stone with a rope over the low-hanging limb of a tree just above the first one, and when Marsh gave the word, they let go of the rope. Every window in the house rattled when the charge went off, and then the guns and the saw and the cowbells let go in a din they could hear way down to Turkey Creek.

Wash came to the door in his nightshirt to see what was up and before he could say a thing, Welt Francis and Ted Coplin pulled him outside. What they'd really come for was to see the bride, they said. By that time Anna had got herself dressed and come on downstairs and while Wash himself pulled on a pair of breeches, they lit the pine-knot torches in the yard. They sat the bride and groom on the porch and the horse fiddle cut in with music. After that they had some speeches, Marsh getting up on the porch and telling Wash he was a right lucky fellow and how they all wished him well, and Wash told them how he had some red currant wine in the cellar he'd bring up if Perry would help him, and then they all let out a whoop and holler for Wash and his bride.

It went all right until they took to drinking heavy and some fellows, like Ted Coplin, carried a big load.

"By god," he says, "I come to kiss the bride and I'm goin' to."

He made a dash for the porch with a dozen fellows right after him, and it would be a hard thing to say what might have happened—they were all that drunk—if it hadn't been for Marsh.

"By god, you're leavin' Anna alone," he says.

"The hell," says Ted Coplin, "she can't come it over me."

The whole thing turned into a fight, Marsh and Ted and

a dozen others squaring off on the porch and then out in the yard and going round and round, milling over and under, gouging and kicking until some of them gave out and stopped to have another drink. If the wine hadn't held out, someone would have gotten hurt sure—but it did and after a while they were all dead drunk and lying in the yard. It was then that Perry got hold of Pete Martin.

"Let's get the stone-boat and haul 'em home," he says.

They went out to the barn then and yoked the oxen, poled them to the stone-boat, and brought it alongside the yard. Every time they found a fellow from down Mud Corners way, they piled him on. They had quite a load when they started out, but some fellows kept rolling off, and they left them scattered all along down to the corner and then on east to Minot's. When they got there, they carried what they had into the barn and bedded them down in the hay.

The next morning Perry drove the ox team back to Wash's place. Wash was out in the barn when he got there and came over to help unyoke.

"Howdy, Perry," he says, proud-happy as a young Adam.

"Howdy," says Perry.

"Well," says Wash, "I reckon we got a new boss in the kitchen now."

"Is that so?" says Perry. "Where's Hattie?"

"She left for Kendallville right after the wedding," says Wash, kind of sober-like. "Swore she'd never set foot in this house again."

"Hattie know you had all that currant wine down cellar?" says Perry.

"No, that she didn't," says Wash. "I'd been savin' that up fer quite a spell."

Sometimes all an old maid can see is nettle in a crop of wild oats.

[*193*]

Chapter 18

HOW ELIPHALET WATERHOUSE *helped the runaway slaves, and the whole neighborhood joined
in to pay his fine*

FOR OLD Eliphalet Waterhouse, right was no up-and-down
saw—up today and down tomorrow. Right was right, and
Eliphalet worked at it seven full days a week. Many a fellow
in the neighborhood used to think the old man crazy as a coot.
But for Minot he was just a Sunday-School fellow who
worked at it some.

*Betwixt Sunday and Monday fer a lot of fellers buckle
and tongue don't anywheres meet.*

The first time Perry came to know about Eliphalet was in
the fall of '59 when he went to stay with the Cooney family,
one of Elph's elbow neighbors on the post road. Sam was an
orchard man and gone a lot every spring and fall grafting
trees, and what he wanted Perry for most was just to do the

chores when he himself was away from home. Perry hadn't been there more than a week or so when one morning, bringing the cows up from the meadow, he saw Eliphalet go driving by with what looked like a load of wheat. You could see the tops of the sacks sticking up above the wagon box and Eliphalet, with his old broad-brimmed hat and full gray beard, sitting on a cross-board up in front giddapping the horses.

"Eliphalet must of had a lot of wheat," says Perry, sitting down to the breakfast table. "That's the second time I see him go by this week."

Sam looked up at his wife before he answered; then he says, quiet-like, "I don't know whether it's wheat or not, Perry. I wished it was."

Perry couldn't figure that out, so he just sat there and didn't say anything for a spell.

After a while Helen looked up at Sam and says, "I don't see how they stand it. I was sitting there yesterday in the kitchen talking to Alice, and all of a sudden it come to me I was smelling something."

"More 'n likely not," says Sam. "I figger he keeps 'em in the barn."

"He'd never of gotten into it if it hadn't been for Alice," says Helen.

"I don't know," says Sam. "His brother up to Coldwater is in it, too."

Perry still couldn't make head, tail, or fiddle-end out of it, until he bit in.

"What smells?" he says.

For a moment Sam looked at Helen before he turned to Perry. "Niggers," he says. "I reckon you'd best know."

"Niggers!" says Perry. "What fer?"

"That's what I said," says Sam. "But you keep your clam

[*195*]

shut, young feller. They'll make it mighty hot for Elph if they ever catch him, and everyone else in the neighborhood, more 'n likely."

"But what's he doin' with niggers?" says Perry.

"I said to keep your clam shut," says Sam.

Perry did, but he kept his ears open. And after that a lot of things he heard down at Captain Barry's saloon or edging up to fellows talking at Abar Cain's store, began to make sense. They were running slaves right through the neighborhood, just as they did over in Ohio and Pennsylvania, and some fellows like Hoss Martin and Wash Butterfield were all out for it, and others, like Minot and Seth Talbot and Phil Beisel, were dead set against the whole thing.

Later on that fall they held the first open anti-slavery rally in the township. Seeing as how everybody from Mud Corners and Applemanberg and Mongoquinong was likely to be there, Sam and Perry hustled through the chores and went on down. There were a good many speeches that night, but the most fiery of all was by a young fellow, Caleb Larkey, from Oberlin, Ohio.

"Oh, my people," he cries out, "let slavery perish from under these heavens; let it cease forevermore. It is like a beast, dreadful and terrible, and strong exceedingly, whose teeth are of iron and whose feet are of brass. Let us rise up now, well-armed, and strike off the chains and shackles which enslave our darker brethren. May God speed the time, when by our own generosity and by our unceasing toil the oppressed of every land shall be free and the yokes of servitude lie broken."

After the speeches came some singing by the girls. The one Perry could mind best was Alice Waterhouse. Eliphalet had three daughters, but Alice was the only one left at home. She was a girl of about eighteen or twenty then, fawn-slender, with blue eyes and hair like the gold of ripe wheat in harvest time. She had lived down South and had seen the darkies in their chains, and she could sing until a fellow could feel all the blood and trouble, just as if he'd been there himself. Perry couldn't remember the verses, but the chorus everyone in the meeting house knew afterwards and sang in the neighborhood for a long time to come.

> The baying hounds are on my track;
> Old Massa's close behind.
> And I'm afraid he'll take me back
> Across the Dixon line.

At the end of the meeting, they passed around a cash box. If they got enough money, Caleb said, they could free a thousand slaves willing to make a run for it, and he asked everyone in the hall to stand, as he put his money in the box, for a testimonial to the abolitionist cause. When Eliphalet, who was passing the box, came down the aisle as far as Seth Talbot, Seth just kept his seat and never got up at all.

"I can give what I'm goin' to, settin' down," he says right out in meeting.

"Ain't you with us, Seth?" says Eliphalet.

"I don't know whether I am or not," says Seth.

"Surely now," says Caleb Larkey, "not a single one of us will sit idly by while this monster of iniquity feeds on the vitals of our land. Surely now, this gentleman is against slavery?"

"Maybe I am," says Seth, "but I figger on mindin' my own business."

"Slavery's everybody's business," says Caleb.

"That it is," says Minot, breaking in, "but we won't settle it by stirring up more trouble."

"You ever see 'em cat-haul a nigger?" says Eliphalet, getting roused up.

"No, that I didn't," says Minot.

"Well, I did," says Eliphalet. "Down to Tennessee one time, I see 'em tie a fellow belly down on a log so he couldn't move and then bring out a big tomcat and set him on this fellow's back till he got his claws set and then drag the tom back and forth till his back looked like a skinned coon. And then they up and slopped salt brine over him and let him lay there screamin'."

"Fer doin' what?" says Seth.

"Fer runnin' away," says Eliphalet.

"That's what I was talking about," says Minot, getting to his feet. "Every time you help a slave run away, it makes it worse for the rest of them down south. Up here we don't believe in slavery, but that happens to be the law down there. And it won't help them to change the law any—raising money to steal their property."

"God's law is higher than man's law," says Caleb.

"That it is," says Minot, "but it don't hold in court, not yet. We've got to get them to give up slavery, but the only way to do that is to pass a law recompensing them for the loss of what the law now says is their property, same as we do up here when we're building a dam or a millrace. All you're doing here tonight is stirring up a fellow till his heart acts for his head."

That came pretty nigh to breaking up the meeting, until the Elder Gibson got up and told them all men were brothers in the sight of God, black as well as white, and then they hurried up the collecting and came to the benediction. There was a grist of argument after the meeting, though, and for a good many days to come.

On the way home Seth told Perry about the underground

railway. It had been going on for a good many years, he said, and he'd heard the way-stop down below Eliphalet's was a fellow's place by the name of Whitford. Whitford would bring them up to Elph's place, mostly at night for they had to come through South Milford, and Elph would hide them out somewhere for a day or so and then take them on to Mongoquinong or Orland. He didn't know where the other fellows hid them, but he'd heard say Elph had a cellar dug out for them under the barn with a drop door going down through the haymow and kept a lot of hay banked on top.

About a week after the rally, Sam rigged up his wagon and left for his fall trip. Perry helped load up the buckboard with the wooden case of grafting tools, the round gums full of whittled splints, and the bundles of green shoots to be used as cions wrapped up in gunny bags against the weather. Sam would be gone a month or so, traveling all over the country and staying at night at any place he happened to be working. Perry would have given his right arm to go along, but he couldn't since, as Sam himself said, he was now the full hand on the farm.

He was cleaning out the cowbarn with the old homemade wheelbarrow a day or so later, when he saw a rig come up the post road and turn into the farmyard. A thick, heavy-set fellow, wearing black riding boots, got out of the buggy and came over to the barnyard fence.

"Come over here, bud," he says, calling out to Perry.

Perry set down the wheelbarrow and went over.

"Howdy," he says. "Is this the Cooney place?"

"That it be," says Perry.

"Mr. Cooney at home?"

"No, he's gone on a trip," says Perry.

"Are you his boy?" asks the fellow.

"No," says Perry, "I'm just workin' here."

"Been here long?"

"A couple of months now."

"Come now," says the fellow, sudden-like, "tell me, you seen any niggers around here?"

"No I ain't," says Perry.

"You ever hear 'em talkin' about niggers?"

"That I never."

"Who lives the first house down the road?" says the fellow.

"Eliphalet Waterhouse."

"You seen any niggers around there?"

"No, sir," says Perry.

Perry was that scared his knees were playing ticktacktoe on the fence, but he couldn't tell whether the fellow knew he was lying or not. The man turned around then and went back to the buggy and got in alongside of another fellow who had been holding the reins and together they drove off, turning north. He saw the same rig come back later in the day, but they didn't turn in that time. That night, though, Wash Butterfield told Helen he'd heard that one of the men was a United States marshal from down at Fort Wayne.

The very next morning Alice Waterhouse came running down to Cooney's. The two men had been there and scramble-scratched the whole place, she said, but they hadn't found anything. Papa was sure they were being watched. He was down sick in bed with the ague, and Wash and Hoss Martin were there now figuring out what to do. She had come to see if Perry would ride over to Minot's and ask him to come down right away.

Perry felt mighty anxious and as soon as Helen allowed that he could, he saddled a horse and hurried on over. When he got there, he told Minot what he'd come after.

"Well," says Minot, "Elph's a good man, but I've told him many a time I'm against the whole thing."

But he saddled a horse and rode along back. When they got to the Waterhouse's, Alice showed them into where Eliphalet was lying sick in bed. Wash and Hoss were still there holding counsel. Eliphalet was sick all right. He had the ague bad, he said, and when the shakes came on it took him like a pack of wildcats clawing up his back. For a spell he could hardly talk at all for coughing.

"Minot," he says, "I'm in trouble."

"So I hear," says Minot, looking at Wash and Hoss.

"It ain't that I'm mindin' what they'll do to me," says Elph, "but I got two poor fellers here now—"

"Niggers?" says Minot.

"That's right," says Elph. "And a United States marshal and a feller from Kentucky come in here with a search warrant and ransacked the place from cellar to garret. I was prayin' to Almighty God they wouldn't find 'em and they didn't, but they'll be back. I reckon they've gone down to South Milford now to get some more men."

"Is that so?" says Minot.

"That's what I figger," says Elph. "They've got a line on this place, and sooner or later they'll move in and tear the rafters apart till they find 'em."

"That is, if we don't get 'em out of here," says Wash.

"And what'll they do if they catch 'em?" says Minot.

"They'll send the niggers back," says Elph. "One of them's got big welts all over his back and arms where they beat him with a rawhide, just because they figgered he got uppity after they'd sold his wife down river and split up his family."

"And Elph, here, like as not, will go to jail or have a big fine," says Wash.

[*201*]

"Well," says Minot, just sitting there thinking it over for a spell. "I'm against this thing, that I've said a good many times, but you've got the fellows here now and something's got to happen. What are you figuring on doing?"

"Wash says he ain't seen anybody," says Eliphalet, "but I figger the place is bein' watched and the fellers from South Milford will know the whole neighborhood. If Wash or Hoss here or Seth Bulmer was to make a move, they'd be after 'em. We figgered you bein' agin it, if we could get them over to your place—that would be the best thing."

"How'll we get 'em over there?" says Wash.

"We can manage that all right," says Hoss.

They worked out a plan then to throw the marshal and the fellows from South Milford off the spoor, and afterwards Wash and Hoss and Minot went on home.

As soon as it got dark that night, Wash and Hoss came back to Eliphalet's, rolled out the wagon, loaded on the sacks of wheat just as he usually did, and hitched up the team.

To make it seem a sure-go thing, they went through a lot of pitch and hustle, running in and out of the barn and up to the house until they were all set to go. Then Wash climbed up on the seat and picked up the lines, and Hoss got up on the wagon with his shotgun. When they were all set, Wash giddapped the horses and the wagon tore out of the yard and up the road.

They'd figured on some fellow seeing them, if they were being watched, and giving out the word, and sure enough before they'd gone more than a mile, they could hear a buggy and some riders coming up full chisel. Wash whip-lashed the horses and made a race for it, up past his own and Sam's place, and then on towards Mongoquinong. It was close-papers for a while, but they were doing well enough till they hit a stretch of plank. The old plank road had been torn out three or four years earlier, except for a stretch or two on past Gilbert's Corners where the roadbed was soggy and the planks had been left in against the heavy going in the spring. It was dry now and the planks rumbled as Wash drove over them, and now and then where one of them was broken, a wheel would hit a chuck hole and come down hard. That scared the off-gelding and once when he jumped ahead about four feet and took the wagon with him, the plank he came down on broke and a piece flew up and hit him on the flank. From then on there was no holding in the team. The gelding kept dashing ahead of the mare and that ran the wagon over to one side, and when the left wheel went up the bank, the wagon toppled over, dumping Wash and Hoss and the sacks out onto the road. That was the end of the race all right.

Wash was still dragging hard on the lines trying to hold in the team, when the fellows who were following came on up. The first thing they did was to jump down and grab the horses and help steady them, and then they started in looking over the wreckage. By that time the United States marshal had come on up in the buggy.

"All right," he says, "where are the niggers?"

"Niggers?" says Hoss. "I ain't seen any niggers."

"Goddamn you," says the fellow from Kentucky, "you givin' us the go-around?"

"No sir," says Hoss. "We was just makin' a quick trip to Mongoquinong. Old Eliphalet Waterhouse is plumb out of bread and the flour bin is bottom-board empty."

The fellows knew they were beaten then, body and breeches, and some of them were mighty riled up, but the marshal told them there wasn't a thing they could do, so they got on their horses and rode on back. Wash and Hoss were scared flat the men would get back to Eliphalet's before Minot and the Negroes had made their getaway, but they didn't know what to do about it then—it had all happened too fast—so they straightened up the wagon, hitched the team again, and drove on home to Wash's place. What had happened, they never knew till afterwards.

Just about the time, though, that they started out for Eliphalet's earlier that night, Minot said he was going out coon hunting in the woods along back of Colonel Cochran's place, and he and Marsh had shouldered their guns, called the dogs, and started out. He left Marsh out in the woods with the dogs as a decoy, and then came on over to Eliphalet's the back way. As soon as he saw the chase was on, he led the two fellows out the same way he'd come in, back to Marsh and the dogs, and the four of them had then high-tailed it through the woods and along hedgerows back to the farm. They got there along about midnight, never having seen nor heard anything along the way, and after Nancy had given them all something to eat, they bedded the fellows down in the front parlor. The last place on earth, Minot said he figured, anybody would be looking for a runaway slave was in the front parlor of Minot Gilmore's home.

He kept them there till just about daylight, and then he hitched up a team to a light buggy—the only one he had with a top on it—told the two fellows to get in, got in himself and sat on their laps, and picked up the reins. They made it in record time to Clark's wagon shop in Orland, and after the fellows had thanked him for what he'd done, he never saw them again. They were well on their way to Canada, he took it.

The fellows from South Milford and the marshal came on back to Eliphalet's that night and searched the place once more. But when they never found a thing, not even the hideout in the barn, they gave up and went on home. The whole neighborhood was mighty uneasy for a day or two, but when nothing happened, everyone figured it was all over.

It wasn't, though. How the story got out, no one ever knew. Maybe some of the neighbors talked too much, the way they often will, and the story got noised around. At any rate a month or so later one of the fellows down at South Milford swore out a warrant against Minot for violating the law in helping two Negroes get away. Minot was ready to plead guilty, but what no one had figured on was old Eliphalet. As soon as he heard about it, he rode right down to the marshal's office at Fort Wayne and gave himself up. He was the real fellow that was guilty, he said; he had done it regular and Minot had only done it once to help him out. He was ready to stand trial if they'd let Minot go.

Seeing as how Eliphalet was the fellow they were really after, the marshal agreed to it and took him down to Indianapolis. He had his trial there and was fined three hundred and fifty dollars. That was a lot more than old Eliphalet had in cash; so to keep him out of prison the neighbors chipped in, and that's why some of them always said Elph's giving himself up was a crazy-fool thing to do. Minot could have got off for a lot less, being it was the only time he had ever done it and the neighborhood ready to qualify that he was against slave-running.

But when they came around to see Minot, he cashed in a full fifty dollars.

"For old Eliphalet I'd do that much any day," Minot says, "but sooner or later you fellows will get the whole country into trouble."

And he was dead right about that.

Chapter 19

How Marsh Gilmore *went off to war, and* *Minot was called a copperhead*

Wᴴᴇɴ ᴛʜᴇ ᴡᴀʀ broke out, Minot was dead set against it but he was no copperhead, though some fiddle-minds came to call him that.

Fer some fellers it's all blue sea or the devil with no in-between.

The first big war meeting in the township was held down at South Milford in front of the Trindle Building. The township was about half Democrat and half Republican then, and there in the open square in front of the building the two poles erected during the campaign the fall before were still standing, the one flying the names of Douglas and Johnson and the other the names of Lincoln and Hamlin with the maul and wedges still dangling from the top.

All morning long folks kept coming into town on foot and horseback, and in dearborns and farmwagons. After a basket-picnic in the square, Francis Henry pounded on the big bass drum, and the meeting got under way.

Jeremiah Bartlett, a justice of the peace for the township, was the first speaker. He had come to tell them, he said, how the rebels had fired on Fort Sumter, how President Lincoln was calling for seventy-five thousand volunteers, and Governor Morton had issued a proclamation calling for six regiments of soldiers from Indiana.

"My fellow citizens," he cries, "we are at war! The enemy has fired the first round! I trust every fellow here is ready to respond to the call of duty."

Then he called upon anyone who wanted to, to have his say.

"I'm all for this war and the next one when it comes," says Lew Shingle, who had moved over to La Grange and was now one of the high moguls in the new Republican party. "I say, let the bloody hand of war reach into every home and village of the south till we drive them to their swinish knees in surrender!"

"Huzza! Huzza!" says a lot of fellows in the crowd.

"We are ready for the battle of the Lord," says the Elder Gibson. "May the bolts of divine wrath descend upon the iniquities of the enemy till the idols of inservitude lie shattered and broken. This is a holy war. Who will not fight for the Lord is against Him."

"Hold on a minute," says Minot, coming up to the platform when the Elder had finished. "I figure no war is holy. I say it's an evil thing for hate and bloodshed to sweep over a land. War never has and, I reckon, never will settle anything—excepting maybe the dust on a lot of fellows' graves."

"Hear! Hear!" says Phil Beisel and one or two of the other Democrats.

"I hold," says Minot, "in a government of free states you've got to give all the people, south as well as north, the right to stand up for what they believe."

[*207*]

"Not when they're in the wrong," says Hoss.

"Even when they're in the wrong," says Minot. "If you've got a faith in your fellowman at all, you've got to have a faith in him even when he's wrong."

"By god, they started this," says Abar.

"After we gave 'em cause," says Minot. "Shooting back won't show them they were wrong."

"What will?" says Hoss.

"Talking it over," says Minot.

"It's too late for that now," says Abar.

"It's never too late," says Minot, "not with enough give and take. The real trouble is you abolitionist fellows—you and the hot-bloods down south. You've been shouting for blood and slaughter that long the human talk's got lost in the babble. Four years ago up to Cleveland I heard Elihu Burritt say the north was just as responsible for slavery as the south, and the way to settle it was for us to talk the whole thing over and to pass a law recompensing the south for their slaves. If we'd have done that, or were willing to do it now, we could settle the whole thing. The trouble is, for some fellows money comes a lot dearer than human blood."

"Hold on, Minot!" says Andy Morrison, with a lot of other people joining in. "May I say something?" he says to Jeremiah Bartlett, coming up to the platform.

"That you may," says Jeremiah.

"I am a Democrat," says Andy, "but I didn't come down here to hear a lot of fine talk. My fellowmen, we already are at war. The Confederate States have levied soldiers and equipped them with arms stolen from national armories. They have fired upon our flag. I say the time has come for all citizens, Republicans and Democrats alike, to unite as one people in support of our government and in the defense of our country!"

"Huzza! Huzza!" the crowd shouts out. "Huzza for Andy Morrison!"

"I tell you what," says Andy, "let's take those flags down and run up a new one, a Union pole with a Union flag on top."

And that's what they did. Francis Henry shinnied up the Democratic pole and brought down the names of Douglas and Johnson, and Hoss stepped in to lay an axe to the pole. Asa Blackman shinnied up the other pole and ripped off the maul and wedges and brought down the names of Lincoln and Hamlin. Then they ran the Union flag to the top and let it unfurl.

"Three times three cheers for the Union!" says Andy, waving his arms, and everybody joined in.

It was at that rally that a good many of the Democrats of the township, men like Phil Beisel and Seth Talbot, changed over to the Republican side, though not Minot.

"Maybe I'm wrong," he says to half a dozen fellows who gathered around when the big meeting broke up, "but I figure not. Getting you fellows to listen to reason now is just like using your hat to stop a blue wind."

"Well," says Hoss, laughing, "I hear say, spitting into it, all a fellow's likely to do is foul his own beard."

It wasn't more than a week or so later that the first volunteer company for the county was organized over at La Grange, and some of the boys from Milford township, like Asa Blackman and Buck Latta, rode on over and joined up. It was a brand new thing and people used to come from miles around to see the men drill. Old Jim Bingham from La Grange was the drill master. He walked up ahead flourishing his cane and calling out, *hay foot, straw foot,* and the fellows, some of them carrying guns and others just empty-handed, tried to keep in step along behind. The boys were pretty awkward and about the best old Jim could do was swing his cane or stop and swear at a fellow for being clumsy as a three-legged cow, until Captain William Roy, who was in the regular army, came home from Indianapolis on furlough and took over. He gave the boys some regular drill and in about two weeks they were ready to set out for Fort Wayne, the nearest railway station, to report to Indianapolis and the governor.

On the day before they left, the people of the county held a big farewell rally for the boys. There was singing and marching and bands playing and fireworks. Captain Roy made a short speech praising the boys, and Lew Shingle himself talked for a full hour. Afterwards there was a wave of cheers from the crowd, and when the boys set out, dozens of people on horseback and in farmwagons followed along, laughing and cheering halfway down through the county to Wolcottville.

It was the first and biggest send-off that any of the boys ever got, though there was a kickback to it in the end. For when the company got down to Indianapolis, the governor told them the six regiments were already full, and all the *La Grange County Tigers* could do was to disband and sit around waiting for vacancies or come on back home, as a good many of them did.

Everyone was thinking then that the war would be over soon, but it wasn't. In the middle of the summer Hoss stopped off at Captain Barry's saloon with the news of the battle of Bull Run. The Union men had been beaten, he said, and the rebel soldiers were on their way to Washington. Ten thousand men lay dead on the battlefield and ten thousand more had thrown down their arms and fled along the roadways and up into the hills. Abe Lincoln was calling for 300,000 more volunteers.

Later on that fall and during the winter, volunteer company after volunteer company left for Indianapolis, and in the end even that wasn't enough. By the next year well over five hundred men from the county and thirty-one fellows all told from Milford township had gone off to war, and there was hardly a family from South Milford to Mongoquinong or from Applemanberg to La Grange where one or two boys hadn't shouldered their muskets and joined up. Some of them who had gone off earlier were already dead, like George Harman, Perry's half brother, and Sam Ream, or taken prisoner like Welt Francis and Buck Latta, or had come back from the battle at Shiloh, like Asa Blackman, with an arm shot off and crippled for life. And when in the winter of 1862, the Union armies needing still more troops, Governor Morton issued a proclamation calling for a state draft of men between the ages of eighteen and forty-five in all counties unable to meet their quota, an anti-war fever began to spread throughout the neighborhood.

It was then that many a fellow, who had been all out for war in the beginning, began to grow dubersome and called for peace and compromise. *The Constitution as it is and the Union as it was*, was what they called for now. And the louder the secesh talk grew, the hotter the kettlefires of fear and anger burned. Scare talk began to come into the neighborhood. All day long down at Jim Ball's blacksmith shop or Captain Barry's saloon or in at Abar's, fellows kept flying the eagle. Over in Illinois, so the stories ran, an angry mob had hanged a fellow, and it no more than served him right. Down at Fort Wayne a Democratic rally had been broken up and the men beaten. And more than one fellow over in Ohio and up in Michigan had been arrested and taken away and jailed without any warrant or ever coming up for trial. It wasn't everywhere, Abar said, that they were taking all of this treason talk without backcapping, the way they were right there in the neighborhood.

For a long time then Minot hadn't been saying much one way or another. He had been against the war, but now that the country was in the middle of it and Marsh old enough to go and field-dog anxious, it was a lot harder knowing the right thing to do. He was against slavery and always had been, though, seeing as how the slaves hadn't been freed in the border states where the Union army was in control, the war seemed to have little enough to do with that. And if a fellow was going to lose his right to stand up for what he believed and speak his mind, what was the whole country coming to, he asked.

A week or so after the governor's proclamation for a draft, Luke Babcock and Lafe Klingerman and Jim Ball came over to see Minot. They were getting mighty scared of the draft, Luke said. What would a fellow do with a big farm and family, like him or Lafe, and no one there to look after things, and what with the draft and volunteers, no hired men to be had at any price. They had all been thinking about it, he said, and they had figured out something. He and Lafe and Jim and others still young enough to go were getting up a pool. They were putting in one hundred dollars apiece and if they could get ten men, they would have a thousand dollars. And any one of them in the pool could use a part of that to hire a substitute to go for him if he got drafted. What they wanted Minot to do was take out a share for Marsh.

"No," says Minot, thinking it over as he sat there, "I reckon not."

"By god," says Luke, "it ain't any more 'n a forehanded thing to do."

"You figger they won't be draftin' Marsh?" says Lafe.

"No, I figure they will more than likely if the war goes on," says Minot, "but even so I'd be against it."

"A lot of fellers are doin' it," says Jim.

"And it'll only cost you a hundred," says Lafe.

"No, it ain't the money," says Minot, "but what I'm not willing for Marsh to do, I'm against hiring some other young fellow to go and do for him."

For a while, though, it looked as if they might not need a draft at all. Earlier that summer the county had organized an enlistment committee and the county commissioners now doubled the bonus for any young man who would volunteer. Lew Shingle had been appointed chairman of the committee and that winter he and other members drove all over the county holding war meetings and urging the young men to go. On the night they held a meeting down at Union Hall, Minot and Marsh and Perry, who was spending the winter at Minot's, went on over.

What he had to say Lew had said that often he could have done it with his eyes shut, but that wouldn't have been like Lew. He stood there banging the table with his fist and flailing his arms. Ending up, he was telling them what a noble thing it was for a young fellow to die for his country.

"His name shall be forever numbered among heroes," he cries out, "cherished in song and story. And someday when the battle clouds have lifted and the flags are all unfurled—"

It was then that Liza Ream spoke up right from the crowd.

"Hold on a minute!" she says, and it was that startling it stopped Lew right in his tracks.

By the time people got to see what was happening, there was Liza, holding her baby in her arms, standing up right down front and shaking a fist at Lew.

"Hold on a minute!" she says. "Are you goin' to have your

name numbered among the heroes, Lew Shingle? Why don't you go and die for your country?"

"There's one for you," says Seth Talbot, laughing aloud and some people joining in and others getting up to look.

For a moment Lew was that set back he couldn't say a word; then he says, "My dear woman, you are disturbing the peace."

"Peace?" she says. "I thought you was talkin' about the war."

"That I am," says Lew.

"Well, I can shuttle-mouth about that," says Liza. "Sam died six months ago and there ain't been any songs written about him."

"Well, not yet," says Lew.

"No," she says, "and iffen they was, it'd be no salt in the hominy fer me and the baby."

For a minute that came nigh to breaking up the meeting, what with the noise and talk that broke out, some joining in with Liza and others ashamed of what had happened and asking for everyone to be quiet.

Lew just stood there, pounding the table with his fist.

"Hold on! Hold on!" he says.

"I say Liza's right," Seth breaks in again. "It's an easy thing fer a feller to talk war when he hasn't got enough spit 'n hustle to have any boys of his own."

"Hold on!" says Lew, still pounding the table and shouting for them all to be quiet. "I ask the constable of this township to arrest that woman."

"For what?" calls out Phil Beisel.

"For disturbing the peace and breaking up the meeting," Lew fires back.

"Just a minute," says Minot, getting up then.

"Shut him up, too," calls out Abar Cain. "He's a Democrat!"

"Just a minute," says Minot. "All I was going to say—"

"We don't want to hear what you was goin' to say," says Abar.

"Well, you're going to," says Minot, raising his voice that loud he could drown out even Abar. "Liza's not disturbing the peace. She's got a right to speak her mind."

"Minot Gilmore, I call on you to support the forces of law and order," says Lew.

"That's what I'm doing," says Minot, "but I've got something to say to you, too. We're in the war and I figure we'd best get on with it, but people have a right to say what they're a mind to. And Liza's right; what you're doing is going around the country inciting young fellows to join, just so you and a lot of other fellows can beat the draft. War is a terrible thing—"

"By god, that's treason," says Lew.

"And no songs and stories will ever make up for it. I hold—"

"That's enough!" says Lew, pounding the table again. "We didn't come here to listen to any copperhead talk."

"Copperhead?" says Minot. "Call names if you're a mind to, but I came to a free and open meeting to—"

"By god, no!" says Lew. "I'm the one that's doing the talking here."

"Well, then," says Phil Beisel, jumping to his feet, "I hold this isn't any meeting at all. It's just Lew Shingle gassing off and some of us have got a lot better things to do. Come on, men," he says, moving towards the door.

And for a minute it looked as if the whole meeting might break into a fight right then and there. There was a babble of shouting and backcapping then, Abar calling for them to

[215]

throw all the copperheads out, and Seth and one or two of the others with their fists doubled ready to stand their ground.

"Get out!" shouts Lew. "Get on out! You too, Minot." He stood there sputter-choking mad. "By god, we got a United States marshal to look after fellows like you."

"Well," says Minot, when they got outside, "I reckon it's come to that pass now a man can't even speak his own mind."

It wasn't more than a week or so later, though, that Marsh looked up at his father while they were eating the noonday meal.

"Well, pap," he says, "I figger on goin' over to La Grange and joinin' up this afternoon."

"You've got your mind made up?" says Minot.

"That I have," says Marsh. "I've been thinkin' it over and I've come to see it's the only thing to do."

"Well," says Minot, studying him a little before he answered back, "I won't be the one to gainsay you."

"It's my country," says Marsh, "and we're still losin' the battles."

"All right, then," says Minot. "God bless you, my boy, and bring you safe home."

When the story of Marsh's going got around, many a fellow was ready to forgive Minot for everything he'd said, but there were a good many others like Lew and Jim Ball and Abar Cain, who, when the draft really came, still held it against him. First and last, they said, that's all Minot was, just a goddamn copperhead. It was a brand new word and came easy on the tongue and in it a fellow could put all the spit and hate for something he was afraid of and didn't quite understand.

It's an easy thing just to call out copperhead when you don't agree with everything a feller says.

Chapter 20

How Uncle Perry *worked for John McNutt,*

and John Reed came looking for a substitute

THE SPRING after Marsh left, Uncle Perry went to work for John McNutt over in Springfield township. John was a mean, snug-fisted fellow and tough as a piece of tug-leather. That summer Perry got his keep and a full shilling a day, but he earned it, he said, down to the last grain of noonday salt. He was the main hand on the farm, on the get-up all summer long, hanging onto the handles of a big bar-share plough, swinging a scythe, raking the platform and binding after the reaper, pitching bundles and cutting corn. Even so old John docked his pay every time it rained.

"Sunup to sundown makes a full day," says John, the first time an April shower cut off the spring ploughing.

"By god, a feller can't help fer a thundershower," says Perry.

"God Almighty can," says John. "I save on the wages and you get to rest."

"But I already worked half a day," says Perry.

"I don't pay lessen it's a full day," says John.

And he never did.

Every morning a half hour before sunrise old John would rouse him out and they'd do up the early barn chores before they sat down to breakfast. By full daylight they were at work in the field and except for half an hour at noon they'd stay there till sundown. After supper would come the evening chores before a fellow, dog-tired and all petered out, would get to turn in.

Many a time that summer Perry thought of enlisting. He was only fifteen and under the legal age, but all he had ahead of him this way was working out, and he'd been doing that year after year ever since he was seven and had run away from old Leazer's. Down at Minot's, where he'd gone now and then during the winter, helping Marsh do chores and cut up rift timber and split fence rails for his keep, was as near as he'd ever come to hanging up his hat and calling it home. But Minot and Nancy had enough mouths to feed all around the table without filling his.

The best friend he had that summer was Pete Martin who worked for Lem Cooper on a neighboring farm. Pete was older than Perry and sometimes of a Sunday afternoon with their chores all done, they would get together and talk about what they were going to do when they were both old enough to join up. Pete had a mind-set for the cavalry.

"Look at all the fun a feller could have ridin' his own mount like a general," says Pete.

"That'd be mighty handsome," says Perry.

"Besides, I figger it'd be a lot easier rustlin' a little calico iffen a feller was on horseback," says Pete.

Pete was a fellow with a good weather-eye for the fun and frolic of a thing. As for Perry, ever since he had seen his own half brother, George, go marching off, it wasn't so much the fun he was figuring on as the glory.

That had been two years earlier and George was already

dead now, killed at the battle of Shiloh, but Perry would never forget how he had felt the day George left. Captain Crocker had been organizing a company over at La Grange, and when the men were ready to go, they had come marching down through the county to Fort Wayne and the nearest train. The news that they were coming got ahead of them and everywhere in the villages and crossroads the people gathered to see them go by.

Down at South Milford the ladies of the township had laid out a basket-picnic for them in Trindle Square, and long before the company got there the streets were cram-jamb full. Perry was working for Seth Bulmer and had gotten leave to light out right after the morning chores. He had beaten the company to South Milford by a full two hours, and after the long wait he saw the men come swinging down the street, all eighty-one of them, carrying their guns and knapsacks, and Captain Crocker up ahead flourishing his sword. When they came up even with the square, the captain shouted a command and the company fell out for the picnic.

After they were through, the full company and all the crowd joined their voices in the *Red, White, and Blue,* and you could have heard the singing halfway up to Mud Corners. Then the captain had the men fall in and give an exhibition of their marching skill, letting them fire a volley or two up overhead. A good many of the women of the township had gotten together and made a flag for the boys, and Alice Waterhouse had been elected to make the presentation speech. Alice was the prettiest girl in the township, and Uncle Perry could still remember how she stood up on one of the tables for a platform that afternoon, her sundown tilted back over her golden hair, and talked to the boys.

"In behalf of the patriotic daughters of the township," she says, reading a speech Judge Carnahan had likely written for her, "I present to you, our brave volunteers, this glorious banner of liberty, this flag of the free, this proud emblem of loyal hearts, yours and ours. Be it yours to fight fearlessly to maintain its honor, to preserve it from insult at the hands of foes and traitors, even at the cost of your own dear lives. Be assured of our warmest sympathies and our most fervent prayers. Live nobly up to every duty, face bravely every danger until that time when right and humanity shall triumph and peace be restored, and may Almighty God grant you a safe return to rejoice with us in the blessings of eternal liberty."

It was a fine speech everybody said, and as soon as she had finished, the boys of the company broke out in three cheers for the ladies and the crowd gave back three cheers and a tiger for the boys. Then, being short of a full company, Captain Crocker got up and asked for more volunteers.

"Who else?" he says. "Who else will step right up and volunteer to serve his country? Who else? Rally round the flag, boys; she's yours and she's mine."

As soon as he had finished, a lot of babble-talk broke out in the crowd, some urging others to go and some mothers and wives pleading with their menfolk not to. It wasn't more than a minute or so, though, until right through the crowd he had seen his own half brother, George, raise his hand and go on up. Captain Crocker leaned over to shake his hand and then had him come up on the table and stand beside him, while wild cheers broke out from the crowd.

"Huzza! Huzza!" says a lot of fellows. "Huzza for George Harman!"

Then Captain Crocker had Alice come back up on the table and she shook George by the hand and gave him a kiss on the cheek and the crowd broke out in more cheers. One other fellow volunteered and then Judge Carnahan got up and gave the boys a rousing farewell, and with a lot of hand-shaking and backclapping and the women wiping tears from their eyes, the company went marching off, George waving to Perry and Lucinda and Nancy, as he went by.

It was a thing to remember, Uncle Perry said. George was twenty-one and a strapping big fellow, and Perry wasn't but thirteen, but he knew then that someday he was going to go.

It's a funny thing how all-fired fast a young feller's heart can beat to go and lay down his life fer a cause.

In the end, though, it didn't really happen that way at all. Late in October he was shucking field corn with snow already on the ground, when one day two fellows came driving along the road and seeing him in the field pulled up their horse and stopped. When they got out of the buggy, Perry recognized one of them as Ed Hern, a deputy draft commissioner, from over at La Grange.

"Howdy," says Ed, climbing over the fork-and-rail fence, "is your name Perry Harman?"

"That it is," says Perry, getting up from where he was kneeling and brushing the snow off his pants.

"The name's Hern," says Ed, "and this here is John Reed."

"Howdy," says Perry.

"Mighty good to meet up with you," says Reed.

"Perry," says Ed, "we're out lookin' fer some young fellers like you."

"Is that so?" says Perry.

"Yes sir," says Ed, "the country needs all young fellers like you in the army."

"I ain't but—" *fifteen* Perry was going to tell him, but before he ever got it out, John Reed came biting in.

"And we got a right handsome offer fer any feller that'll join up right now."

"How much?" says Perry.

"Three hundred dollars," says John. "Half of it in good hard cash and the rest in six months with interest from the day you sign."

Perry had heard of bounties all right. Pete had told him they were paying seventy-five or a hundred dollars maybe, but he had never heard of three hundred. That was a lot more money than he could make in three years scratching for old John.

"Fer a bounty?" he says.

"Well, sort of," says Ed. "John, here, belongs to a pool and he's lookin' fer a substitute."

For a minute Perry just stood there open-mouthed.

"I reckon I couldn't go," he says finally.

. "Why not?" says Ed.

Perry was going to tell them then that he wasn't old enough, but he hadn't said it right away and afterwards he just couldn't bring himself to it.

"I figger Minot wouldn't like it," he says.

"Minot Gilmore?" says Ed. "He ain't your legal guardian, is he?"

"No," says Perry, "Leazer Grimes is that."

"That's the way I figgered," says Ed. "I figgered Leazer wouldn't mind one way or t'other, and as for Minot, you just tell him a feller old enough to work out is old enough to tend his own ash-hopper. Feller up the road here, Pete Martin, says he'll go if you will."

"Is that so?" says Perry.

"Right here's where he signed," says Ed, showing him the papers.

"What company?" says Perry.

"Cavalry," says Ed, "the Twelfth Indiana Cavalry."

"All right," says Perry, "I'll go."

He signed up and after the men had driven off, he finished husking the shock of corn he was on, bound up the fodder, and carried it over to the gallows-stalk. It was getting on towards quitting time then, so he rounded up the cows in the nearby meadow and drove them up to the farmyard.

"Goddamn you, what you quittin' early fer," says old John, when Perry came up towards the house. "You run out of corn?"

"I'm fixin' to go," says Perry.

"Be daylight another half hour," says John. "Get on back there or you'll make it up tomorrow."

"I reckon I won't be here tomorrow," says Perry. "I just signed up."

"Signed up?" says John.

"Yes sir," says Perry, "I'm goin' off to war. Twelfth Indiana Cavalry."

"Well I'll be goddamned," says John, "a little shitepoke like you joinin' up to ride a jackass."

"I figger it'll be easier 'n workin' fer one," says Perry.

"Hold your sass," says John. "By god, what with the war and the bounties and all, you fellers are gettin' too stinkin' big fer your britches."

"I'll help out with the chores," says Perry. "I ain't goin' till after supper."

"Forage fer your supper," says John. "By god, you quit half an hour early. Go get your fixin's and haul butt out of here."

"I'll just stop long enough fer my pay," says Perry.

"How much you figger you got comin'?" says John.

"Eleven dollars and sixty cents," says Perry, "countin' today. You ain't paid me since the end of August."

"By god, I ain't got that much," says John. "I'll just be owin' that to you till you come back, I reckon."

He could see right then, Uncle Perry said, that old John was chancing him never to come back, and for the first time it came to him that maybe he wouldn't, just like George and Sam Ream and a lot of other fellows. But it was too late to think about that then. So he just went in and got his pack, said good-by to the old lady, and set out on foot for Mud Corners.

All the way down there he kept thinking about what he'd done and would he ever come back and could he tell the whole thing to Nancy and Minot. It was late, though, by the time he got there and the family had all gone to bed; so instead of waking up anybody he just shinnied up the kitchen lean-to roof and crawled into bed with young Frederick.

"Howdy, young feller," says Minot, looking up from the breakfast table as Perry came walking into the kitchen the next morning. "Mighty good to see you."

"Howdy," says Perry.

"How you making out with old John?" says Minot.

"I ain't workin' fer him any more," says Perry.

"He fire you?" says Lucinda, laughing, "or just lay you off for a day or two while the snow melts?"

"I quit," says Perry.

Minot didn't say anything for a minute and Perry began to feel uneasy. Then he got up his grit and spoke out.

"I'm enlistin'," he says.

"Oh, Perry," says Nancy, breaking in. "You can't do that."

"Well," says Perry, talk coming easier the minute he'd told them. "I ain't makin' much this way. John ain't paid me since August and these fellers came around and offered me three hundred dollars and Pete Martin signed up."

"But Perry," says Lucinda, "you're only fifteen."

"They never asked me how old I was," says Perry.

"And so you didn't tell 'em?" says Minot. "You think three hundred dollars is a good price for telling a lie and going off to kill other fellows?"

For a spell after that nobody said a word. Lucinda sat there with a down-look, and the younger ones kept busy eating.

"It ain't really the money," says Perry.

"No?" says Minot. "Well, that might be better 'n some fellows making out they're doing it for Almighty God. Who you substituting for?"

"John Reed," says Perry. "He and Ed Hern come over yesterday and I signed up."

"What I got against the whole thing," says Minot, "is their picking on young fellows like you."

"Perry," says Nancy, "you've got to tell them you're only fifteen."

"I reckon they wouldn't really care as long as they get another fellow in," says Minot.

"Promise me," says Nancy.

"Perry," says Minot, "I want you to think this over."

"I already done that," says Perry, "and I've made up my mind."

"You talk to Leazer?" says Minot.

"I figger Leazer won't be carin' one way or another."

"Well," says Minot, "even if Leazer don't, I do. I've always figured on you being one of the family."

"I don't figger it that way," says Perry. "I ain't really got a home or a family. I just work out, and Ed Hern says a feller old enough to do that is old enough to make up his own mind."

That hurt Minot, Perry could see, but he had hammered in the nail that Ed had told him to.

"All right, then," says Minot after a minute or two. "I

only got one thing to add. I take it a fellow big enough to make up his own mind is big enough to stand up to his own lick-log whatever comes of it."

And with that Minot got up and left the table. Perry sat around for a little while talking to Lucinda and playing with the younger children, and then he went over to see his half sisters, Esther and Lissa, and on to Old Leazer's to say good-by. The very next morning he was ready to set out for Kendallville. But he felt mighty low.

"Well, good-by young fellow," says Minot, shaking hands.

"Good-by soldier," says Lucinda, her brown eyes teasing him. "Bring me back a handsome young rebel."

"That I will," says Perry, laughing, though he felt like crying inside.

"Good-by, Perry," says Nancy. "May the good Lord bring you back to us."

Perry swung on his heel and started down the road.

Sometimes a feller'll do a mighty big thing just fer the glory, leastways he will, when there's money in it.

Chapter 21

How THE MEN *trained at Camp Mitchell, and Lucinda took care of Perry when he came down sick*

T HE SIXTEEN MILES from Mud Corners to Kendallville, angling through the woods along the east shore of Long Lake, could be lost-dog lonely when a fellow walked them all alone. What Perry kept saying to himself on the morning he set out for Camp Mitchell was that he really didn't give a holy church damn. Being a soldier in the federal army couldn't be any harder than working for old John McNutt. His leave-taking hadn't been quite the way he'd planned it, but then maybe nothing ever was.

Sometimes the only place a feller ever really gets to be a hero is in his own dreams.

Later on he came to see that he had no right to be, but at the time he was bitter even at Minot. "You think three hundred dollars is a good price for telling a lie and going off to kill other fellows?" That still rankled like a sandbur. All his life Old Leazer or Laura or Isaac or Sam or Minot had been telling him what a fellow could and couldn't do, and what had he ever got for paying a tinker's cuss of mind to any of them. He'd show them all, and even Minot, that he could work his own ash-hopper, let the drippings run lye.

It was late in the afternoon before he got to Kendallville, where he met Pete at the Calico House just as they'd agreed to, and then they both went on out to Camp Mitchell. Perry felt mighty uneasy when Captain Williams began filling in the full papers.

"How old are you?" says the captain.

"Sixteen," says Perry.

"Sixteen," says he, writing it down. "When were you born?"

"December 18, 1846," says Perry, making it a full year earlier, since he figured a plain unfancy lie would be the easiest.

"Now your father's name," says the captain.

"I ain't any pap," says Perry.

"Your mother?"

"She's dead, too."

"Next of kin?"

"I ain't any family at all," says Perry.

"Well, who do you want notified in case you're hurt or killed?" says the captain.

"Nancy Gilmore up to Mud Corners is my half sister," he says.

The captain wrote down the name and then he called a sergeant to take the boys over to get them their blankets and an army tent.

The only building Camp Mitchell had was a long, low barracks, set out in the middle of the commons, with some wooden sheds for the horses off on the far side. Right out in front of the building, where they had come in, was the camp well and the watering trough and over on the right the parade and drill grounds. Stretching along behind the building were two rows of wall tents for the enlisted men. There were close to a hundred men in camp then, and only the officers and some of the old vets slept in the barracks.

The first thing they had to learn right off was how to set up their own tent.

"There ain't no better way to teach a greenhorn he's in the army," says Sergeant Ritter, "than to let him freeze his backside right outen his pants."

Four men to a tent was the regulation, and Perry and Pete and Jim Mooney from over near Rome City and Albert Halper from Albion, all newcomers, set theirs up together. None of them had ever set one up before, and they made a poor fist at it, what with all the flaps and strings. And the very first night they were rained out like a pack of ground squirrels.

The next day the sergeant showed them how to dig a trench around the outside to carry off the water and pile the dirt up inside for a high floor. Some of the other fellows, too, had brought in planking for a wooden floor, and after a week or so on the damp ground, Perry and Pete made a raid on the village sawmill and lumberyard one night. Then one of the old vets showed Jim Mooney how to drive stakes into the ground for bedposts, nail some slats across, and pile hay on top of that for the ticking.

But even then they never slept warm. The fall rains and snow had set in, and they'd come off the parade grounds soaked to the skin. The inside of the tent would dampen up like a hen house, and likely as not if the night turned colder, you could scrape the hoarfrost off the walls by morning, big enough in handfuls for a snowball. And later on, when the winter really set in and a blue wind with a raw edge on it swept across the drill ground, it was as drafty as sleeping in an unfilled corn crib.

Every morning after long roll the camp greenhorns had to clean up the horse sheds, and Perry hand-pitched more dung every week than he'd barrow-hauled out of Sam Cooney's barn in a whole winter. While they were doing that, the older fellows would be watering, grooming, and saddling the horses. The old vets would go off riding then with the cavalry, and the newcomers would fall in for foot drill and spend the rest of the morning marching, counter-marching, shouldering and stacking arms, until a fellow had a regular plough-handle ache from swinging the old carbine. By eleven o'clock they'd fall out, and then one of them, Perry or Pete or Jim or Albert, would go over to the commissary to draw their rations for the day.

The four of them did their cooking together, most of it in an old dutch oven with a broken lid rigged up on a tripod right in front of the tent and with a flat stone to set the coffee pot on or an extra pan. They had to rustle their own firewood, too, and though for a day or two it was just like a field-picnic and they cooked up some good meals, it soon got to be an old thing and easiest of all was just to throw everything, the bacon or side pork and whatever potatoes and vegetables they had, into the dutch oven and serve up a pepperpot stew. They got so they even ate right out of the dutch oven, each with his own spoon, seeing as how that way there were less dishes to clean up afterwards.

After dinner a fellow might get an hour or so to lie around and rest or play a game of *old sledge* or *chuck-a-luck* if he was lucky enough not to get himself detailed to clean up the captain's quarters or have to take his turn at the pump filling the watering trough or at redding-up the parade grounds. Then came afternoon drill, heavier than in the morning, and with maybe a long march out into the country, and back from it you would wind up the afternoon cutting firewood or cleaning the muck from the carbine and sabre and your own clothes for the next morning's inspection after long roll. After supper was over, you were on your own, leastways you were when you weren't detailed for guard duty.

Day and night Captain Williams kept sentries posted all around the commons, each fellow with about a forty-yard beat, just as if the enemy was camping right across the street or leastways right over the next hill. When you were detailed for that, you were on for a full twenty-four hours, two hours on the beat and two hours off. In the daytime it was pleasant enough. A fellow could always watch the other men drilling and be happy he wasn't one of them, or talk to some fellows come over to see the camp, but the nights were chilly and a two-hour stretch, belly-cold and foot-sleepy, always seemed forever.

Along about the first of January they had an early spring thaw and a lot of sickness broke out in camp. Blear-eye and nettle-rash they'd had all fall and a lot of ague and dysentery; but now they had an outbreak of the mumps and a good many cases of the measles.

Camp Mitchell had no hospital or sickrooms, and if a fellow got down, he just lay there in his bunk or tent bed until nigh everybody else in camp had it, too. When some of the cases got too bad and a couple fellows died, Captain Williams and Doctor Roberts from Kendallville got busy and rented some rooms uptown, where they hired a fellow by the name of Moore who was handy with the sick to take care of the men they sent over. Perry was up there for four days when he had the measles, but then they needed the room for other fellows and sent him on back to camp.

He felt too all-overish when he came back to stand drill, so Lieutenant Rerrick detailed him for guard duty. He stood his turns for two or three days, but he didn't seem to pick up any and, the weather turning colder, one night he got a bad chill. A morning or so later when Sergeant Ritter came to rouse him out because he hadn't got up for long roll, his throat was that sore he couldn't even swallow.

"Sergeant," he says, "I got an awful sore throat and I'm feverish."

"You want to be on sick call?" says Ritter.

"No," says Perry, "I figger that ain't necessary."

"Well," says Ritter, "stay where you are. I'll tell the lieutenant and when the doctor gets through up to the sickrooms, he can drop by and look at you."

Perry lay there, dozing off and then waking up when the cold chills came on, till about eleven o'clock, when the doctor came in along with Pete. By that time he could hardly talk, let alone swallow. The doctor sat down on the turned-up nail keg and looked him over. Then he turned to Pete and told him to bring Captain Williams.

"I figure this fellow's got a case of putrid sore throat," he says to the captain, "and we've got to get him out of here. I don't want him up to the sickrooms, either. The thing to do," he says to Pete, "is to go uptown and get a livery rig and take him on home. And you'd best hurry up about it."

Pete swung off without saying a word, and the doctor stood there a moment talking to the captain.

"It's the only thing to do," he says. "He's got a bad case. It'll hustle him to make the riffle."

For a minute Perry just lay there, trying to make it all out.

So that's what his soldiering had come to in the end. He would have been willing right then to settle for a bullet wound or even an arm shot off like Asa Blackman and going home a hero, but he couldn't go back, not to Minot's, not with putrid sore throat.

"Captain," he says.

"Yes?" says Captain Williams, coming back in.

"I ain't no place to go," says Perry.

"Why not?" says the captain.

"I ain't goin' to Minot's."

"Who's he?"

"By god, I ain't goin' there," says Perry.

"Well, you're like to die here," says the captain.

"It's my own lick-log," says Perry.

The captain stood there a moment as if he didn't know what it was all about. Then he tucked in Perry's blankets, gave him a pat on the shoulder, and turned to go.

Perry didn't remember very much after that, though later on he could call to mind how two or three fellows had come into the tent and carried him outside wrapped up in his blankets and bedded him down in the front end of a bobsled. He was too sick to talk at all by that time or to really care what happened to him, though even at the time he had a feeling one of the men was Minot, and he remembered wondering how he happened to be there and what was really going on.

When he came to, they were out at Mud Corners, and Minot and Lucinda and Nancy were carrying him upstairs. As soon as they got him into bed, Perry heard Minot tell Nancy to get out quick for it was a dangersome disease, but he and Lucinda stayed right on working over him. Lucinda was a mighty handy girl, with a lot of pitch and hustle just like her father. She put blistering hot flatirons at his feet and

Minot poured some hot whiskey into his mouth; then he rubbed his chest with bear grease and covered it with hot rags that Lucinda brought from the stove downstairs. Every half hour, too, they would rouse him up and make him gargle his throat with hot salt water and make him swallow down some more whiskey.

How long he lay there sick, rousing and falling off into a nightmare of dreams and fever, Perry never knew. One morning after he had coughed up a lot of phlegm, he began to feel better and later on, the skin peeling off his throat like birch bark, his swallowing eased up and he took to eating again, and a day or two later he was sitting up in bed.

"How did I come to get here?" he says to Lucinda.

"Pap brought you home in a bobsled, and it was a mighty lucky thing he did," she says, her eyes lighting up like a fire-bob.

Then she told him on the day he had come down sick, Minot had gone to Kendallville to do some store buying for the family, and how he had run into Pete on his way up to the livery stable.

"Pap was meaning to look you up anyways," she says. "Abar Cain told him he'd heard say you had the measles."

Lucinda was full of fun and frolic, and lying there in bed at Minot's there was a world of time for him to laugh and talk with her about the old days, about the wonder of his finding them when he had run away to Pretty Lake, or the days when they had gone to school at Mud Corners, or gone berry picking or swimming down at Turkey Creek.

When it came time for Perry to go back to camp again, his heart was that full there wasn't really anything he could say.

"All I hope to do," he says to Lucinda and Minot, "is to

[*234*]

live long enough to someday pay you back fer this. I sure wasn't deservin' of it."

"Don't you go to worry-mind about that," says Lucinda.

"Well, I'm thankin' you," says Perry, "and I'd like you to have my bounty."

"I thought the bounty was why you joined up in the first place," says Minot, laughing at them both.

"I ain't lookin' at it that way now," says Perry.

"Oh, Perry," says Lucinda, "I don't want your bounty. You're a brave young fellow for joining up, and all I want is for you to come back to us someday."

"That I will," says Perry.

Going back to camp that time, Perry felt all washed clean inside. It was a good thing to have happen to a fellow before he went off to war.

Human kindness is a mighty big thing, bigger 'n the glory, come any time a-tall.

Chapter 22

HOW THE TWELFTH CAVALRY *fought the bush-whackers, and Alonzo Metzger was killed by a mine*

ALONZO METZGER was a big jimber-jawed fellow weighing upwards of two hundred pounds, though he didn't stand but five feet six. He was deep-chested, broad-backed, and big around as a barrel in the belly. Alonzo was the butt of a good many jokes and maybe that was one thing that made him feel mean. Perry himself was a small-made fellow and the company shavetail, and it wasn't long after he'd come back from Minot's, till Alonzo took to badgering him.

Alonzo hadn't been in camp more than a month before he got the itch, and seeing as how on a cold morning he wouldn't any more than dip a lead finger into the washpan to daub his eyes, it soon spread all over his body, so bad that whenever he wasn't busy doing something, you'd see him sitting down somewhere, holding his hands out in front of him with his fingers stretched wide apart, just to ease the tickle, as he said. One day when Perry was sitting on the south side of the barracks in the sun chunking away on an apple, Alonzo came over and sat down beside him. It took the edge off his appetite, but it was warm there, so he just stayed where he was, holding the apple in his hand.

"Iffen you don't aim to eat that," says Alonzo, reaching for the apple and getting his hand all over it, "give it to me."

"Damn you," says Perry, "keep your dirty hands offen me."

"Who you swearin' at?" says Alonzo.

"You," says Perry. "I ain't wantin' that itch. Here, you can have the goddamn thing." And with that he threw the apple on the ground and got up.

"You goddamn little shitepoke," says Alonzo, grabbing hold of Perry's arm before he could get away. "I'll learn you somethin'."

They had a fight right there. Perry took a side-winder at Alonzo and butted him in the stomach with his head, but Alonzo hung on like a grappling iron. He got Perry down and tearing open his shirt, rubbed his hand all over him, up and down his belly. As soon as he got away, Perry went over to the tent and washed up good, but it wasn't good enough, for it wasn't any time at all before he broke out with the itch. Before he ever got rid of it, he said, he had to boil every rag he owned, bedclothes and all, and rub himself down night after night with a homemade salve Doctor Roberts gave him that burned like nettle.

One day two or three weeks later, just as they had come in from drill, Alonzo called out to him from where he was sitting down on a bench right out in front of the entrance to the barracks.

"Harman," he says, "come on over here."

Perry turned and started walking towards him.

As he came up to him, Alonzo reached out as if to shake

hands and for a moment Perry thought he was going to say he'd been sorry for the whole thing. Instead of shaking hands, though, he grabbed him by the wrist, Perry pulling back too late.

"You ain't quite as quick as you thought," says Alonzo. "Now then, just bend over and ease off my boots."

"Ease 'em off yourself," says Perry.

"I told you to," says Alonzo, giving his arm a twist and half turning him around and then shooting out his foot so Perry fell over it backwards. By the time he had picked himself up, there were a lot of fellows watching. So he just bent over as if he were going to do it for Alonzo, got a good hold on the right boot, pulled it away, and then turned trigger-quick and flung it over his shoulder into the watering trough.

"Goddamn you," says Alonzo, making a lunge for him, "I'll beat the dog outen you fer that."

"Iffen you catch me, you big belly of hog lard," says Perry, ducking away.

Alonzo kept hobbling after him, one boot off, the other on, all the other fellows and Captain Williams, too, standing around laughing and joking about it. Mad as he was, even Alonzo could see he'd fouled his own beard. He hobbled on over to the trough and stood there shaking the water out of his boot.

"Fair enough, nicktail," he says. "We'll just call it quits." Then he tried taking the whole crowd in with his laugh. "I'll tell you what," he says, turning back to Perry. "You stand guard fer me now and I'll do your fightin' fer you when we get down south."

"Goddamn you," says Perry, his dander still up, "I'll do my own fightin'. I'd just as lief shoot you down as a rebel."

It was no Sunday school thing to say, Perry said, but he didn't figure on its ever coming back on him, though it did.

They broke camp early in May and by late June they were down at Hunstville, Alabama, where the Twelfth Cavalry, now members of the 127th Indiana Regiment, was sent to guard the Memphis and Charleston Railway against bush-whackers. Mostly the bushwhackers were small bands of fighters and night riders, sometimes twenty or thirty and sometimes well over a hundred older men and farmers or maybe even regulars, who would come riding down out of the hills or up from the bottomlands of the Tennessee River and burn out a culvert or tear up a stretch of track, anxious to wreck a train of cars for whatever spoils they could get or at least to block off the traffic on the road.

Huntsville was the base camp for the regiment, and Perry's own group, Company C of the Twelfth, was assigned to blockhouses five and six with patrol and picket duty at all points in between. The blockhouses had been built earlier and stretched all the way from Decatur to Paint Rock at the time, guarding the larger trestles and bridges, but in between them lay miles of track cutting through the hills over smaller fill-ins and culverts. To guard the in-between places, small detachments of troops were sent out for patrol and picket duty night and day.

It was something new for them all right and not like Camp Mitchell, lying out there, a dozen or so men rolled in their blankets right under the trees or maybe down in the thick underbrush next to a creek, heads pillowed on their saddles, or a fellow walking his beat, waiting while the others slept, watching and listening for any movement or a sound that might be a bushwhacker. There had been plenty of trouble, too, so the boys of the 121st Indiana said. A week or so before the 127th had come there to relieve them, the bush-whackers had burned out a big trestle down near Greenbrier, and two nights later another band had wrecked a half mile of track between blockhouse six and Brownsboro, tearing up the iron rails and fire-bending them over flaming piles of crisscrossed railway ties.

"Keep your eyes skinned," says Captain Williams, when they stood to horse, waiting for their first detail of picket duty, "and stay together. Likely as not there's a rebel hiding behind every tree just waiting to pick off a straggler."

There wasn't a man in the company that wasn't scared right down to his boot tops, and before the week was out, more than one of them had heard the whee-ang of a minie ball all right.

It was along about the third night that a band of bush-whackers surprised some of the fellows at a culvert three miles below blockhouse six and held them off with snipers and rifle fire until they'd piled brush around the timbers and set flames roaring tree-high. The very next morning Perry himself was detailed along with Pete and Jim Mooney and a dozen other fellows to rebuild the trestle, while the captain set out with a scouting party of thirty men to give chase. The scouting party was gone two full days and covered fifty or sixty miles, so Albert Halper said later, though they never caught sight of any bushwhackers till on the way back and within ten miles of camp when, riding their horses single file down through a pasture and dismounting to water them at a brook, they ran into an ambush.

The first thing they knew, Albert said, was when they heard rifle fire crack out from higher up on the hillside, and on the first shot, right there beside him, Les Haskins fell down in his tracks shot through the heart. For a minute it was a bad scramble. Then ducking down where they could behind some outcropping boulders near the creek, they stood them off, firing back volley for volley until it got dark, when they all made a run for it, leaving their own dead and losing nearly all of their mounts.

They came wandering back into camp later on that night, sometimes in groups of two and three and some fellows all alone, clothes torn and gashed by brambles, footsore, and wounded.

At daybreak Captain Williams was still checking up on his men.

"I figure we must have lost three men," he says, "Les Haskins, Abe Newman, and Alonzo Metzger."

"Alonzo?" says Pete. "Alonzo ain't lost. He came ridin' into camp last night well before dark."

"Riding?" says the captain.

Then he walked over to Alonzo's tent.

"Alonzo Metzger?" he shouts.

"Yes, sir," says Alonzo, coming out rubbing his eyes.

For a moment the captain stood there dumbfounded. "Well, I see you're back," he says. "Now tell me what happened."

"I just eluded 'em," says Alonzo.

"Eluded them?" says the captain.

"Sure," says Alonzo. "They went one way, and I went the other."

"By god," says the captain, "you know what happens to a fellow that'll turn his back on his own men?"

"No, sir," says Alonzo.

"Sometimes he never lives to find out," says the captain, turning around and walking away.

It was quiet after that for a spell until one night about a month later when the bushwhackers wrecked a long Memphis freight train down at Moore's hill by loosening the rails and toppling the engine and a half dozen cars down over the grade. Likely as not, it had taken only a handful of men, Captain Williams said, but once the loaded cars of wheat and salt and supplies for the Federal Army lay there on the hillside, two hundred rebels swarmed in from the countryside and down out of the hills to help guard and unload the train.

When that happened, Major Blake came up from Huntsville to take command and for the next two days they fought a regular pitched battle. To the right of the wreck, where the land dropped off down a steep hillside, the rebel sharpshooters and snipers could cover the whole valley. On the left, rose a ten- to fifteen-foot embankment beyond which the land rolled away in a long, half-timbered knoll. Up on top of the embankment the rebels had thrown up a breastwork of brush and felled trees and torn-up railway ties to protect the wagons and teams and oxcarts busily unloading the train.

On the first day Perry's own company was ordered to make the attack from the left, charging in over the top of the knoll and through the open field leading up to the breastworks. Before they ever got anywhere near, a hail of bullets and rifle fire cut down their ranks like a reaper, standing grain. A dozen different fellows had their horses shot down from under them. Right next to him Jim Mooney rolled headlong out of his saddle with a bullet wound in the shoulder. Riderless horses came charging across the battle line, rearing and plunging into the ranks. Halfway through the open field, Perry could see Captain Williams up ahead wave his sword and swing off sharply to the right, leading his troop over into the woods to cover their retreat.

Back at the starting line at the other end of the knoll, the captain called a halt to rest, and to check and re-form their lines. When they came up, they saw Alonzo sitting there on a stump, cleaning his gun.

"What are you cleaning it up for?" says Captain Williams. "You didn't use it."

"I did too," says Alonzo. "Right at the edge of the field I see two fellers off to the right in the brush cross-firin' at us, and I rode over there and run 'em out. Killed 'em both."

"Like hell you did," says the captain. "I figure you just eluded 'em, you goddamn bounty-jumper."

"I thought he was the feller that was goin' to do Perry's fightin' fer him," says Pete, laughing.

"By god, from now on everybody'll do his own fighting," barks the captain.

It was the next morning, right after daybreak, when they were ordered in again.

"All right, men," says Captain Williams, when they were ready to go, "there'll be no turning back today. Harman," he calls out.

"Yes, sir," says Perry.

"You're riding behind Metzger," he says. "If he turns back, you shoot him dead in his tracks."

One or two fellows were for laughing then, but Captain Williams snapped right back at them.

"Did you hear that, Harman?" he says.

"Yes, sir," says Perry.

"By god, there'll be no feather-bedding in this company," he says, turning his horse and leading the men off.

Perry swung his horse in behind Alonzo, sitting kind of pale there on a big raw-boned black.

"You wouldn't shoot down a feller on your own side?" Alonzo says, as they went riding down through the woods.

"Captain's orders," says Perry.

In a few minutes they came to the open field where they spread out and formed their lines ready for an attack. Then an orderly from Major Blake came riding across the field. Captain Williams was to take his men down through the woods to the right, circle the knoll to the mill road, cut his way through to the roadbed, and come in for a flank attack.

Captain Williams raised his sword and they swung off to the right, breaking into an easy gallop. Then a party of bushwhackers that must have been waiting over in the woods ahead of them opened fire. They hadn't been counting on that, and you could feel a recoil in the men. The captain turned and rode to meet them head-on.

On the second volley Perry's horse, a little bald-faced roan he had gotten from the federal cavalry depot at Nashville, was hit in the shoulder and crashed headlong. Lucky for him, Perry rolled free as they went down and picked himself up still swinging his carbine. Alonzo had turned in his saddle as the roan went down and seeing what had happened, reined in as if to help, and then, wheeling again, started galloping off the field.

"Hold on!" calls out Perry.

But Alonzo never stopped to look back. It was the devil's own pickle to be in and all Perry had to make up his mind was a split-trigger time. Sighting along to the middle point between Alonzo's shoulder blades, he pulled the firing lever. Then he just stood there, he said, hot iron whizzing by, shots ringing out up ahead, wounded horses screaming, cursing Alonzo and himself and the whole damn war. When he came to, he swung around and set forward on foot, and a few minutes later when a big bay came running across the field, he managed to lay hold of the reins and swing himself up. Reining in, he cut along the edge of the field and down into the woods where he could hear his own men well ahead.

By the time he had caught up with the rest, they had driven the rebels off and Captain Williams was stopping to rally his men. A quarter of a mile farther on they came out onto the mill road and swung left. Far off, higher up on the knoll, they could hear the fire of the first cavalry charge on the breastworks. Captain Williams kept hurrying them along.

Suddenly as they swung around a gooseneck in the road, they ran head-on into a party of rebel horsemen, waiting there likely to guard the rebel flank.

"Charge!" Captain Williams calls out, setting spurs to his horse, and the rest of them followed, clattering down the hillside, stone and dirt flying. Up ahead Perry saw the captain rise in his stirrups and fire his rifle at the lead horseman, and then as they came closing in, swing the butt end around and bring it crashing down on his head. Perry got one shot with his carbine, but he missed the fellow he was aiming at. Then they were horse to horse, swinging sabres. Pete's horse went down and as he saw Pete jump clear of the saddle, still swinging, a fellow charged into his own bay and Perry lashed out with his sabre. The jolt of the horses swung them both around, and Perry felt the slow-up of the blade as it caught the fellow's flesh above the shoulder. Turning back, he could see the blood spurting from the cut jugular, the rebel's arm going limp. For a second the young fellow sat bolt upright; then, his head falling back, he side-slipped to the ground.

Perry reined in and turned his horse. Many of the rebels had already been cut down and killed or were lying wounded and being trampled by the horses. Two or three of them, still mounted, had swung around and were trying to make a break for it. Two of them jumped their horses across a gully on the right of the road, one of them clearing it, the horse of the other stumbling and falling short of the far side, horse and rider together rolling down into the ditch.

"Come on men!" shouts Captain Williams, dashing his horse over the fallen bodies, right through the thick of it. "Come on!"

Perry set spurs to the bay and dashed after him. The road led down to the tracks and as they swung left on the roadbed, ahead of them they could see the wrecked train, the cut-in shelf of the roadbed, and the embankment swarming with rebels. Up ahead on the left Major Blake and his men were crashing through and leaping their horses over the barricade. On the right Company D, dismounted as infantry, were coming up the long slope. Perry and the others rode forward on a dead gallop, shouting and yelling. Seeing they were trapped, most of the rebels threw down their arms and raised their hands in surrender, or running down the hillside, tried hiding in the wreckage.

It took them all the rest of that day just to round up prisoners, care for the wounded, and bury the dead.

They had seen action, though, and won a victory. That night back at camp Captain Williams praised his men.

"By god," he says, "I figure every one of you will make a soldier. I saw Perry here cut down a fellow twice his size."

For a long while they all sat around camp that night talking about what had happened to them and what they'd heard about who had been killed or wounded, and even after Perry rolled into his blankets there was no sleeping. He just lay there, he said, living the whole thing through half a hundred times. He could still see the face of the young rebel, the blood spurting out, the arms dropping, the blue eyes and brown curly hair under the gray cap. He was a fine-looking fellow and a brave fighter. By god, he might just as well have been on their side—as Alonzo.

Goddamn Alonzo. All day long the thing had been riling in his mind. Had he really hit him, he lay there wondering. Alonzo had been carried off the field, so a hospital orderly had told Jim Mooney, with a stray bullet wound in his shoulder. Even if he had, there were some fellows in the company for whom the whole thing would be no more than a good joke on Alonzo. But for Perry there wasn't anything funny in it, not any more, not in firing at a man for doing what he himself had felt like doing a good many times.

As for Alonzo, he turned out to be a right good soldier in the end. His wound was no more than a scratch, and later on he went with them all through the war, from Huntsville back up to Tullahoma and Murfreesboro and over to Pulaski, and then on to Vicksburg and down the Mississippi to New Orleans and Mobile, where Perry's company, deployed as infantry, helped to take the last fort in Mobile Bay.

It was there, two days after the fort had fallen and the white flag had risen over the southeast bastion, that Alonzo, with a number of other men, walking around on the earthworks, was blown-broken like chaff in a circle wind as a rebel mine let go. Standing inside the fort, Perry could feel the heave as the earth burst upward, hurtling dirt and water and splinters of bone and flesh over the earthworks and up over the parapet.

Sometimes a feller'll have courage and sometimes luck and sometimes he'll turn tail and run like a dog, but a minie ball or a mine don't stop to pick and choose.

Chapter 23

How THE FEDERALS *foraged off the land, and*

Perry borrowed a greenback from the captain

SOMETIMES the federals lived by the rules of war, Uncle
Perry said, and sometimes just by their wits.

Belly hunger is bred mighty deep in the bone.

Throughout the state of Alabama and central Tennessee,
Union and secesh families lived side by side, and after three
years of war all of them were down to lean scratchings. A
Union family was always ready to share whatever they had
with the federals, but they had to be mighty careful of their
neighbors lest the bushwhackers get wind of it, raid their
place and burn it to the ground. And many a good rebel let
his crop, if he had any, rot in the field or even burned his own
nigh-empty bins and graneries if he figured they were likely
to fall into Union hands.

Many times the men of the Twelfth Cavalry were down to
half rations or none at all. Sometimes all they got for days on
end was a half-dozen pieces of pilot bread and, if they were
lucky, a half-pound strip of salt pork. A fellow could make

a shift of that for a week if he was good and hungry, but after a while the frying grease would gag him like a dose of castor oil. And sometimes there wasn't even any salt pork.

Down at Huntsville one time the whole camp was out of food for three days and the men that hungry they took to picking up the kernels of shelled corn that had been spilled into the dirt from the horse troughs days earlier, washing them off and chewing them, or maybe if they found enough, grinding them up in a homemade mortar and baking a hoecake.

When the supply trains couldn't get through at all, Major Blake would send out forage wagons with a party of troops to stand off the rebels and act as guard. One time down near Hartselle, Perry's company pulled up at a white house set well back in the trees with a white post-and-bar fence all around the yard. The fence was falling down here and there, and when a fellow got nearer he could see some of the windows in the house had been broken. Over to the right were a lot of out-buildings, though the big barn had been burned and the charred timbers were still lying there. Captain Williams halted the company in the roadway at the front of the house, sent a guard around to the rear of the buildings, and detailed Lieutenant Rerrick and four men to go inside the house and bring out the occupants.

The men rapped at the door and when no one answered, they opened it and went on in, pistols ready. When they came back out, they were leading a broken old man of seventy, walking with a cane, and a young woman of about thirty and her three ragged, half-starved children, the youngest one a baby in her arms. Captain Williams rode up.

"I'm sorry, sir," he says, "but we're in need of provisions."

"We ain't a thing to spare," says the young woman, her chin high and her back stiff as a ridgepole.

[*249*]

"Nothing?" says the captain.

"Nothin' fer yankees and mudsills," she says.

When she said that, the old man stepped forward. "Please to excuse my daughter, sir," he says. "She has a husband in the army and feels strongly."

"And how do you feel?" says the captain.

"I am loyal to the Confederacy, sir," he says.

"What have you about?" says Captain Williams.

"Nothin' that we ain't needin' fer ourselves," the woman says.

"Well, speak up," he says. "What is it or we'll search the place."

"I have a mule," says the old man, "with a halt in his shoulder, left me by one of your troopers who took the last horse in its stead."

"All right," says Captain Williams to his own men, "bring out the mule." Then he turned back to the fellow. "What else? Any cattle?"

"I have one small pig," he says.

"Fetch the pig," says Captain Williams to his men. "Any corn?"

"There's a bushel or two of corn," he says, "just about enough to feed out the pig."

By that time the men had brought out the old mare mule, and Pete Martin was coming across the yard holding the squealing pig by the leg. Captain Williams dismounted as if he meant to look them over. The young woman stood there, her eyes flashing fire, the children wide-eyed and clinging to her skirts. The captain circled the animals, gave an order to the wagon train, and then remounted his horse.

"Yankees and mudsills do not rob the needy," he says, touching his cap. "Remount, men. Let's go."

It hadn't always worked out that way, though. One of the

stories the men used to tell on Captain Williams was about the time he had come up to a big plantation in Virginia, a red brick house with chimneys at each end, a dozen well-built stables and barns, and a long row of Negro quarters down towards a creek. The yard was torn up, and tables and buckets were strewn around as if troops had been camping there. The grass was long and uncut, and some of the mortar was chipped off the pillars. The big house and all the barns stood empty and there didn't seem to be a living soul around, until the captain, riding on down to the Negro quarters, found a half-dozen families still living there.

At first the darkies all seemed slow of speech and mighty hesitant, till one of the older ones came over and started talking. The mistress of the house and her daughters had gone down to Richmond, he said, and all the menfolk had gone off to war. There were plenty of provisions stored on the place, hidden out and buried, if the federals could find them. They had been forbidden themselves to look for them and threatened if they did. But they were free Negroes now, he figured. Some of them had already gone off, though the rest of them were staying, for there wasn't really any place to go, except to join the hundreds of wanderers and beggars daily driven off and beaten out of nearby towns.

Captain Williams set out a guard and the men scrabble-scratched over the grounds, and before the afternoon was out, they'd unearthed a lot of supplies from an old stone cellar hidden in a grove, well covered with grass growing on top. The men all hustled around and pitched in, and after they had loaded up the supplies, for the kindness done the federals, Captain Williams gave the old Negro two or three sacks of corn meal and a half-dozen hams for the families. In the end that was what must have given them away.

At any rate about a week later one of the young men of

the family came back to the place and, seeing what had happened, got together a posse of neighbors and they rode in and rounded up the Negroes. They tied the old Negro to a tree right out in front of his own cabin, threw a pile of pine knots at his feet, set fire to them, and burned out his vitals. Then they turned on the other Negroes, beat them with their gun stocks, cut them down with their sabres, and left the bodies lying there as they rode off in the breaking dawn.

When the news got back to the Union camp, Captain Williams went out with a detail of men, and after they saw what had happened, they buried the bodies, and set fire to every building on the place, burning them all to the ground.

Captain Williams could be flinty as a piece of bar iron when he had a call to be. Give him a cavalry charge with the men riding in face to face and he was ready to lead with carbine and sabre, but looting and burning out the countryside, he wanted no hand in that, he said. Raiding a berry patch was all right, maybe, or even stealing a bushel of apples from a fellow's orchard for eating and pie, but slipping out of camp at night, as the men sometimes did, stealing hogs or cattle, breaking into a smokehouse, or setting fire to a building, he was dead set against.

In the fall of 1864, when the whole regiment was moving up from Huntsville to Tullahoma, the turnpike dusted up that dry the men tied handkerchiefs over their mouths until the whole regiment looked like a gang of highwaymen. Early in the evening Colonel Anderson called a halt and sent the troops into a roadside bivouac, and as it happened, Perry's company came to a stop right alongside a big farmyard.

Captain Williams rode into the yard, dismounted, and went up to the house. In about ten minutes he came back and spoke to the men. They could water their horses at the farmyard trough, he said, and roll their blankets in the orchard. He had given his word that there would be no fires, no molestation of the livestock, and no snooping around any place where a fellow wasn't wanted. Then he detailed some of the men and set a guard for the buildings.

Perry and Pete watered their horses, filled their canteens, and led the mounts over under the apple trees, where they tied them next to a high board fence shutting the barnyard off from the orchard. Then they sat down with their backs to the wall. They were down to half rations and all that was left were a few hardtack biscuits. For a spell they just sat there, nibbling. Then Perry sat up, sudden-like, listening.

"You know what's behind that fence?" he says.

"No," says Pete.

"Chickens."

"By golly, I think you're right," says Pete. "A roast hen'd taste mighty good."

Perry got up, went over to his horse, and dug a few kernels of shelled corn out of the feed bag. Sitting down again with his back to the wall, he threw them up over the fence. You could hear chickens come cluck-running to pick up the corn.

"That's a high fence," says Pete. "I reckon a feller couldn't reach over."

"They'd likely see us," says Perry, "and Captain Williams give us strict orders."

He sat there a moment, thinking. Then he got up and dug an old fishline out of his haversack, slipped a kernel of corn over a hook and threw the line over the fence. Pretty soon he felt a tug and, starting to pull away, he could hear the hen flutter. He kept the line taut till he had her well over towards the fence and then, giving a heave, he swung her up and over. Pete caught her as she came down and wrung her neck before she'd ever let out a cackle.

One hen would have been enough for them, but seeing it

was that easy, they caught two more and passed one of them down the line to Albert Halper and Jim Mooney. Then some of the other fellows caught on and rigged up their own lines—they'd all been fishing down on the Tennessee River a couple of weeks earlier—and in less than twenty minutes they had caught over a dozen hens. It wasn't long after that till they had them dry-plucked and the fires built and sat there with the birds turning on the spit.

As soon as Captain Williams saw the fires, he came charging down the line. When he saw what was happening, he gave the order for an assembly in the farmyard.

"Goddamn it," he says, "I told you fellows not to forage."

Then he told them the old lady was secesh all right, but that was no call for robbing her of the last mite she had. She was living there alone with her four grandchildren and all the slave-niggers had left her, even the house-help. Her husband and her two sons had been killed in the war and her daughter-in-law was gone, doing sanitary work in the Confederate Army. She'd allowed them freedom to use the premises, but she'd asked to have the buildings undamaged, and the chickens in the walled-up yard were all she and the children had to live on.

"I want to know who's responsible for this," he says.

For a moment no one said a word. Then Perry stepped forward.

"I figger I am," he says.

"Goddamn you, Harman," says the captain. "You heard my orders."

"Yes, sir," says Perry.

"Yes sir, hell," says the captain. "I want those fires put out right now. Any man disobeying my orders will be under military arrest. As for you, Harman, tomorrow you'll apologize. Men dismissed."

The next morning Captain Williams marched Perry and the others into the farmyard and lined them up in front of the house like a row of schoolboys. He went inside, had the old lady come out, and then he called Perry to the porch. Perry just stood there for a while like a comb-cut rooster.

"I—I figger we're sorry, madam," he says. "Can we pay you fer them hens?"

What in the world he would have done if she'd said yes, Perry hadn't quite figured out.

"No," she says, standing there, quiet-like, in a gray shawl and white lace cap. "No, boys, you can't."

She turned to the captain. "I reckon my own boys might have done the same thing."

For a few days Perry felt mighty foolish, what with all the men laughing and joking him about it, but before the war was over he figured he got to even up the score some with the captain.

That was a long time later when the war was nearly over, and the whole regiment came up through Montgomery and went on a long march across the state into Georgia and then back again through Alabama into Mississippi. General Grierson had given strict orders against foraging and the word had been passed down all along the line that they were to pay for everything they got.

It was that that got them into trouble. Perry and the others hadn't been paid since they left Vicksburg and many of them were out of money and there was little enough to buy, with prices sky-high. Perry could remember paying as much as a dollar for two small biscuits and a small piece of spoiled bacon, and when their money ran out they took to bartering what they had with the people along the road, an old pair of shoes or an extra blouse or a haversack or canteen for a loaf of bread or a handful of potatoes. Many of the people didn't have anything to sell, though some of them were that bitter that even if they'd had the horn of plenty, they wouldn't have given a shelled peascod to a damyankee. They went on for days without enough to eat, and some fellows got that weak they toppled from the saddle. Every day added to the stragglers.

One noon over in Georgia, already on the way back, Perry saw a big white house, setting well up in a fringe of trees a mile or two down a lane from the turnpike.

"Jim," he says to Jim Mooney, who was riding alongside, "I'll see if I can get somethin' to eat, iffen the captain'll allow it."

He dug his spurs into his horse and trotted ahead till he came alongside of Captain Williams.

"Captain," he says, "see that house over yonder? Well, I figger on goin' over to see if I can get somethin' to eat. All me and the boys have had fer three days is a little dried corn bread."

"All right, Perry," says the captain, "but no foraging."

"No, sir," says Perry, starting to turn around.

"Hold on a minute," says the captain. "You got any money?"

"Some," says Perry.

"How much?" says the captain.

"A shillin' or two."

"You can't buy very much for that," he says.

Perry turned his horse again and started riding off without saying a word.

"Hold on," the captain calls out, reaching in his pocket. "Here's a greenback. You can borrow it from me."

"Thank you, captain," says Perry, taking the money and then galloping off.

When he got to the house, he rode up to the front porch,

dismounted and knocked at the door. It was opened in a minute or two by a peak-nosed, sharp-eyed woman.

"Well, what do you want, you dirty Yankee," she says, looking hard at Perry. "Do you have to beat the door down?"

"Madam," says Perry, "I'm lookin' fer to buy some victuals."

"Buy?" she says.

"That's what I said," says Perry.

"You got money?"

"That I have."

"Well, then, hand over your haversack and the canteen," she says, as if she weren't for wasting words on a mudsill.

Perry reached them up and she disappeared into the house. In about ten minutes she came back with the haversack and the canteen full of milk. Perry looked into the haversack. There was half a ham, two or three loaves of white bread, a small sack of black-eyed peas, and a strip of bacon. That was more food than Perry had seen in a month.

"Madam," he says, "you've been very good. How much am I owin' you?"

"Nine dollars and fifty cents," she says.

It would come high but Perry felt proud that he had enough money for once in his life to pay for it without haggling. He took the greenback from his pocket and handed it to her.

"Here you are, madam," he says.

But she never touched her hand to it.

"What are you trying to do," she says, "rob me? I don't want any of your filthy Yankee money. Give me that haversack back."

As he was handing it back to her, Perry thought of a Confederate note he was carrying. Three weeks earlier down at Montgomery, where they were camping in the courthouse square, someone inside had taken to throwing away greenbacks—they weren't worth a cornshuck then any more. A whole bundle of them had come pitching out of a courthouse window.

"Think I'll pick me up a hundred, just to feel it bulgin' in my pocket," says Jim.

"It won't do you no good," says Perry. "But I'll take me a twenty fer a souvenir."

He had picked it up then without thinking it would ever come in handy.

"Hold on, madam," he says, reaching in his pocket. "I got some of your money on me."

"Thought you could beat me out of it, you damn Yankee," she says. "Well, maybe you'd like your change in your own money?"

Perry wasn't one to argufy. "Madam," he says, "it's good enough fer me."

He turned back towards the turnpike and caught up with the column about midafternoon. That night in bivouac he laid out his fixings.

"Now fellers," he says, before they sat down, "I'll just take a slice of this ham and a loaf of bread to the captain."

He walked over to Captain Williams and gave him the victuals, and while the captain was still thanking him, he looked him square in the eye.

"Here's the greenback I'm owin' you," he says. "I'm much obliged."

"Perry," says the captain, looking a hole right through him, "did you pay for this food?"

"Yes, sir," says Perry.

"But you said you didn't have any money," says the captain.

"I didn't," says Perry.

"Then where in hell did this come from?" says the captain.

"You give it to me," says Perry.

"Goddamn you, Perry Harman," says the captain, "one way or other you're a liar."

Perry couldn't hold back any more, so he told him the story.

"And she gave you change?"

"Yes, sir," says Perry.

"I ought to be confiscating that," says the captain, laughing.

But he never did.

That night, for the first time in many months, Perry and the others sat down to the fat of the land.

Chapter 24

How THE TWELFTH CAVALRY *fought the battle of Wilkerson's Pike, and Pete Martin died like a soldier*

PETE MARTIN was clear grit for a tussle come any time at all. He'd had a horse shot from under him down at Moore's hill, but he had lit on his feet, swinging, and stood off a rebel charging right at him, dodging this way and that until Albert Halper's revolver had brought the fellow down with a ball through his head. And in a picket skirmish down at Lily Flagg he brought in three prisoners single-handed, walking along behind them carrying their rifles and sidearms, laughing and talking to them as they came.

"I brung you three visitors," he says to Captain Williams, "just waitin' to inspect a federal camp."

"Mighty fine," says the captain, "and what is it you think they ought to see first?"

"Breakfast," says Pete, "if the boys will cook up some conglomerate. All I had on me was a fistful of soda crackers."

"How did it all happen?" says the captain later on.

"Oh, they just come up and surrendered." says Pete, laughing.

"Ambush," says one of the rebels, hearing him, "and down-right falsification of numbers. I allowed there were ten men the way he called halt."

Pete was a fair fighter and against bloodshed, leastways when it wasn't necessary.

In the fall of 1864 a good many of the men in the regiment were furloughed home for the election, though not Pete or Jim Mooney or Perry, since they weren't old enough to vote. And while the men were at home seeing their friends and relatives, the number in the regiment being cut well below half, those who stayed on were assigned to the Second Tennessee. Colonel Spargus was in command—a burly, black-mustached fellow, hard-driving, and full of hate and fury towards the rebels. The regiment had moved up from Huntsville to Tullahoma then, abandoning the Memphis and Charleston line to the rebel Forrest and his regulars.

The men from the Second Tennessee were fierce fighters, every one of them. They were tall, strapping fellows from the mountains of eastern Tennessee who had worked their way through the rebel lines into Indiana and Kentucky to fight in the northern army, and the nearer back home they got, the more cruel and bloody they became. All around Tullahoma the countryside looked as if the plagues of Egypt had struck it. Down in the valleys and the meadowlands lay the burned and blackened timbers of the big houses, the tall chimneys still standing like lone markers in a burying ground. Up in the Coffee Hills even the cabins looked unlived in, doors and windows broken, barns and fences burned down, ragweeds and briars growing in the corn patches. Sometimes out on scouting duty they rode half a day without seeing anyone around, except maybe now and then a lonely woman, barefooted and in rags with a pipe in her mouth, trailed by half a dozen children and a long, sharp-nosed hound.

They used to say that the Second Tennessee never took a prisoner, and there were plenty of times, Perry figured, that was true. Out on a scouting party one day up towards Coalmont they ran head-on into a party of rebel horsemen. They outnumbered the rebels three to one, and it was no trick at all to turn their flank and drive them up a crooked country lane with a steep bank on one side and a high, well-staked-up rail fence on the other. It was too close for the rebels to jump their horses and get away; so they turned and took to fighting it out, man to man. Pete and Perry were well up in front, and when Pete got one of the rebels backed into a corner so he couldn't fight any more, the fellow surrendered. He was young, slender-built, and didn't look a day older than Pete himself.

Both men swung off their horses and the young fellow reached Pete his pistol and sabre. Just then one of the big fellows from the Second Tennessee came dashing up.

"Draw blood on him," he says. "We ain't takin' any prisoners without drawin' blood."

"This one we are," says Pete. "He surrendered."

"By god," the fellow says, "iffen you won't, I will."

He set his spurs and rode a step nearer, leaning forward in his stirrups to swing.

"Hold on," says Pete, raising his own sword to ward off the blow.

"Goddamn you," says the fellow, "get out of the way."

But Pete stood his ground. "Leave him alone," he says. "He's my prisoner."

With that the fellow swung at Pete himself, sabre in hand. "You goddamn rebel," he says, "I'll get you first."

When Perry saw the big fellow swinging at Pete, he was that mad, he said, he could have run him through from the back.

"Hold on!" he says, riding his own horse in close and rapping the fellow's mount a good one on the rump with his sabre. The big fellow's horse jumped about six feet and carried him well away from Pete and the prisoner.

"Goddamn you," he says, looking back at Pete, "I'll settle with you fer this."

Perry swung off his horse, and he and Pete took the young rebel with them and started walking back down the lane. The fight was all over by that time; nine rebels lay dead on the roadside, ten or twelve of them were wounded, a half dozen had gotten away, and the rest had surrendered.

Back at camp the next day Pete got a call to report to Colonel Spargus.

"You draw on a fellow on your own side?" he says.

"Yes, sir," says Pete, "defendin' myself and a prisoner."

"Poppycock," says the colonel. "You're in this war to kill rebels. One week in the guard house on bread and water. By god, I'll make soldiers out of you Yankees."

Drawin' blood is one thing; havin' blood drawed on you is another. It takes a mighty good man to be a soldier.

Give him a tough fight, and Pete was hard as flint and ready as a spark in a firing-pan. He cut down a color bearer in the battle of Wilkerson's Pike, and that helped to turn the whole tide of battle.

That was after Captain Williams and the other men were back again and the company had moved up to Murfreesboro. For a good ten days before the battle, they had been out on scouting parties and sentry duty, feeling out the approach of the enemy as the rebels under General Forrest came pushing up from Pulaski and other times carrying dispatches to Columbia and over to General Schofield at Franklin. On the afternoon of the battle of Franklin they could hear the roar of cannon and heavy artillery a full twelve miles away. Then came news that General Schofield was falling back. Two days later their own communications with Nashville were broken, General Forrest having by-passed Murfreesboro and taken the railway blockhouses at Mill's Creek and La Vergne.

Out on a scouting party two nights later some of their own men had a skirmish with a party of cavalry in advance of Forest's main troops. It was clear then that Forest was turning back and encircling the city of Murfreesboro. That night the order came through to be ready to move; ammunition was issued to the troops and three days' rations. Twice before morning the order was countermanded and then reissued. Finally at ten o'clock the next morning Perry's company got under way, moving out from the city on Wilkerson's Turnpike in the rear of their own infantry.

A mile behind their own lines the order came to dismount and proceed as infantry. The ground underfoot was a sticky red clay and it took them a full hour to slide and stumble their way forward through the jack oaks and cedar brakes, in and around the swamp holes. The whole company to a man hated to fight on foot.

"Goddamn," says Perry, picking himself up from where he'd stumbled full length into a mud hole. "And I figgered I was joinin' the cavalry."

"That you did," says Pete, laughing, "only right now you're ridin' shank's mare."

Right where they came up, the line passed through a farmyard where the stone and the half-burned timbers of the house and some old farmwagons and wheels had been used in throwing up a breastworks. Just ahead of them towards the rebels lay a half mile of open field with a ditch a hundred yards ahead of the abatis, filled with their own sharpshooters and snipers.

It was quiet enough when they came up, and the first thing Perry and Pete did was to throw off their knapsacks, find themselves a place to sit down in the shelter of the breastworks, and eat their rations. Some of them even rustled around and lit small fires to heat their coffee. Perry and Pete were still sitting there scraping the heavy, sticky clay from their boots when the first boom of cannon fire cracked out of the hills.

Lieutenant Rerrick came down the line summoning the men to their positions. The first shots passed well over them, crashing down through the oak groves and popples, branches and splinters flying in every direction. Then a slow one came in like a winged quail just over the breastworks, landing twenty or thirty feet to their rear.

"Down!" someone calls out, and all the near men fell flat on their bellies in the red clay.

"Watch out sharp!" says Lieutenant Rerrick, running down along the line.

The artillery fire came heavier and heavier and to the left and rear their own guns thundered back. The whole countryside broke into a long rolling roar. The shells kept dropping nearer, digging up the earth and spraying the water and mud and broken iron over the men. Clouds of gray smoke hung over the battlefield, broken by flashes of fire, like chain-lightning in a sultry summer sky. Then as it got darker towards the west, quail and partridge came flying over the breastworks, and rabbits ran across the field.

"Get ready!" shouts the lieutenant.

In a minute Perry could see the rebels come charging across the field in a line straight as standing grain after the first swath. The guns of the sharpshooters and snipers in the ditch ahead cracked out. The federal battery on the left raked their lines with grape and double-charged cannister. But they still came on. Breaking into a run, they charged the snipers in the ditch, fighting hand to hand, and driving the federals back into the shelter of the breastworks. Then a second line could be seen moving onto the field.

"Fire!" calls out the lieutenant.

They opened up then with muskets and rifle fire all along the line, reloading quickly and firing again and again, with every volley dropping dozens of rebels onto the field. Within forty yards of the breastworks, the rebels broke rank, dropping their guns, turning and running back across the field. Then the second wave came across the ditch on towards the breastworks, and the federals went to reloading again with their guns still smoking hot. They were tired and anxious now and fired more wildly. On and on came the graycoats, firing and running, dropping down, and then firing again. Fifty yards away, then twenty-five, then ten.

"Sabres!" shouts Lieutenant Rerrick.

Just ahead of Perry a rebel color bearer sprang up on the breastworks, a young fellow, shouting and waving to his men. In a split second Pete had leapt up and cut him down with his hatchet. The colors falling, the rebel line halted, giving the federals time to reload and fire again, as the men turned and fell back towards the ditch.

Before the rebels had time to try it again, it was dark. Perry and Pete and the others sank back in the sticky, churned-up clay, thankful they were still alive and breathing, scraping the mud off their clothes, and chewing the uncooked corn in their knapsacks. Then Captain Williams came rousing up the men and sent them to work seeking out and helping their own wounded. There was no relief and all night long, while some of them stood sentry, others sat huddled together against the freezing cold or stretched themselves full length in the mud behind the shelter of the wall, beyond which lay the rebel dead and wounded, calling out now and then for help in the still night.

At daybreak the battle broke out again, fire belching from the hills and the artillery roaring once more, shells dropping out of the sky thick as hailstones. By nine o'clock it was all over, though, the rebels having withdrawn under the cover of their own fire, swinging around to the right and crossing the turnpike back towards Nashville, leaving their dead and wounded on the field.

Two weeks later, after the battle of Nashville, with the rebels in full retreat down through Lewisburg and Lillard's mill, the Twelfth Cavalry, now attached to General Wilson's corps, was sent out to overtake and harass the rebel rear. For almost ten days they were in the saddle then, riding forced marches fifty to sixty miles a day, swimming and wading streams, cutting overland through the hills, skirmishing with the rear guard, sometimes cutting off a wagon train and other times taking hundreds of ragged, worn-out men.

Down at Anthony's Hill which lay like a bent-open horseshoe, with the open prongs pointing north and a high ridge like a center calk towards the south, the rebels made a stand. A narrow road led up between the two wooded ridges and swung off towards the west over the hill, just to the right of the highest hogback. The night before, so the scouts reported, a rebel wagon train had gone lumbering up the long dusty road, and the next morning the Twelfth Cavalry set out in pursuit. As they came up the defile to where the road angled towards the right, Major Blake called a halt. He could see that the towering ridge just above them to the left commanded the road and the valley and would be a likely place for the rebels to make a stand or lay an ambush.

Ordering the men to dismount, he sent two companies up through the oak groves and cedars and around the outcroppings of rock to take and hold the hogback. Perry and Pete and the other men spread out and began to work upward. It was a steep hillside and they went slowly, dodging from tree to tree, dropping down behind boulders, and then going on. There was no sign or sound of the enemy, not until they were within fifty paces of the top. Then suddenly the guns broke loose.

Grape and cannister came pouring down into the oak groves and thickets. Musket fire cracked out from the wooded ridge on the right of the road. Captain Williams could see that the hill was full of armed men. He called for a retreat, and they began to fall back down into the valley, from oak grove to oak grove and outcropping to boulder, the hot iron whizzing and tearing into the trees, ricocheting from the stone and digging into the hillside. With a shout the rebels themselves began to charge down the steep incline, falling and sliding, resting their feet on outcropping stones to fire, then coming on again, stumbling and rolling, and then picking themselves up again and firing.

It was every man for himself from then on. Perry fell and rolled into the open fire, crashed into a boulder, felt a sharp pain in his ankle, picked himself up and stumbled on. Almost down at the road, he saw Pete come running over from a cedar thicket.

"Come on there," he says to Perry, seeing he was limping and then stopping to grab him by the hand.

Together, hand in hand, they started down the road. Dozens of their own men were up ahead of them; others were breaking out into the road to their rear. A big twelve-pounder up on the ridge began to shell the road. Up ahead of them a shell landed among the running men. Perry and Pete kept on, caught up with the wounded, and went on.

A second shell lit in the road ahead of them. Then one came in just to their rear. The roar of the explosion swept over them, dirt and iron flying. Pete stumbled headlong and went down. For a moment, unable to stop, Perry kept on. Then he saw that in his own left hand he held Pete's right, severed at the wrist. He stopped and stood there, holding it. He opened his hand. His knees gave way and on all fours he crawled back to where Pete lay by the roadside.

"Goddamn," says Perry. "Oh goddamn."

He ripped the sleeve from his own blouse and tore it into shreds. He wound it about the arm above the elbow, grabbed a broken stick, and twisted it up tight. The blood stopped. Pete lay there moaning. Perry looked around at the men running by him and called out, but no one stopped. The fire from the twelve-pounder slackened off as most of the federals cleared on down the road beyond range. Perry tried to bring Pete to his feet, but he was that weak from the loss of blood, his knees buckled under him.

"You go on, Perry," he says, sinking back down on his shoulder. "You go on."

"No, by god," says Perry, unbuckling his canteen and giving him a drink. "I'm stayin' right here."

"Hand to hand, Johnny Rebel is a clean fighter," says Pete, "but a man can't hold his own against a shell."

Farther to the rear even the musket and rifle fire was dying down then, but Perry could already hear the rebels moving among the dead and wounded, shouting and hallooing, looting the bodies of shoes and clothes. He lifted Pete to his feet, swaying, ducked his shoulder down under Pete's belly, and swung him over his back. Ten rods farther on he came to a lane leading off the main road, running alongside an open meadow. Halfway down he could see a building in a clump of trees. He came up to it, a weathered, frame cotton gin, standing there by the roadside. He eased Pete off his shoulder into the grass and looked for a hiding place. The gin stood empty. Inside he found a loose puncheon and lifted it up. Then he went outside where Pete lay, white and still. He carried him in, lowered him down through the floor, and worked the board back into place.

It was hours later and long after dark before Perry, stumbling and crawling along across country and through the woods to avoid the rebel cavalry patrols on the road, came upon a federal sentry, and was passed along the line to report to Colonel Anderson of the Thirteenth Illinois.

Perry told him what had happened. Some of the other men had come back, Colonel Anderson said, but the losses were heavy, and there would be no wagons going out until morning.

"Better get something to eat and drink," he says.

"I ain't wantin' anything," says Perry. "Can I go now?"

"Where to?" says the colonel.

"Back after him," says Perry. "By god, I can't let Pete Martin lie there and die."

He started limping away. Colonel Anderson looked at him hard for a moment. Then he called an orderly.

"Find this fellow a place to sleep," he says, "and have a look at that leg. He's not to leave camp tonight."

By the next morning the roads were all clear, the rebels having moved on, but when the wagons brought in Pete, he was dead. For Perry it seemed then as if they'd lost the whole war.

But Pete died, just like a feller ought to live, without any hate in his heart.

Chapter 25

HOW UNCLE PERRY *met his cousin Hiram, and the
bitter war came to an end*

BEFORE THE WAR was ever over and Perry got back to
Mud Corners, there was a blue moon of time to think about
things.

*Hindsight is better 'n foresight but a man comes by it
harder.*

After they had helped General Wilson chase the rebels
down through Pulaski, the Twelfth Cavalry went into winter
quarters up at Murfreesboro, and that was the longest winter
Perry ever lived through in his life. Late in November they
took over some log-built cavalry huts left from the year before, cleaning them out and fixing the stick-and-clay chimneys, though even then they didn't draw well in the heavy
winter air till Jim Mooney figured out how to knock the
bottom out of a salt pork barrel and rig it up on top. It was
a cold, wet winter of rain and snow, then a heavy freeze, and
then more rain and snow.

All winter long the chill never left a fellow's bones, except now and then when he was out in the saddle, and then he'd sweat and steam up and have the damp in his clothes to keep warm when he got back. And the old log huts were full of fleas and body lice that would get into a fellow's clothes and bed blankets. On Saturday Perry and the others would set up a boiling kettle at the spring down near the river and beat out the wash on flat stones, but it didn't help much, for likely before there was time to build a fire for the drying-out, it was raining again and they'd have to put the clothes on half wet and crawl into bed to keep warm. And by the time the clothes were dry, they were full of fleas and lice once more.

But the worst thing was just lying there day after day in the winter rain and snow, minding what had happened, or dreaming of Mud Corners, and waking up at daycrack home-sick beyond what a fellow could ever say. Sometimes of a morning he would just lie there cursing the whole goddamn war. What were the rebels fighting for anyway? They didn't have anything left.

After the battle of Wilkerson's Pike, Perry's company had helped to carry off the wounded and bury hundreds of dead. Most of the rebels were in rags and looked half-starved and many of them lay there without any shoes on their feet. On the night of the battle a heavy freeze set in, and many a time they had to stop and break away the frozen mud before lifting some poor fellow onto a stretcher. Hacking through the frozen crust, they buried the dead in shallow pits, some-times half filled with water. The federals they wrapped in blankets whenever they could find any, but the rebels they just rolled in. Alonzo wasn't even for turning them over, face up.

"They're human same as we, I figger," says Perry.

"No," says Alonzo, "they ain't but goddamn rebels. Let 'em scratch their way down to hell."

But Perry could never quite reconcile himself to that. Later on that winter he had an experience that he figured few federals ever had. Leastways it wasn't likely, for it was just a happen-to, that's all.

Early in March, about two weeks before they broke camp and left for Vicksburg, Captain Williams took them out on a scouting trip up near McMinnville. They had been gone from camp three or four days, though they hadn't seen a regular or a bushwhacker, and were camping that night in a cedar grove near a small creek, three miles below the village. Jim Mooney was standing guard just along about sundown when he saw a farmer come walking down the road. As he came nearer, Jim could see he was a middle-sized fellow, dressed in butter-nut homespun and an old felt hat.

"Howdy," says Jim, as he came up.

"Howdy," says the fellow. He stood there for a moment looking at Jim and the camp. "You Union fellers?"

Jim didn't answer for a minute. Let him figure it out, he thought. No fellow could tell offhand, seeing that a rebel scouting party or even bushwhackers wore Union clothes every time they could lay hands on them. The old man kept looking him over. "I figgered you'd be Union," he says.

"Been any rebels or bushwhackers around?" says Jim.

"Two days ago," he says, "there was a party through here pickin' up stragglers."

"Which way was they headin'?"

"Down towards Sequatchie."

"Did they get many fellers?"

"A good many, I hear say."

They kept on talking for a while and the fellow got real friendly-like and pointing out the way to his own house, higher up on the ridge, he told Jim his name was Jake Harman.

"By god, that's funny now," says Jim. "We got a feller in camp, his name's Harman, too."

"Well, I declare," says the fellow. "And where does he hail from?"

"Indiana," says Jim. "La Grange county."

"Is that so?" says the fellow. "Well I reckon I just might have some kin up there. I'd like to meet this feller, Harman."

When the time came for Jim to be relieved, he brought the old man along to camp and they both looked up Perry.

"Here's a feller says his name is Jake Harman," says Jim.

"Harman?" says Perry.

"Yes sir," says Jake. "I hear say you're from Indiana and I figgered out maybe we was kin. What was your father's name?"

"Jeremiah," says Perry.

"You know where he come from?"

"From over in Ohio—Owensville, I hear say. That's where my grandpap lived."

"What's his name?"

"Jonathan, I hear my sister, Nancy, say."

"Jonathan Ebenezer Harman," says Jake. "Now ain't that a humdinger. I figger your father and me might be cousins."

"Is that so?" says Perry.

"Yes sir," he says, "I figger that may be right. I had an uncle by name of Jonathan Ebenezer. The last time I see him was back in Connecticut before he left for Ohio. I wasn't more 'n a shavetail of ten or twelve. I can even mind me of his oldest boy, Jeremiah. He was older 'n me. There were some girls, too. Let's see—"

"I got an aunt livin' over in Owensville, though I never come to see her," says Perry.

"Hannah, as I mind me," says Jake.

[*274*]

"No," says Perry, "Selina. But I hear say one of them died."

"Yes sir, your pap and me is cousins. My father's name was Samuel and he came from Madison, Connecticut, down here to Warren county when I was fifteen. He died the next year, and I never heard a dang word of what happened to Jonathan or any of his family. Be your father livin'?"

"No," says Perry, "he died before I ever knowed him."

"Well, I declare," says Jake, "your name's Perry Harman and you're kin. By golly, you come right up to the house with me and pay us a visit."

"I'd be mighty glad to," says Perry.

They went on over to see Captain Williams then, and seeing what a wonder it was, the captain allowed Perry might go along and spend the night. They were breaking camp early, he told Perry, and he could join them again down at Hollow Springs the next day.

Perry and Jake left camp, Perry leading his horse, and began climbing a winding road heading up the hillside. About half a mile up, after they had gone through some limestone outcroppings, heavily timbered, the land opened up and leveled off some and, taking a right fork, in about a half mile they came to a little clapboard house, two or three unpainted outbuildings, and the charred timbers of a barn.

"Here we be," says Jake, leading the way in.

Then he showed Perry where to stable his horse in one of the empty barns, took off the saddle and bedded the horse down with some dry cornshucks, and together they walked towards the house.

"Clara, I brung you a visitor," says Jake to his wife, as they came up the back porch into the kitchen. "Perry Harman, a cousin of mine, from up in Indiana."

[275]

"Howdy," she says, shaking hands, but looking hard at the Union blue and the buttons.

"He's a soldier," says Jake, "but he ain't meanin' no harm to his own kin. You set out a mess of victuals that'll make him feel to home."

Jake took the new Spencer rifle Perry had been issued at Murfreesboro, looked it over carefully, rubbed the stock with the palm of his hand, and set it in the corner of the kitchen. Perry washed up and sat down and they all started in talking, while the old lady kept working away at the kitchen stove. She was a fine-appearing woman with gray hair parted in the middle and gathered up in a bob at the back, dressed in homespun well-washed and worn, her hands and face seamed with lines. The house itself looked mighty clean but bare, much as Esther's or Lissa's up in Milford township. It wasn't long till Perry came to feel right at home.

The puzzling thing was the victuals she set on the table. First a bowl of baked potatoes and then some cooked Indian corn. Then she went back to the stove and piled a blue platter high with sausages—with pork selling for well over a dollar a pound if a fellow could get any at all, that Perry knew. Then came a loaf of white bread from the pantry, and the kettle hissing, she poured out four cups of coffee, the first coffee he had seen in any house in Tennessee since he'd been in the war. He couldn't figure out how they could give him a welcome like that.

Before they sat down Jake went outside. In about ten minutes he came back, and as he came up onto the porch, Perry could hear someone else following along.

In a minute a young fellow stood there in the doorway, young, though he looked old and sick, with a heavy beard and untrimmed mustache, dressed in a torn and patched uniform of the rebel troops.

"Here's my son, Jeff," says Jake. "Jeff, this here's Perry Harman. He's kin."

"Howdy," says Jeff, holding out his hand.

"Howdy," says Perry, getting up and standing there that dumbflustered he couldn't think of anything to say at the time.

"Well," says Jake, "let's set down to our victuals."

After they had all heaped up their plates with food, talk came easier. Jeff was home on a furlough, Jake said. He had been in the war for nearly three years. His older brother, Ben, had been in before him and had been killed at Lees Mill. Jeff himself had been at the battle of Shiloh, where he'd had three bullet holes through his sleeve, and a charge of cannister had blown off his hat and torn it into chitterlings at Fredericksburg.

"You seen much action?" says Jake.

"Some," says Perry. "I had a brother, George, killed at Shiloh."

"Jeff was wounded at Chickamauga," says Clara, laying a hand on his arm.

"Just a rifle ball that lodged in my thigh," says Jeff, making light of it. "Take Fredericksburg. By golly, I figger that was the best lickin' we ever gave you. We took two thousand prisoners."

"Well," says Perry, laughing back at him, "I don't figger I'm to blame fer that. That was before I ever come to join up."

"What'd you fellers ever come down here fer anyway?" Jake says, turning serious-like. "We never asked fer a thing except to be left alone."

"Well I figger it was because you fellers seceded from the Union," says Perry.

"Seceded?" says Jake. "By god, we had to. And that don't

[277]

give you any call to come down here killin' our people and carryin' off livestock and starvin' out the countryside."

"Starvin'?" says Perry.

"That's what I said," says Jake. "I traded the last mule I had on the place fer the sausages and bread you're eatin' right now just to give Jeff a decent welcome home. I lost over twenty head of livestock to your own foragers, the time they burned down the barn. I'm flat on my back. I got the place mortgaged down to the last fence post and outhouse."

"Well," says Perry, "you fellers brung it on yourselves."

"Brung it on ourselves! Fer what?"

"On account of niggers."

"Niggers!" says Jake. "I never owned no niggers and I ain't aimin' to."

"Then what are you fightin' fer?" says Perry.

"By god, any feller'll defend his own home down to the ashes of his floor sills," says Jake, "as long as he's got that much."

"But you're fightin' fer the slaveholders," says Perry.

"No," says Jeff, biting in. "I've been fightin' fer my country, same as you. I don't give a damn fer the big planters. They've lost all their niggers anyway."

"That's because we freed 'em," says Perry.

"Yes," says Jake. "And let them overrun the countryside. Who's goin' to feed and take care of 'em now? We could have handled the whole thing if you fellers had stayed out of it. It had gotten so a white man couldn't get a job as a wheelwright or a blacksmith or a carpenter, nor do any work at it, not fer the big planters—not with slaves to do it fer 'em. What we were aimin' fer was a law to hold the niggers down to field work. That would have taken the money out of it and given all of us a chance, and slavery would have died out in the end. But your own hot-heads wouldn't stand fer that.

They goddamned every feller in the south who wouldn't swear he was a greater friend to a few niggers than he was to his own family. And your president took a Bible oath he wasn't agin slavery, only secession, and now he's turnin' around and armin' thousands of our own niggers and settin' 'em agin us."

"Hold on a minute," says Perry.

"And for three years you fellers have been down here burnin' down towns, tearin' up our railroads and burnin' out bridges, and drivin' off livestock, just to set loose a gang of niggers. By god, I hope they all foller you back home."

"Well," says Perry, "iffen that's the way you feel about it, maybe I'd just better be gettin' along."

But Jake wouldn't hear of it. He'd asked him up for the night and he meant what he said. "No," he says, after a while, "I ain't really faultin' you, Perry. Likely enough, iffen my own father had gone to Owensville instead of comin' down here, Ben and Jeff would have been fightin' on your side."

After that the conversation turned more friendly. They sat around a while longer, Perry telling them about Mud Corners and Minot and Nancy, he and Jeff trading war stories, and Jeff looking over his accouterments and hefting the fine Spencer Jake had set in the corner. Along about ten o'clock they were all ready for bed and Jeff, taking a candle, led Perry upstairs to a long, low-ceilinged room with a four-poster flock-bed standing at one end. They both undressed and got into bed, lying down side by side. Perry didn't feel like sleeping and for a long time he just lay there thinking, and Jeff, too, racked with a dry cough, kept turning from side to side.

After a while he says, "Perry, I'm figgerin' on givin' up."

"Is that so?" says Perry.

"I ain't on any furlough," he says. "I just plain deserted,

though I ain't ever told Mom that. I'm sick inside. They were after me but Pap hid me out in the woods, and with you fellers up this way I reckon I'm safe fer a day or two."

"You could take the Union oath and be paroled," says Perry.

"And be shot fer a traitor the first time my own neighbors catch me?" says Jeff.

"Well, you could give yourself up as a prisoner," says Perry.

"And be sent to a prison camp up north to live on bread and water in the raw cold and dirt till the flesh falls off a feller's bones? No, I've been thinkin' about that. I just want to quit. I'm plain tired."

Perry didn't say anything at all for a spell.

"All I done fer three years now," says Jeff, "is march and camp and fight and dog on through the mud on half rations or none a-tall, fightin' off the ague and dysentery, and fer what? I figger the country's all gone to smash and a hundred years of buildin' won't bring it back. I'm fer quittin' now."

"Maybe you're right," says Perry.

"Take you and me, now, lyin' here side by side. What have we got against each other?"

"Nothin' a-tall," says Perry, "exceptin' we're on different sides."

"And if they caught us, by god, they'd shoot us both fer spies."

"More 'n likely."

"I just want to quit," says Jeff, "and go away somewhere. I was thinkin' when you were tellin' us about Mud Corners. By god, I'd like to live alongside of a feller like Minot. I figger he'd understand."

"He would that," says Perry. "He's the finest feller I ever came to know."

[*280*]

"I could start in all over again," says Jeff.

"Maybe I could get you a pass through the lines," says Perry, "and you could go."

"Could you?" says Jeff.

"I don't know," says Perry, "but, by god, we can try."

They talked on for a while, but well before daylight they got up and went downstairs. Jake was still sitting there in the kitchen in his day clothes, just where they'd left him when they'd gone to bed, and after they had told him what they were up to, he went in and woke up Clara. They all sat there talking for a time, and then she got a few things ready and tucked them in a carpet bag, and gave them a breakfast of hot coffee and the white bread that was left from the night before.

Then she turned to kiss Jeff. "Be good to my boy, Perry," she said.

Cousin Jake never said a word at all. He just stood there in the doorway and shook hands with Perry and then with Jeff. When the boys turned to go, he moved over to Clara and stood by her and put his arm around her waist. Many a time afterwards it came to Perry: an old man, barefooted and in butternut homespun, standing by a gray-haired lady, tears trickling down the seams of her face, saying good-by to all they had left to live for. That for him was the picture of the whole south.

Jeff knew all the country byroads and lanes and they made their way down the other side of the ridge. They were in heavy timber by daylight and before noon they came to the outskirts of Hollow Springs. They waited there under cover until Perry saw Captain Williams and the scouts come riding into sight. They all thought he had taken a prisoner, then, but on the way to camp Perry told Captain Williams what they were up to. Captain Williams shook his head, but when they got back to Murfreesboro, he talked to Colonel Anderson, and two or three days later, the colonel called Perry in and gave him some dispatches for General Grierson over at Columbia, and allowed Jeff to go along, dressed in some castoff federals.

General Grierson was a tall man with full black sideburns and chin whiskers, but the thing Perry marked about him, as he stood there in the high-ceilinged room, was the sadness of his eyes. He was a stern man, so many fellows said, but Perry found him kindly. He read the dispatches Perry handed him, and then he called them both back in and asked Jeff to tell his story. He had an orderly bring him some paper and a pen to write a safe conduct, and after that Jeff took the oath of loyalty.

"You willing to stake your life on this," the general says to Perry, "your life for his that he will never turn spy?"

"That I am," says Perry.

They left then and Perry went along with Jeff halfway to Nashville before he turned back to Murfreesboro. It might take weeks, Jeff said, but he'd keep on going. After he'd passed through the lines at Nashville, he ought not to have any trouble.

"Good-by," says Perry, "and good luck."

"Good-by, cousin Perry," says Jeff, "I'm mighty grateful."

"Say hello to Minot and Nancy and Lucinda," says Perry. Then something that had happened a long time ago came back to mind. "Tell her I sent the rebel she was askin' fer. But mind you, Jeff, she's mine. I'm comin' back fer her myself."

"I pray Almighty God that you will," says Jeff. "We'll all be waitin' fer you."

Perry would have given his own right arm and maybe a leg thrown in to have gone along back to Mud Corners with Jeff, but it wasn't to happen that way. Between that day and the end lay the long trip down the Mississippi River to Mobile and all the fighting there and the long raid over into Georgia and all the way back to Columbus, Mississippi. They were hard days, filled with cold and hunger and blood and death and a loneliness that kept gnawing at his heart.

All the way through Georgia and Alabama the nights were damp and cold and the days burning-noonday hot. For miles the countryside lay like a spent battlefield, the air heavy with odors of decay and rot. Weeds and bush laurel grew lush along the bottomlands and maggot scum and wiggletails covered the streams. On the way back Perry came down with dysentery. First would come the chills and then the fever and then he'd break out in a drip of perspiration. His lips turned blue. And after a while he was that weak he could hardly stay in the saddle.

At Columbus Captain Williams took to looking over his men.

"Perry," he says, "you're sick, and the war is over anyway. I figure we'll all be discharged in a month or so. Why don't you go home on furlough and rest up?"

Captain Williams talked to Colonel Anderson, and the next day Perry, without waiting for the mustering-out pay the regiment would get up at Vicksburg, set out on foot for home. All the way up through the state and across Tennessee and Kentucky, walking along in the early morning, resting in the hot afternoon, and then setting out again at night, he kept thinking of Minot and Mud Corners and Lucinda and home. He had had a letter waiting for him at Columbus from Minot.

Jeff had died of consumption less than a month after he had gotten there, but his coming had been a wonderful thing for all of them, Minot had written. It had helped them to forget and even to forgive Marsh's death in the rebel prison down at Andersonville. Nancy and Lucinda and all the family were well and waiting for him to come back home. Lew Shingle

and the Republicans had held a big victory celebration down
at South Milford, though Eliphalet had died—just like Abe
Lincoln—and never lived to see how the war came out. Some
eastern capitalists were building a railroad through the county,
but it would cut through from Kendallville to Rome City
and Wolcottville and by-pass the township. That would likely
bring a whole rift of changes to Mud Corners.

Nothing would ever again be like it was, Perry thought.
Life was like the moon hanging low over the Tennessee hills—
now dark, now full. Deep in their hearts, though, under the
hate and bitterness of war, under the fierce pride of victory
and in the loneliness of defeat, people were friendly.

That was the thing to remember.

*Any feller—and a whole country fer all that—is as
strong as his fist but never any bigger than his heart.*

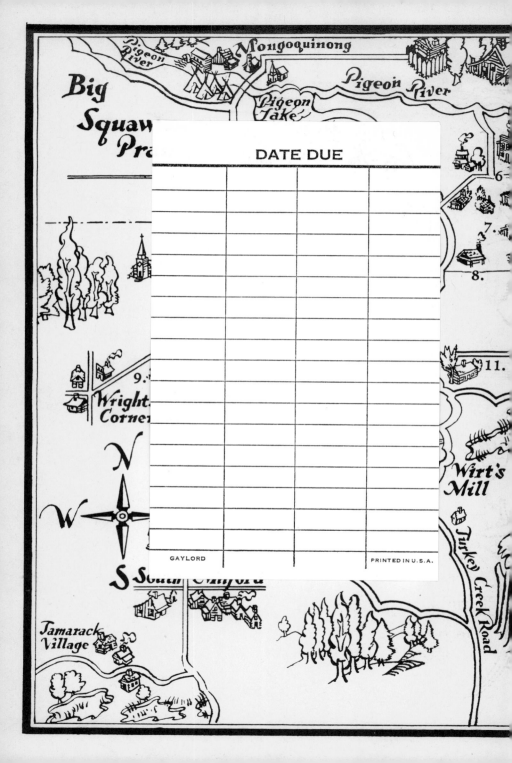

DATE DUE